Pasanen

Interview with Death

Interview
with
Death

Tales
from
the
Afterworld

Book 1

V. K. Pasanen

Editor
Marie Anne Cope

Cover
JDandJ.com

Author contact, updates, and more
www.vkpasanen.com
v.k.pasanen@vkpasanen.com
v.k.pasanen@talesfromtheafterworld.com
Amazon.com: V. K. Pasanen: books, biography, latest update
https://www.goodreads.com/vkpasanen
Also check out **Spotify** playlist: Tales from the Afterworld.

Welcome to my tales
from a place out of time
about realities you may not have known.
So much has passed since I knew one reality
and the narrow confines of a vast universe
beyond my mortal world.
So much death since then.
Untold billions gone in a senseless apocalypse
and the purge that followed
to save what could not be saved.
Now the heavens are at war
and the end of everything is near.

I write these tales not for the realities we knew,
but for the rebirth beyond the prophecy
when all will be made right
and the Master Creator begins
the next turn of the wheel.
May these tales be a warning
to those who follow in our footsteps.

The following is the story of how I came to know Death
and became a Reaper of Souls.
It is also an overview of events that led to the Apocalypse,
told from the outside looking in.
This is the prologue.
Future volumes will guide immortal readers
from the beginning of the end,
through thirteen years of hell,
and the bitter peace that followed
in the Age of Ethereal.

N. Reaper

One

0630, Wednesday, October 27, 2004. Almawt Lilkifaar, Iraq.

Corporal Toby Almaraz told another joke as the packed Bradley lumbered down the street in one of the two secured sectors in the ancient city. Other than Toby, everyone was as quiet as the street outside. Too quiet. Toby said something about three hookers and a pimp, but I didn't catch the punchline. I was too distracted by a presence I'd felt many times before. He was close, and that was never a good sign.

This wasn't my first ride in a Bradley, but the heat and rancid smells made it more claustrophobic. I cracked a shaky grin at Travis, my cameraman. He glanced at my hands and fingers that were tapping away. Travis nodded back. No smile. Just his customary *let's-get-this-done* look as his camera rolled, catching anything he could edit for this week's episode of *Berets*. Sweat trickled down his cheek. A stream ran down mine.

Packed inside the mobile oven were four Army Rangers who were like brothers to us. Besides Toby, John the Giant, Kyle, and my good friend, Ryan, were along for the ride. The rest of Ryan's unit (or chalk as they say in Ranger lingo) was in front of us, split between two Bradleys mixed with Marines. Our three heavy vehicles led the convoy to the target.

The eyes around me were focused, intense, but strangely relaxed as sweat dripped like rain from the hair poking out from my helmet. I wiped my forehead and took a deep breath. Something didn't feel right.

1

What was I worried about? *Stay calm*, I told myself and took another breath. General Cornelius Adamson assured me the hospital would be a cakewalk while Travis's camera caught everything. What viewers wouldn't know was that the mission was orchestrated for maximum ratings. But I did, and it gnawed at me. Chewed at me. Uncle Frank would've been so ashamed.

The entire episode was the General's idea to salvage the show that rumor mills whispered wouldn't be renewed for another season due to the war's waning popularity. The truth is, it was shameless hubris for a photo-op to raise the General's star higher and maybe add another to his uniform. The premise was simple. Ryan's men would capture the hospital containing an enemy stronghold towering over the Bridge of Death. It would be an iconic moment for General Adamson.

A year earlier, the bridge was a scene of unbridled carnage during General George Levinson's retreat across the Euphrates during a rout of U.S. forces. The city's inhabitants savagely tore apart wounded soldiers, decapitating four. The insurgents displayed their severed heads on bobbing AK47s to cries of "Allahu Akbar!"

After throwing their heads in the river, the decapitated bodies were dangled from meat hooks from the bridge and left to rot while repeatedly shown for several months on Al Qaeda-sponsored websites. The images, colored in a dull rainbow of death and decay, were tattooed in my head. Ryan Mender and the rest of the guys smelled revenge. Sweet revenge. But none knew the mission was unnecessary, except Travis and me.

The night before, Captain Martin Rice and his SEAL team had cleared the hospital, leaving a few Wahabi insurgents trapped inside. Still, much could go wrong for Adamson's photo-op in an unsecured city, for which I had incrementally sold my soul for more riches and fame. Travis knew it, and it was killing him.

But it was more than that. I'd seen too many people die in this hellish place the year before, and I was close to Ryan and his men. Too close and I had lost my objectivity. They had made it this far without any life-threatening or life-altering wounds, and, like I said before, they were the brothers that neither Travis nor I ever had. If I could pull strings to bring them home alive and whole, then that's what I would do. I pushed aside anxious thoughts and focused on the episode about to unfold.

Let me pause and rewind. This was only the start of my downward spiral that led to the pinnacle of success and excess and drove me to suicide and an interview with Death. There was much that led to that day of infamy in 2004, but it began with my first encounter with the Man in Black when I was thirteen. No—it was before then. The path to that spiral began the day I was born, because of where I was born. And then there were forces that shaped my destiny that no mortal could've comprehended before my one on one with the Reaper.

I'm not writing this to excuse my actions or shift blame for the pain I have caused so many. I will eternally live with the bloodstains and bear the burden, like I do with the job I accepted as penance. I do not ask forgiveness for things that can never be made right. I only ask that you hear me out as I start from the beginning.

I entered my reality on June 13, 1960, in Oak Park, Illinois, the hometown of Ernest Miller Hemingway. If not for the location of my birth, I wonder if I'd have ever become a writer. I was an only child and have few memories in Oak Park besides playing with army men at the park near my house and trips to the Lake Michigan boardwalk to get ice cream. Pink Bubblegum with the little blue gummy pieces was my favorite. There was also the Ackerman Tower Massacre, which created my early boogie man. My father, Jonathan Leslie Miller, worked for Lester Ackerman and was in the building when the massacre occurred. The event is something I won't speak of now. Its significance will become clear later. But few living then or born in my reality since haven't heard of or seen Ackerman's murderous extravaganza that played out on live black and white TV on Christmas Day in 1964. My father sheltered me as best he could, but that wasn't easy since he lost his job.

The following February, my family moved to Williamsport, Pennsylvania, where my grandfather, Milton Leslie Miller, worked as a manager for a small aircraft engine company. Grandpa Milton lived in a yellow Victorian home where my father and uncle Frank grew up. By then, it was a lonely home and had been since Grandma Dorine passed away before I could remember her. My father tried to find a new job in the defense industry but after months without success, he settled for a job working with Grandpa Milton alongside his brother.

Shortly after we moved, Frank was drafted into the Army. Once enlisted, he volunteered for the Seventy-Fifth Airborne Regiment and became a Green Beret before shipping off to Vietnam. That year while Frank was overseas, Grandpa Milton died of a massive heart attack and my father replaced him as manager.

Frank returned in 1970, right before Nixon began covert operations in Cambodia. The Army begged him to stay, but he was done fighting a war no one would allow him to win, if it could be won at all. What followed his return was a nightmare for his wife,

4

Dorothy, as much as it was for himself. Frank told me years later that my father and mother tried to help, but something had broken inside him. He couldn't get the faces of the dead out of his head, whether they were friends or enemies or collateral damage. So, Frank drank until he blacked out to make the faces disappear. When he opened up years later and told me his stories, he admitted to hitting Dorothy. But she stuck it out because she believed in old-school marriage, up to a point.

One morning, Uncle Frank awoke to find Dorothy crying on the porch steps of the Victorian home willed to him by Grandpa Milton. Her right eye was black and swollen. When he reached to console her, she pulled away and told him she was leaving. Frank ran inside, grabbed every bottle, and smashed them on the sidewalk in front of Dorothy. He said he'd get help for his drinking and what would soon be called Post-Traumatic Stress Disorder, not that Frank was one to blame what he did on anyone or anything but himself. He was made of tougher stuff than that and always said, *"You own it when you do it, no excuses. You're responsible for what your hands do and what your mouth says. Don't matter if you're drunk or anything else. And you're responsible for making it right or carrying that burden to your grave."*

Frank swore he would do anything for Dorothy if she wouldn't leave. She reluctantly agreed to stay. And unlike most abusive husbands, he owned it and made it right. He never drank again or raised his voice or hand to Dorothy. While her broken heart didn't mend overnight, in time, they found tranquility in their eternal love. I'm glad my parents never told me any of this. Kids need heroes to give them something to strive toward, and I wasn't ready to know the real Uncle Frank back then.

5

On October 15, 1972, four months after my twelfth birthday, my parents were killed by a drunk driver who veered into their lane. They were diehard Eagles fans returning from Philadelphia after a short trip to celebrate their thirteenth anniversary. The Eagles lost big to the LA Rams like they did to the Cowboys a month before, which was the last thing we did together. I wanted to go to the Rams game, but Uncle Frank and Aunt Dorothy insisted I stay with them so my parents could have a rare date. After midnight, I learned my parents wouldn't be picking me up in the morning.

In their living will, my parents gave custody of me to Frank and Dorothy. Other than that, my parents had little of value other than a heart-shaped pearl locket, wedding rings, and a watch Grandpa Milton gave my father.

Who knows what would've become of me if not for Uncle Frank and Aunt Dorothy taking me in after the third offense drunk driver killed my parents and stole my innocence. I still remember their faces at the funeral, all made up to give the impression of life, but their foreheads were cold to my warm lips. Frank and Dorothy held me up when my legs were too weak to stand.

For several months after the funeral, I rarely left my upstairs bedroom that had belonged to my father. Frank and Dorothy always told me they loved me and that Grandpa Milton and Grandma Dorine's house was too big without me. Once, they'd hoped for children, but Dorothy was barren, so they considered adoption. Then Frank got drafted. When he got out, sobered up, and they considered adopting again, my parents were dead, and I was dumped in their laps.

Six months passed before I started coming downstairs for more than meals and school. I seldom spoke unless spoken to, and my responses were no more than a word or two. During those first difficult months of our life together, Frank and Dorothy tried to crack my heart's stone-casing. They wanted to see their happy, carefree nephew again, but I felt immune to joy. Every waking moment oscillated between tears and anger toward the man who stole my parents. I hoped for nothing more than to find him one day and end his life.

The loneliness was unbearable, and the nights were worse. I dreamed about my parents as if they were alive, only to have them taken away again in the morning. But Frank had lost his only brother and much more in Vietnam, and soon, Dorothy and Frank's love softened my heart. I learned to smile and laugh again when the waves of grief weren't crashing down on me.

For my thirteenth birthday, Frank and Dorothy twisted my arm into going to the Harrisburg County Summer Fair. It was a sunny day, and I remember eating blue cotton candy and too many chili dogs. I felt sick, but we were finally happy. It was as if I had forgotten my parents were gone.

After the belly cramps passed, I told Frank and Dorothy I wanted to go on some rides. I rode every single one twice. My favorite was the *Enterprise*. It was a spoked disk with two-person pods attached around the wheel. It rose to ninety degrees, spinning at eye blurring speeds, making me dizzy.

Shortly before closing, I asked to ride the Enterprise one more time. After I got in line, a soft breeze blew, and the ride to my left caught my eye. It was called *The Loop* and looked like a single loop of a loop-de-loop roller coaster. I eyed the Enterprise again and then The Loop. The breeze picked up, and the wind seemed to whisper, *"Ride that one instead."* I listened.

I bumped into a hazel-eyed girl behind me as I exited the line. She had short blonde hair and looked a little older than me. I said, "Excuse me." She smiled sweetly enough to make me blush and look away.

Before snaking through the crowd to my destination, I brushed by the man behind the girl. He was old and wore a fancy black cowboy hat. He had wild silver hair poking out from underneath. Hard etched lines aged his face further. He looked out of place, dressed in his black trench coat, matching shirt, slacks, and cowboy boots. It was night, and it was dark, but his blue eyes were luminous when they met mine. He solemnly grinned like a mortician. I shook my head as a chill danced along my spine and moved swiftly through the crowd to The Loop's shorter line.

To this day, I can't remember being on that ride. I only remember hearing the screams when I got off. I ran toward the crowd to see what happened and pushed through. In the center was a crumpled pod that had broken off a poorly maintained ride. Crimson dripped from the cobalt metal pod into a red puddle. A candied apple floated in the middle next to the lifeless face of one of the four victims. It was the hazel-eyed girl. I wondered if the old man was among the dead until I saw him look my way with fathomless sorrow. He turned and disappeared into the crowd. I never forgot him, though it would be many years before I saw him again.

Two

The day at the fair set me back. I couldn't get the girl's smiling face and hazel eyes out of my head. And then there was the old man with the brilliant blue eyes that cut through the darkness. I would often think about those chilling eyes during the day and dream about them at night. After a while, I began believing that there was no Man in Black at the fair, especially after asking Uncle Frank and Aunt Dorothy about it. They had been standing right next to me and had the same vivid memory of the girl, but not the out of place man with the remarkable eyes that couldn't have been missed. Memory is a tricky thing and some of the greatest fallacies we hold dear are memories of things that never happened or happened quite differently than we remember. Soon, the old man became nothing but an embodiment of guilt for living when someone died in my place. It probably didn't help to experience faces of death so soon after my parents were taken from me.

Time heals most wounds, even if scars remain, and Uncle Frank and Aunt Dorothy refused to let me curl up and die. That's when Frank told me what he'd seen and done and how he survived to become whole again. Uncle Frank was a religious man but never zealous. He found hope in the Good Book, but more than just faith in God saved him. It was Dorothy by his side that led him from the darkness into the light. After learning the truth from Frank's lips, I thought of him whenever I faltered. My last wife as a mortal was Finnish and she called it *Sisu*. Frank was loaded with it like an alcoholic on Friday or Saturday night or both. I tapped into his fountain, drank my fill, and found strength to navigate the ups and downs of my teen years.

That's when I started keeping a journal to work through the loss of my parents and the death of the hazel-eyed girl. I also recorded Frank's stories about Vietnam, my parents, and other relatives going back to before the Revolutionary War. He was a virtual encyclopedia of mostly correct facts to the best of his knowledge. I

9

also became obsessed with the memory of the Man in Black who I turned into the Grim Reaper in a short story for my sophomore creative writing class.

The tale was inspired by a nightmare I had near my sixteenth birthday about the hazel-eyed girl. In every dream before, she was dead and staring at me. Not in this one. I was in line and she was behind me like usual, but this time, I heard no voice on the wind warning me not to ride the Enterprise. And so, I continued on. I looked back. I still saw the hazel-eyed girl behind me and the Man in Black behind her. He looked sad. He caught my eyes, but I didn't hold his gaze, because I couldn't. I wouldn't hold his gaze. I felt something was wrong, but I didn't know what. I had no knowledge outside the dream.

I got on the ride and sat in the pod with the boy that had been in front of me. The hazel-eyed girl got in the next pod. And the ride started. I had the same excitement and anticipation as the first time I rode it early that day. As it sped up I felt the exhilaration as my stomach fluttered. It sped faster, and faster, and faster again. And then I heard the buckling of metal. A screech. A snap. A bolt came loose, and rattled around, and banged against the outside of the pod. And then I was flying. Flying. And then I was not, and everything went black.

I woke up, opened my eyes, and I felt wet. I felt like I had fallen in a pool of water, but the water was warm and sticky. Then I realized it wasn't water. It was blood. I was lying in the crimson puddle. I saw the apple, and I looked up. The hazel-eyed girl was looking down with tears in her eyes. The Man in Black had his hand on her shoulder. He was crying, too. But his tears were fluorescent blue, falling from those mystical eyes. Then I opened mine. I swiped

10

my hand across the ocean of my forehead. I was drenched in sweat. I thought, *Why me*?

I hopped out of bed and feverishly began writing about a war correspondent, like Ernest Hemingway, who gets the chance of a lifetime to interview Death. But my Reaper was kind rather than scary and looked like the country legend Johnny Cash. Johnny was the real Man in Black—the everyman's song writer. Uncle Frank loved his stuff and played it all the time. I knew almost every song by heart but *The Man Comes Around* was my favorite. Anyway, the story got me an A+ and a *Wow* from Mr. Brands, who wasn't a teacher who handed out *Wows* willy-nilly. He even gave me the crazy idea that I might be able to write for a living. From that moment on, there was nothing I dreamed of more than to write a book about Uncle Frank and then maybe, just maybe, become the next Ernest Hemingway from Oak Park, Illinois. Shoot for the moon. I mean, what's the worst thing that can happen? End up dead and become a monument to failure?

Three

My junior year I joined the school newspaper. My teacher quickly recognized my writing talent, and upon graduation, I received a full-ride journalism scholarship to Penn State in 1978. The first day of my freshman year, I met Travis Wright. Funny guy. He would become my partner in harmless crime and be my best friend until he was bumped a notch by the first love of my life.

I remember the first time I saw the eyes that would change that life. Travis and I were at a Phi Beta Epsilon Halloween party in 1980.

I was dressed as Elvis and he was dressed as Dr. Groucho Marx in a white lab coat with a fake mustache, round rimmed glasses, a stethoscope, and a fat cigar. The frat back porch was filled with brothers and sorority sisters in various costumes. One brother in a gray and tan werewolf costume held a water hose to his mouth, attached to a funnel. His neck was craned back as he gulped behind a mask and Frankenstein's Monster poured beer into the funnel. The crowd laughed and chanted, "GO, GO, GO."

Blondie's new smash hit, *Call Me*, blared over the speakers. I held a red Dixie cup filled with cheap beer and smelled reefer from a couple passing a joint on the couch. The girl pinched the blunt, pulled hard, created a bright orange glow, and coughed hard enough to bring up lung chunks.

I scanned the room. Sauced guys and girls were draped on furniture and counters. The girl on the couch had stopped coughing and was making out with the guy. She grabbed his hand, and they spirited upstairs.

Across from me, three bombshells dropped into the room—two blondes flanking a brunette, all bobbing their heads to the beat. The blondes were dressed as flower children wearing mini-skirts, but the one in the middle with the piercing gray eyes won my undivided attention. She was dressed as a prisoner in a black and white jumpsuit with a round-top prison cap. She carried a plastic sledgehammer and a black ball attached to her right leg by a silver chain. My heart tingled and electricity rippled over my skin as I saw the woman I wanted to be with more than any other. Then the cold shower of self-doubt drenched me and brought me back to earth.

"Nathan. Man, check 'em out." Travis leaned into me with a bent finger to his lips. He subtly motioned at the trio as if I were blind. "Damn, that one on the left is uhh, smokin' hot!" His eyes were comically directed up and to the right as he fiddled with his cigar like a vintage clown.

"Shit, man. They're way out of my league. They'd never talk to me," I said as I ignored the knockout blondes and studied the gorgeous prisoner. She looked like a cropped-brunette version of Blondie's Debra Harry mixed with Diane Spencer, who would soon become the Princess of Wales. Her lips were thin, shiny, and flawless, ending in little dimples. Her teeth were almost perfect, with a subtle gap between the upper two incisors accentuated by laughter after the flower child on the left said something funny. She looked in my direction. I glanced at Travis, who was smiling like a horny wolf. I looked back. The brunette was eyeing her Dixie cup as the chilling opening chords of Blue Öyster Cult's *(Don't Fear) The Reaper* boomed through the room. She was wearing just the right amount of base to lift her cheeks. Her eyeliner was dark, but not too much. A pair of black tears were drawn, falling from each eye. She had beautiful hands with long fingers and nails, painted half black and half white. She could've been a princess in a different life. To me, she was a goddess in this one and, as I said to Travis, entirely out of my league. I caught her gray eyes, and she caught mine undressing her. I glanced away and turned to watch Frankenstein hit the beer bong outside.

"Dude," said Travis with a disappointed chuckle, "I swear, you are never gonna get laid. You're on your own tonight. I got somebody I wanna meet."

Thank Gaia that wouldn't be the last time I saw that gray-eyed bombshell who would be the mother of my children.

That Monday in a large physics hall for a required class that had little to do with my major, the room was full except for the seat to my left. The guy on my right smelled like he hadn't bathed in a week. He was hungover and reeked of alcohol, weed, and body odor. I tried not to gag.

The beautiful brunette from the party shuffled into the hall as the doors closed. She saw the open seat, strolled to my row, and worked her way toward me. She bumped a few knees and said several *excuse-mes* before arriving at the empty seat. Her gray eyes and smile shone down on me.

"May I sit here?" she asked as she crinkled her nose. She retched adorably.

After class, we hurried to distance ourselves from *Smelly Guy* (whose name I have forgotten). We agreed that someone should tell him, but neither of us wanted to be that someone.

As I stepped from the hall, the gray-eyed princess grabbed my shoulder. "Wait, I know you. You're that shy guy from the Halloween party who dressed as Elvis. You were a terrible Elvis, by the way."

I laughed. "Yeah, I was, wasn't I?"

"Yeah, you were. Travis told my friend Candy you didn't think I'd talk to you. I was over there wishing you would, but you turned away. Kind of sucked. I figured you didn't like me, or that maybe you were gay. So, I was like, whatever."

"I'm not gay. I'm just socially awkward, I guess. Not good with the approach, you know. Not like Travis. I love the guy, but he's a dog."

"Yeah. I told Candy to watch out for that guy, but I think she already digs him too much. But hey, he seems to dig her, too. But I warn you, if he hurts her, I'll cut his dick off."

I chuckled. "That would suck. Seriously, though, Travis is a good guy. I've known him since my freshman year. Your friend has nothing to worry about. He's a good dog. Anyway, my name is Nathan Miller. I'm a journalism major."

"Vanessa Richardson," she said and shook my hand, "anthropology with a minor in Scandinavian studies. You wanna get some coffee or lunch or something?"

"Yeah. Sure. That'd be cool," I said, nodding my head a bit too enthusiastically.

Four

Vanessa was amazing—a true angel—and she was mine and I was hers. Why she chose me—I'll never understand. But she did and I was blessed beyond measure to have such a kind, compassionate lover of life as a girlfriend, and soon, fiancé, after she agreed to spend her life with me. Travis also settled down after he started dating Candy, who had been Vanessa's best friend since childhood growing up in Bangor, Maine.

After graduation in 1982, we had a double wedding at the Philadelphia Museum of Art. Travis and I stood atop the stairs as Vanessa and Candy did the slow walk up the *Rocky* steps. The location was a must since the movie was our favorite. *Rocky II* was good, too, and our quartet had recently been to the opening of *III* in May to see Rocky make a fool of Mr. T. We even had a ritual. Every

December 3, we commemorated the 1976 U.S. release by running up the steps together in rain, rarely shine, or early snow. We would eat Philly steak sandwiches with lots of whiz for lunch. For a few years after the 1982 VHS release, we added watching the movie to our annual ritual to celebrate each wedding anniversary. I would do a terrible Rocky impression (if that's possible), Travis would do Paulie, Candy would do Micky (which was pretty good and would always have us in stitches), and Vanessa would quote Adrian's lines. It was our Rocky Horror Picture Show and something I missed when Travis and Candy moved to Lake Winnipesaukee. The tradition faded though Travis and I would still get Vanessa's and Candy's attention with a "Yo, (insert name)," for several more years, until even that dimmed with the complacency of marriage.

After they moved, time flew like it does when you're living the best days of life and don't realize it. I held Vanessa's hand as she delivered Franklin Milton on August 9, 1984, followed by Jenna Renee on May 4, 1987. Jonathan Christian rounded out our trio when he entered our reality on July 24, 1990.

During this time, we lived in a small place in Greenwich Village and struggled to make ends meet and feed and entertain the kids. The neighbors above us were to murder for. The manager refused to do anything about the incomprehensible noise they blared at odd hours when the babies were trying to sleep. The only thing that broke the din and sent them to nodland was Vanessa's slightly raised but angelic voice when she read The Tales of Toivo the Bear by Finnish author, Kaisa Jännök. I still remember the little white Toivo bears the kids would run to their room to get (when they'd graduated from crawling) and held whenever Vanessa pulled out that little blue and white book. With strapped finances and a desire to stay in Manhatten, we had no choice but to deal with the inconveniences of New York's vertical rat traps.

Vanessa applied for grants and worked as a teacher while I wrote and wrote and failed and failed. A framed Benjamin for my first paid column hung on the wall. More than once we were tempted to break the glass but Vanessa had faith that it would be the first of many. Besides that column, and a few freelance pieces, I had little to show for my hard work except dusty manuscripts below rejection letters taunting me from a nail on the wall. I knew Vanessa had doubts, but she never voiced them as we barely kept the electricity on while eating mass quantities of ramen and pork and beans. It was all uphill as hope was dashed by false summit after false summit, and there seemed to be no top to this mountain. I worked odd jobs doing whatever I could to bring in the bacon. It was just enough, but we weren't fat.

One day I had a chance meeting at a coffee shop. I was writing about the Lester Ackerman Massacre for another manuscript that would never see the light of day concerning a topic for which there was little left to tell. As I penned away on the third draft, a man walked up and asked what I was writing about. I told him it was a book about my father, who worked at the Ackerman Tower at the time of the incident. I told him I was born in nearby Oak Park. He asked if I'd mind if he read a chapter or two. Against my self-conscious angels at a random request from a stranger, I let the man read the unpolished first chapter. When he finished, he nodded approval.

"That was good. Really good. I'm sorry, I guess I should introduce myself. My name is Nate Murphy of the New York Evening Tribune. I have to ask, are you looking for a job? Because I

17

think you'd be a great columnist. Not sure about writing books, but you got potential."

"Yeah. Yeah, sure."

"Great. You have a name?"

"Yeah, Miller. Nathan Miller, I mean."

"When can you start? I've got some deadlines and have a few people out sick, but I was in the market for a new hire, saw you, and figured what the hell. I'm not opposed to taking risks on new talent. So don't disappoint me. Opportunities like this don't come along often. Fact is they rarely do."

"Don't worry. Tell me what you need and when you need it."

"Don't you want to know what the job pays?"

"Mr. Murphy…"

"Call me Nate."

"Okay, Nate. I'm barely making it with a wife and three kids. How much less can it be than I already make?"

"I like your attitude. And, it won't be much, but who knows, if you play your cards right and keep your nose to the grindstone, you might be the next Ernest Hemingway from Oak Park, Illinois."

Five

The job at the Tribune didn't last long because Nate Murphy found something better at World News Network (WNN) as their managing director. Without hesitation or solicitation, I followed the man that gave me my big break. Soon, Vanessa and the kids were eating better.

I didn't mind the drudgery of writing columns about politics and corruption (or peas and carrots as I liked to quip). It was nice having a steady paycheck. But I craved something more. Adventure. To be like the real Hemingway. Gellhorn. Murrow. Cronkite. Capa. I could go on. I wanted to be in the field. Smell the acrid smoke and feel the ground rumble. Feel the rush of danger while I irrationally believed I was indestructible. What can I say? I was still relatively young and foolish. But I also believed I could tell a story, yet I hadn't finished Frank's tale, though I had many dusty starts. He was the greatest man I would ever know. I just couldn't find the words to do him justice for the pieces ripped from his soul and left behind in the jungles of Vietnam.

Nate saw that I was restless and called me into his office one day and offered me my first assignment. I would be heading to Bosnia where the war was winding down after three years of conflict and ethnic cleansing. I would be covering a newly uncovered Orthodox Serbian-led genocide in Rajza Vjernika where an estimated eight thousand Muslim Bosnians—men, women, and children—had been systematically taken to a field outside town, executed, and left for the carrion. Some women were allowed to live but all had been brutally raped. It was definitely a case of *be careful what you ask for*, but I believed I was ready.

A few weeks before Nate called me into his office, I pulled strings to bring Travis Wright aboard as a camera operator for the evening news. He and Candy now had a few kids and were living in Queens. The timing couldn't have been better since there was no one in this reality I'd rather have as my wingman for my Hemingway pipedream that was about to come true.

19

When we arrived outside Sarajevo, Travis and I were greeted by local journalist, Gavrilo Haus, who was one of the few survivors of genocidal slaughter outside his hometown. I'll never forget the first sight of Rajza Vjernika's war-torn streets. Lying in the middle of the main road was an older man and his three sons (young adult, teen, and child). They were lined up side to side. Each wore a red fez, a white long-sleeve dry-crimson-stained shirt, and a black vest and pants. Their skin was as gray as the clouds above. The mother was on her side nearby with a 9 mm socket in her forehead above hazy eyes. Covering her hair was a blood-stained white headscarf. She wore a splattered white blouse, an ankle-length red skirt, and a belt with four gold bands on white cloth covered with small blue flowers. In her arms was a baby wrapped in a blue blanket gripping a cloth doll. It was nestled to one of the woman's bosoms in a vain attempt to suckle before death.

A wild dog wandered up and began feeding on the empty shell of the youngest boy. Gavrilo (or Gavin as he liked to be called) pulled his pistol and shot the famished tri-color in the head. It crumpled to the ground with its chin resting on the boy's leg as if it were his loyal companion.

The day before, Gavin told me his story up to the place he was taking us. The place was something he said we needed to see for ourselves. He was a Muslim like most Bosnians, but his father gave him a Serbian name to protect him from his grandfather's checkered past during World War II. When Serbs began using the cover of war to settle old scores with their hated Muslim neighbors, his grandfather, Ahmed Hasanagic, volunteered for the Thirteenth Waffen Mountain Division of the SS Handschar. The SS Division, comprised of Bosnian Muslims and Croatian Catholics, was named for a local fighting knife Ottoman police carried during centuries of occupation. The brutality of the Thirteenth was legendary, so much so that the regular SS ordered them to tone it down a bit.

After World War II, Gavin's ancient country was carelessly lumped with Serbia and became Yugoslavia under the communist dictator Josip Broz Tito. Tito purged state enemies, but somehow Ahmed avoided detection, and his family survived to face the 1995 genocide. Only Gavin remained.

We walked to the local hotel. Gavin showed me where his sisters, female cousins, and many others had been raped and/or killed by Serbs. From there, we drove to a field of decaying corpses outside town. The sickly-sweet smell of mass decomposition is something you can't forget. I bent over and vomited. I was embarrassed but Gavin didn't bat an eye. Travis was focused on capturing every detail to do his part so the world would never forget what happened there. Crows flocked and picked at the dead. One had an eyeball in its beak and dodged its head as another murder member attempted to steal the precious morsel.

Gavin spoke with an accent in a raspy, thready, heartbroken tone. "Nathan, this is where I crawled from after it happened. I had been reporting from Sarajevo during Serbia's non-stop bombing. I heard a rumor that Arkan's Tigers were roaming the countryside, killing every man, and raping every woman they encountered. When I heard they had been sighted near my village, I left Sarajevo to make sure my family was safe. They stormed into town shortly after I arrived and found me at my father's house. They raped my mother and sister in front of me, then shot my mother in the chest and dragged my sister away."

I stood silently, listening as I gazed over the killing field. I thought about the man who ordered this atrocity, Zeljko Raznatovic, or Arkan, as he was better known. He was the commander of a black

21

beret-wearing paramilitary group called the Arkan's Tigers. He carried out ethnic cleansing with the blessing of president and war criminal, Slobodan Milosevic. Arkan never faced trial for his crimes thanks to bullets from an assassin's CZ-99 pistol. But most of his Tigers and those responsible for the genocide escaped justice, and those who didn't escape received slap-on-the-wrist sentences. Serbians hailed them as heroes and allowed them to prowl amongst their victims long after the bodies had been cleared from the field outside Gavin's village.

Gavin continued. "They separated the men from the women and shoved us into army trucks. Anyone who resisted was shot or tortured for fun and left to die. We all knew we would not live to see another dawn, but most of us still climbed in the trucks like lambs to be slaughtered. I was one of them since I wanted to be with my father, who had just watched my beloved mother ravaged and murdered. When we arrived at the field, we were pulled from the trucks in groups of ten or twenty or more at a time. We listened to repetitive cracks of machine pistols rip through the air and prayed to Allah and the prophet Muhammed for mercy in the afterlife. Then they came to our truck. My father continued praying as they walked us into the field already lined with rows of my relatives and neighbors. Right there. That is where I was." Gavin pointed a trembling finger. His face was contorted in too many layers of grief to untangle.

In the middle of the field, amidst twisted, decaying bodies, my eyes centered on a man dressed like the father I'd seen in the street earlier.

"They fired and somehow missed me. I fell with the other bodies like I was dead. I breathed as shallow as I could or held my breath until my lungs screamed for air. Then several of Arkan's Tigers began walking the rows, adding an extra bullet to each corpse. After they shot my father again and spat on him, I felt cold steel pressed against the back of my head. I prayed to Allah one last time, and my prayers were answered. The machine pistol jammed. My would-be-murderer lifted the gun from my head, and it exploded in his hand. The Tiger screamed in Serbian, '*My eyes, my eyes.*' How this happened, I do not know. I only praise Allah for his infinite mercy as I grieve the loss of my family, whom I hope to see in Paradise. Another Tiger took the wounded one's place and continued his grisly work but skipped me and shot my brother again. I lay there with my father, brother, and others for hours until I was sure the Tigers were gone. Then I hiked back to Sarajevo."

Travis panned the scene and captured more than I needed while I looked at the bodies and faces around me. I forced myself not to gag as I cataloged every nuance, smell, and taste in the air. I listened to silence broken by a flock of quacking mallards above. I heard the nearby rippling river where more bodies had been dumped. I watched carrion feed and maggots reclaiming flesh as flies swarmed around.

I made a cut motion, breathed deeply, and regretted it as I wiped tears from cracks in my objectivity. The cracks grew. I looked at Gavin's wet cheeks and swollen eyes. The dam crumbled and floodwaters gushed from my eyes, becoming rolling sobs. That's when I saw him again—the Man in Black with the cobalt blue eyes from the Harrisburg County Fair. Memories of the hazel-eyed girl compounded my grief. The question, *Why me?*, echoed in my mind.

I pointed and said, "Do you see what I'm seeing?"

"Other than the obvious, what?" asked Travis.

"The Man in Black."

23

"You okay? I… I don't see anything."

"What do you mean? He's standing right there across the field. Plain as day. You see him, don't you, Gavin?"

"No, I don't," he said, looking confused.

"Nathan, seriously, are you okay? 'Cause I don't see a thing."

"No. I'm not okay. How can anyone be okay with this shit?" I wiped my eyes and looked again. The Man in Black was gone. "Yeah, maybe I am losing it. Seeing things. Brother, I don't know if I'm cut out for this."

Travis put his arm on my shoulder. "You are. And the fact that you feel it like you do will help you tell the world about it." That was the moment my first book was born.

Six

Two years later, I was at my first book signing. A small line stood in front of me. A heavyset white man with thick glasses handed me my first book to sign. I opened the cover of *Ghosts of Bosnia* and signed a nearly legible *N Miller* on the title page. The man told me the book was moving—possibly the best he had ever read. The words were much appreciated by the insecure author.

While my face on WNN helped sales, the story didn't take the world by storm as I thought it would. The only change in my life was that I could move Vanessa and the kids into something respectable that didn't require sharing our living space with rats. I also began seeing the Man in Black on almost every assignment, always before something terrible happened. And every time, Travis and I dodged the Reaper's cold hands without a scratch.

I stopped mentioning the sightings after the first few since Travis, for whatever reason, couldn't see the Johnny-Cash-wannabe. I accepted my imaginary friend as our dark guardian angel. Of course, being that my friend seemed so real, I would often think about my *Interview with Death*. I was now the war correspondent with a growing reputation for my hard-hitting pieces and a respectable book under my belt. Some people even compared me to Hemingway and other greats who I worshipped and wished to emulate. So, I carried the original *A+/Wow* rated paper everywhere and would go through the questions I asked then and imagine new answers. *Insane*, I thought, at least I did then.

A few years and another book later, *Ghosts of Bosnia* caught the attention of one notable person—a rising Three-Star General named Cornelius Adamson, who had recently become head of Special Operations Command (SOCOM). After reading my debut about Gavrilo Haus's family, he invited me to the Pentagon to discuss a project he had in mind. The General knew my life story and my uncle's. He invited Frank to come along, but he wasn't interested. My uncle knew Cornelius from Vietnam and warned me not to trust the snake. I believed I knew better. I guess my better angels were blindfolded by what the General could do for my career and the access such an ally would provide.

I flew to D.C. the next week. Adamson greeted me at the Pentagon with an iron handshake. He walked me through security, asked about my flight, and made other small talk on the way to his office. The General was a cliché gray-haired balding Patton with a pockmarked granite face. I thought him incapable of cracking a grin but he soon proved me wrong. His voice was commanding and charismatic but sounded like he regularly chewed glass and gargled with gravel or was a chronic cigar smoker. From the smell of his office, I went with the latter.

His office blinds were open with a view of the Potomac, Jefferson Memorial, and the monuments beyond. Adamson beckoned for me to sit, and we spent the next hour discussing his idea for a docudrama that would showcase the Seventy-Fifth Airborne Regiment. It would be called *Berets*. All that was lacking now was a war, and on September 11, 2001, we got what the show needed to assure its success, my eternal fame, and the infamy that would follow me into the Afterworld.

Seven

I was intrigued by the prospect of a docudrama about the Green Berets, even if they were wearing brown ones now. By 2001, Travis and I were ready to get started. The only thing that concerned Nate was that the series might detract from my commitments to WNN.

General Adamson kept delaying the start date, saying the timing wasn't right. He could never find time to arrange a second meeting to discuss the finer details of the series. We had the go-ahead from Home Cinema, but the General kept putting us off. By September, I'd put the project on the back burner while working on my third book. Then came the second Tuesday, and the world changed.

I was sitting at my desk when I heard an explosion south of us. I looked up at the clock on the wall. It read 8:49 a.m. (my clock was three minutes fast). Nate ran down the hall to my office yelling, "Nathan, come quick. You gotta see this."

26

I ran with Nate and soon-to-be-legendary reporter, Julie Florid, to a south window where smoke could be seen billowing from the World Trade Center's North Tower. Everyone was packed against the window. If the building were a boat, it would've capsized. Then the phones started ringing. Everyone was in shock. I thought about the 1993 World Trade Center bombing but dismissed the thought. Like many people, I believed a plane had veered off course. It made no sense until the second plane hit the South Tower seventeen minutes later.

With everything I've seen in the Afterworld, the Realities, and all points in between, the memory of that day is sometimes too much. It was a collective trauma that removed a false sense of security for those who experienced it in my reality and any others with similar timelines. It was one hundred and two minutes that no one could forget. And like every other network, WNN stoked the public's PTSD with reruns of the sucker punches to once-proud towers.

Nate told me and others to head south to cover the events from the ground, but nothing was moving. Everyone outside was looking up at the burning buildings as sirens blared, and first responders crawled toward their date with destiny and death.

That's when I got the call from the General. He simply said, "We need to meet ASAP. We're going to war." Then there was an explosion, static, and the line went dead. It was 9:37 a.m. (according to my phone).

After that, it was a while before anyone got any calls out of Manhattan. I hoofed it with Julie as Travis straggled behind, frequently stopping to capture footage. We were getting close when we saw the South Tower begin to crumble.

We stopped, and Julie said, "Oh my God." She started crying. Her sister-in-law worked in the North Tower, and her nephew was in the daycare. She had tried to call before leaving WNN, but her sister didn't answer.

Travis tried to steady his hands for the camera, but he was shaking. His eyes were red, tears streaming. Then a massive dust cloud came our way. Everyone turned and ran north as fast as they could until we were consumed by the gray. When we could see again, we were covered head to toe with what looked like volcanic ash. Our tears made a muddy paste on our cheeks.

Twenty-nine minutes later, we watched the North Tower fall from a safe distance. It felt like the world stopped turning. Like it was… like it was the end of everything. I've seen so many horrible things in my life, before and since that day, but somehow it will always be like an infected wound that never heals. They never found Julie's sister-in-law or her nephew. And like her and everyone else in Manhattan (and many other places), many lost friends and family or knew someone who did.

A week later, Travis and I were on our way to the Pentagon for a pre-production meeting with General Adamson. When I arrived, we were greeted by Marine Corporal Maynard Coltrane. After passing through tight security, he showed us the damaged area. His lips trembled ever so slightly and his eyes misted.

Barely contained fury steadied his speech as he said, "One-hundred-twenty-five lives were lost here not to mention the sixty-four abroad American Airlines Flight 77, counting those Goddamn raghead, sand-monkey motherfuckers. Hope they get syphilis from their seventy-two hookers. We lost good people here, and I lost my best friend, Lindon Fuller. I can't wait to get over there and send more of those cocksuckers to Allah."

"I'm sorry for your loss. I really am," I said as Travis sympathetically nodded.

"Yeah. You know. *You know*. You two were there in New York, I hear."

"Yeah. Yeah, we were," I said, licking and chewing my lips to keep from losing it over Julie Florid's sister and nephew and many more.

Coltrane nodded, patted my shoulder, and escorted us to General Adamson's office. He knocked.

"You may enter," said the General.

Coltrane opened the door.

The General popped up and to attention like I had four stars. He moved swiftly and extended his hand for an over-the-top iron-grip handshake that almost broke something. "Nathan Miller. Welcome. It is an honor to have you here in my office again. I really enjoyed your latest. Just finished it. Gut-wrenching. But then I am somewhat of a gushing fan. Corporal Coltrane, leave us."

"Yes sir, General sir," he said, saluting as he snapped to attention. He left.

Adamson offered a Cuban to Travis and me.

"No, thank you. I'm not a smoker," I said as Travis accepted.

The General chuckled. "Your loss," he said as he lit Travis's cigar with a gold plated Zippo with a bald eagle emblazoned on the front. On the opposite side was a beveled platinum ankh with two crosses rather than the usual single.

Travis puffed. "This is good. Thank you."

"You better believe it is, and you are so welcome." The General fired up, pulled with contentment, and added to Travis's cloud. He continued, "As you know, this isn't a social call, and what has been done cannot stand and will see quick and decisive retribution. In this kind of war, special operations will play a crucial role, as will the Seventy-Fifth Airborne Regiment and all other special operation groups. I want us to move forward with the docudrama, as we discussed in '99. The enemy will undoubtedly use every means at their disposal to fight us. They are masters at Information Operations, and we need to stay ahead of them by getting out the truth about what our boys are doing over there. I can think of nothing better than popular media and a trusted face like yours to get the word out. I have authorized full access to the airborne training program, and I believe following Ryan Mender's progress would be ideal since everyone knows and loves his mother."

Ryan Mender had grown up in the spot light. His mother was Norine Jasmine Jones, a legendary R&B artist best known for her classic, *Hey Baby, I Love You*. Yet, she was no one hit wonder and had a multitude of Grammy winning singles and albums, not to mention award winning projects with the likes of Aretha Franklin, Johnny Cash, and Paul McCartney. Rarely a day passed when her voice didn't grace the airways on radio stations in multiple somewheres. Many considered her the Queen of R&B and worshipped her as such, but there wasn't a more down to earth megastar who never forgot her Texas roots in the Jim Crow South. That being said, Ryan was raised right, and like many sons (and daughters), famous or otherwise, he put his life on hold, and left his family and privileged existence to answer the call to defend his country like generations before.

I wasn't naïve. I knew Adamson wanted to use *Berets* as a propaganda tool. It was no different than what Ronald Reagan, Frank Capra, and other media members did in World War II. We'd been sucker-punched, like at Pearl Harbor. Like everyone else, I wanted revenge as much as the next guy. Yet, patriotic fervor aside, I was a writer and war correspondent and saw an opportunity to do something groundbreaking that would forever etch my name in Hemingway's hall of fame.

Eight

I arrived at Fort Benning a few weeks after Ryan. Already some of the Ranger hopefuls had dropped out and the shining ones, destined to get their jump wings, were panning out like gold nuggets. Ultimately, it was the General who put together the group for the show's focus with a few that would be cut for dramatic effect.

I had met Norine Jones once after a WNN interview and knew what kind of a person she was. Still, I expected Ryan to be like other celebrity kids I'd met. Spoiled. Self-entitled. No, not Ryan. He was a chip off the ol' Texas block, though his parents lived in Grand Junction, Colorado, and had his entire life. No lie—Norine raised a great kid and refused to let her fame turn him into a little monster.

When Travis and I stepped into the barracks, Ryan was talking to another recruit named Toby Almaraz. Back then, everyone knew Ryan was African American on his mom's side. And while I knew Ryan's father was Native American (a mix of Ute and Navajo), I hadn't dug deep enough to know Ryan had Hispanic roots. As serendipity had it, Toby and Ryan had relatives in San Luis Potosi, Mexico. Even a few of Toby's relatives knew Ryan's grandmother's family.

I stood and Travis filmed as they spoke Mexican Spanish. Ryan showed Toby several photos of Alex, his fuzzy-headed one-year-old, and Suzanne, his Anglo, brunette, emerald-eyed high school knockout and wife. I tell you, Ryan had deep love for those two.

Ryan and Toby looked up and noticed Travis holding his camera, recording the moment. Ryan put away the photos, and the two approached as another recruit named Geno Simmons and a giant named John Smith stepped inside. Toby introduced himself, followed by Ryan, who called John and Geno over to meet us. John introduced himself, and introduced Geno as "the Demon."

Geno was a big guy, but nothing like John who was almost as tall as Kareem Abdul-Jabbar with the mass of Michael Clarke Duncan and a mouth that could make a sailor blush. Geno hailed from the Bronx and John from New Orleans though he didn't have a creole accent. I knew everyone's names and bios since Adamson had provided their files a few days before, but John was a mystery I hoped to crack but never did during the docudrama's run.

The other eight filtered in, perfectly timed, but still appearing natural for cable and satellite TV. There was: Jesus Gonzalez from Gonzales, Texas; Ricky Mendez from Park City, Utah; Thomas Jones from Las Vegas, Nevada; Stan McConnell and Kyle Wheeler from South Park, Colorado, who had lived down the street from each other since they were kids; Riley Jameson from Ovilla, Texas, who was named in honor of a friend of his father killed in WWII when their ship, the U.S.S. Fogg, was hit by a torpedo; Max Iverson from Wilmington, Delaware (or Murder City as he liked to call it); and Benny Roessel, a Navajo from the Nation who had lived his whole life in Window Rock, Arizona.

After introductions, Ryan and I had a chance to talk. It turned out that his wife, Suzanne, was a big fan and had read everything I'd written, including a new book I released the week before 9/11. She said I was the Twenty-First-Century Hemingway.

Travis probably caught my blush as I stuttered and said, "I, I hear your grandfather on your dad's side served in World War II and lost a leg."

"Yeah, he did," said Ryan.

"I can only imagine how proud he would be to see you walking in his footsteps. I read he was among the first commandos who became the nexus for the Seventy-Fifth Ranger Regiment and was the group's only Native American."

Ryan grinned from ear to ear. Had it been lights out in the barracks, no one would've needed a flashlight to see with his glowing pride.

"Yeah. Yeah, he was. Amazing grandpa, too. But hey, I hear your Uncle Frank was a Green Beret in Vietnam…"

And that was the beginning of a beautiful friendship. We spent the rest of the day talking about anything and everything as Travis captured video to edit for the pilot.

Nine

The first episode aired on Saturday, November 3, 2001. News of Anthrax bioterrorism, fear of weaponized Smallpox, and the bombing and stalking of our prey in Afghanistan were frontpage stories in the *New York Times*. The country and the free world were solidly behind President Ethan Cranston, like they hadn't been seen since FDR's infamy speech following Pearl Harbor. Like Ryan, many left their families and jobs and put their lives on hold. They feared for the future and wanted to take the fight to the enemy and wipe them off the face of this earth. I felt like I was doing nothing less. I was emotionally invested and, as such, conned myself into believing I was an objective observer.

Everything went well until midway through the third season. That's when Frank got sick. Before that, Uncle Frank had been on several episodes and was my go-to interview for Seventy-Fifth Airbourne history segments.

I remember the moment Dorothy called me. It was Saturday, February 8, 2003. I was finishing some writing and settling down for an uncomfortable night's sleep outside Kabul, Afghanistan, when my satellite phone rang. Aunt Dorothy was crying and trying to choke out words. The static didn't help, but I understood enough to know that Frank had been admitted to the hospital. When I called back during a layover in Germany, Dorothy told me Frank had been diagnosed with pancreatic cancer. True to form, Frank wouldn't give up. After so many close calls in Vietnam, he wasn't about to let cancer take him down and leave Dorothy to face her last years alone.

The news hit me like a sledgehammer—knocked out my knees. I was alone and crumbled to the ground in my tent and sobbed. I couldn't fathom what would've become of me without Frank and Dorothy, like I couldn't fathom how I'd get up the morning after Frank's last.

While Frank was in the hospital, I took a leave of absence to be with him. Home Cinema aired reruns and home-life episodes scripted by General Adamson to humanize Ryan Mender and the lives of the other Rangers. It also captured crumbling lives and the demise of a few marriages for ratings. All the while, Dorothy,

Vanessa, me, and the kids rarely left Frank's side as the cancer quickly spread.

Over the coming months, I watched the greatest man I'd ever known waste away before my eyes. Frank insisted on chemotherapy even though the doctors told him his chances for remission were slim to none, and the slim was unreasonably optimistic. In the end, the poisons only added to Frank's suffering as he stubbornly endured the remaining days of his life. The doctors finally told Dorothy that there was nothing more they could do. That's when Frank gave in to the inevitable.

We brought him home for his final week, where he drifted into an opioid delirium before passing away in his rocking chair surrounded by Dorothy, Vanessa, myself, his grandniece, and two grandnephews. I can't imagine a better way for such a wonderful man to go than to be surrounded by the lives of those he so greatly enriched. Dorothy followed her man into the ever-after three months later.

Ten

Dawn, Tuesday, October 26, 2004. Almawt Lilkifaar, Iraq.

That fall I found myself nervously stroking my graying beard that I'd let grow out after Frank's death. Several people commented that it made me look like an older Hemingway, flattery that I was beginning to let go to my head. I was in a Black Hawk with Travis, Ryan, Toby, John, Jesus, Kyle, and Max, nearing a helipad inside Camp Almawt Lilkifaar. The show's other six stars followed in a second chopper. Moments before this memory, we had a close call

35

when an RPG barely missed our tail. It turned out that a Seal Team Two sniper saved us from catastrophe with a well-placed bullet right as an insurgent fired a rocket.

Ryan was across from me. We had bonded over the past three years. Really bonded. You know, I loved all the guys in the chalk (or stick, which is Ranger lingo for a paratrooper dozen, though we only jumped a few times in Afghanistan). General Adamson picked them well. But Ryan... we were closer than some brothers—maybe closer even than Travis and me.

In 2002 during a series break, Vanessa and I invited Ryan, Suzanne, and little Alex to the Big Apple. I was surprised that they'd never been since Norine Jasmine Jones had played Madison Square Garden to more sold out crowds than I could count—well almost. I put them up in the grand suite of the nearby Plaza Hotel. Alex was a funny toddler—a little clown. He kept Vanessa, me, and our teenagers in stitches. It was recorded by Travis for the show, of course, but I still feel what Ryan and I had was real. Like what Travis and I had. But I've said that. It's not often you find friends like that. And when they're gone... well.

Vanessa and I also visited Grand Junction, Colorado, with Ryan, Suzanne, and Alex (Ryan never wasted leave time away from them, for the show or otherwise). I didn't invite Travis and this trip wasn't for public consumption. While there, we spent time with Norine and James Mender and his horses at their palatial hacienda in the city's most exclusive walled and gated community. When we left Grand Junction with Ryan, Suzanne, and Alex, the first place they took us was Packer City, the most remote town in Colorado, rich with lore from the late nineteenth century gold rush. Ryan loved that town. *Really loved* that town. Mostly because his grandfather *really* loved that town and Ryan *absolutely* worshipped his Grandpa Edwin.

Packer City was also home to a close family friend who was one of Edwin's fellow commandos—a friend who never forgot the man who saved his life for the cost of a leg.

I never got to meet Edwin John Mender. He passed away a few years before 9/11, but I did meet his war buddy, Melvin Anderson (or Uncle Mel as Ryan's family lovingly called him). Melvin even agreed to do an interview for the show. Vanessa recorded the meeting.

We met at a local restaurant called *The Prospector*. Great food then but I never got the chance to return after Ryan and Suzanne bought the place and turned it into a Mexican restaurant named in honor of Ryan's grandmother, Maria Consuela Gonzales Mender.

As we talked and I eased into questions, Ryan politely interrupted to add any details Uncle Mel skipped for stories he knew and add memories of his own. During the interview, a bolt of inspiration crashed through the diner's ceiling and hit me with an idea for a next book. It would be called *The Menders: A First American Story*. It would be a non-fiction blockbuster about Ryan's family. It would focus on his paternal side (specifically Ryan's father James's mixed Ute Indian and Mexican heritage). Of course, Norine Jones would be in the story, but there was so much already written about the music legend. And it wasn't necessary to make her the focus since fans would undoubtedly buy the book. After all, her classic hit, *Hey Baby, I Love You*, about love with rough edges, was inspired by James who she first met in D.C. for Martin Luther King's *I Have a Dream* speech.

When I finished the interview with Melvin, I pitched the idea to Ryan. Suzanne and Alex (who was soundly sleeping) were sitting at the next booth. I still remember that boyish grin growing into a gap-toothed smile. He didn't cry but I could tell he wanted to. Suzanne looked at Melvin who looked equally choked up. Both nodded their approval. Suzanne grabbed Ryan's hand and looked at him with those emerald eyes that could almost stop a heart, like Vanessa's almost did mine at the Penn State Halloween party all those years ago. And they still did at that moment when I caught my camerawoman's eyes and her heart-warmed grin. Vanessa was savoring the moment as much as I was.

"Yeah. Hell yeah. Let's do it," said Ryan. "We can start now if you want." And we did.

The Menders: A First American Story was released on January 10, 2003, which was Ryan and Suzanne's fourth anniversary and would've been Edwin's Seventy-Fifth birthday. It was dedicated to Ryan's grandparents and to all of their ancestors.

The book was my breakout and went straight to the top of the New York Times best seller list and was highlighted on the Oprah Winfrey Show a few weeks later. Everyone in the audience got a signed copy. By the time I was approaching the landing pad in that ancient Iraqi city, the book had sold over five million copies and had not slipped from the New York Times' number one spot since it was released. That was no small achievement since Hemingway's *For Whom the Bell Tolls* only sold seventy-five thousand units in its first year.

Eleven

The Blackhawk dropped us at the base. Ryan regarded me as we stepped away. He placed a hand on my shoulder. "You good? That was a close one, brother."

"Yeah. No shit."

He could tell I was shaken. I thought I was hiding it well, but he could always see right through me when others couldn't. At least, he couldn't read minds because the near miss was the least of my worries. Uncle Frank had been right about General Adamson. He was a special kind of cobra with slow acting venom that poisons the soul. It started with little compromises for the sake of the show to keep ratings booming, which had now begun to sag. After Frank died and before Dorothy's fatal stroke, I witnessed an incident in Kirkuk while filming the show that I couldn't explain at the time. The event irrevocably compromised me.

Jesus was leading a fireteam into a two-story school house with Geno, Benny, and Max. Travis and I followed as the other two teams waited to enter. Kurdish militia had the school surrounded to provide additional support.

Intelligence stated that the building was occupied by insurgents who had reoccupied the city after its fall to Kurdish forces in April while I was away helping Dorothy with Frank. These were the last of Abdullah al-Janabi's followers in the area after bloody house to house fighting. What made the operation tricky was that the insurgents had taken Kurdish children hostage to use as human shields. For days, there had been heavy fire from the building, but it was quiet now thanks to the meticulous patience of Seal Team Two snipers. It was now show time. General Adamson ordered Ryan's chalk to move in, hoping to catch a heroic rescue on camera or else find dead, decaying enemies and no children.

Jesus's team tossed in several flash bangs and entered through the back. They found two insurgents curled on the ground in contorted death poses. One had a black hole where there had been an eye. The back of his skull was missing and he was still gripping his AK-47. The other had a hole through his throat. Both insurgents had been dead for a few days and smelled of it. The fireteam moved forward and stepped gingerly looking for booby traps.

The other fireteams followed. Ryan, Riley, Stan, and Kyle cleared the first floor, while John, Toby, Rick, and Thomas checked the second. All they found was more death but no children. Suddenly, Jesus heard faint Kurdish voices crying for help. It was coming from under a dusty gore-soiled Afghan rug at his feet. He pulled up the rug and found a locked cellar door. Geno stepped up and busted the lock. Jesus stepped back with his carbine ready as Geno lifted the door. The Kurdish voices were now unmistakable. Everyone heard them. The children had been left during the insurgents' retreat. The other fireteams took up defensive positions.

Geno grabbed a flash bang from his vest. Jesus grabbed his arm and shook his head *No*. He turned on his carbine's beam and stepped from the dusty light, down the steps into darkness and a short hall that ended with a tunnel. Travis and I were above, watching the video through Jesus's helmet bodycam. The voices got louder as the team moved down the hall toward a meager low-watt light source. Jesus entered the underground room. There in one corner, eight boys sat shrouded in partial shadow, huddled together. They were dressed in traditional white kaftans and matching kufi hats. They couldn't have been older than ten. One rose, followed by the others, revealing faces with eyes squinting into the beams.

The first boy smiled and said, "Bang, bang." The others lifted AK-47s.

"Sweet holy mother," said Jesus as he fired, hitting the boy between the eyes.

Geno, Benny, and Max put down the others.

"Holy fuck," said Travis. "Why... why'd they fire?"

I looked at the screen again and the eight boys were sitting against the wall, toppled against each other, bloodied, tied up, and gagged. I didn't see any rifles. They looked as if they'd been executed.

"W-what? How?" I glanced out the window and saw the Man in Black. I looked back at the screen and outside again. My dark angel was gone. *Why the fuck me?* I thought.

I know what I saw and what Jesus's fireteam saw. But the video didn't lie. The strange thing is, everyone heard the boys' voices but we couldn't have. Their mouths were gagged. I wasn't going mad. At least, I didn't think so. I wasn't the only witness, but that didn't matter to the General. He was furious. The Kurds at the scene were angry and needed a sacrificial lamb to quell their fury. It would be the end of *Berets*. But I didn't care about that. Okay, maybe a little at first, but I was more worried about Jesus, Geno, Benny, and Max, who would be court marshalled, dishonorably discharged, and forever stained with the massacre of eight Muslim boys. The international outcry was a given. And how many more people would needlessly die from potential collateral damage from extremists and recruiting videos that would take full advantage of the massacre?

Adamson agreed with my assessment and made the video disappear. And though the Kurds were angry, there was never another word spoken of the incident. After we left the scene, I learned Army investigators found the eight boys in the tunnel, unbound and ungagged with seven either gripping AK-47s or laying near a rifle like the fireteam and I had seen in real time.

A few days later, the Kurds at the scene were killed by a massive IED (Improvised Explosive Device) that took out their headquarters. Without eye witnesses, rumors of the incident became hearsay and was discounted as enemy propaganda. I know for a fact it wasn't Ryan's men who altered the scene, but contractually I couldn't say anything and if I did these men who'd become my brothers would be convicted in the court of public opinion based on my reputation. Travis was sick and threatened to leave the show, but I talked him down. That week, *Berets* was a rerun from season two that ended with a dedication to Uncle Frank. It twisted the knife. Yet, I now trusted the snake Frank had warned me about. My faith was unwavering that Adamson would protect my brothers and ensure that they left this hell alive and go on to enjoy healthy productive lives despite the scars.

Twelve

The General had tried to minimize the danger, which was almost impossible with body bags being sent home daily. Still, I feared every made-for-TV mission would be one or more of my Rangers' last. But somehow we pulled through every tight scrape.

The worst was when Ryan took a bullet to his right arm. A Ranger from another chalk near him wasn't so lucky and was shot in the head and killed instantly. When Ryan's wound healed, he covered it in Ranger fashion with a tattoo of a tan beret-wearing skull with the bullet scar centered on the forehead. He added the initials, *RGW*, below the skull in honor of the fallen soldier. Even with the close escape, ratings were sliding and rumors swirled that the show was fake. It was as if the public was bloodthirsty to see one of these boys killed for dramatic effect.

I know Frank would've been ashamed of the deals I made with Adamson. By the time I stepped off that Black Hawk, I was so deep I felt like I was drowning in the bullshit that aired every week, which the public ate up until after Frank died. Now, the Romans were restless and wanted more gore from their war. A growing majority wanted a reason to end the quagmire that developed after Cranston's premature victory ejaculation following the fall of Baghdad that sent Iraqi President Saddam Hussein running like a rabbit into a hidey hole. They wanted it over in one big bang, but that's not how war usually goes. And the last time it did, my reality and those with similar timelines were left with the terrifying specter of worldwide nuclear annihilation.

Ryan didn't know the half of it. He knew the massacre was covered up and that Jesus, Geno, Benny, and Max weren't the same after that day. Yeah, he sensed there was more, far more, and it strained our friendship. But full disclosure wasn't an option, since I knew how he'd take it if he knew the inner workings of the show. It was important that he didn't so the chalk's reactions would be believable with words unscripted. I also knew what kind of man Ryan was. He would've called bullshit on the whole deal. Fuck the General, who he couldn't stand, though he was a good soldier, knew how to follow orders, and respected the hierarchy. Again, my only concern was pulling strings to get these guys home in one piece. Suzanne worried about Ryan every day. Vanessa was a good woman like her and did the same for me. Ryan and I spoke about it often, and it was killing him being away from Suzanne and Alex. I just had to get these guys through the next ten months, but Ryan and others were facing one of the most dangerous fights of the war in a city where every home was a fortress. Urban warfare at its grisliest and it'd already cost many American lives.

The General assured me the way would be cleared for the show when our guys took the hospital towering over the infamous Bridge of Death. The hospital had served as a Wahabi stronghold the year before and was the source of our revenge lust. Capturing it for the General and allowing him to strut in and establish his base of operations would be his crowning achievement.

Thirteen

We passed a checkpoint and approached the General's sandbag bunker. The General stepped from his tent to greet us. Corporal Coltrane was by his side with two Army Privates flanking the entrance like Praetorian guards.

"How was your flight?" asked Adamson.

"Good, except for that close call. Nearly shat myself. I wanna hug that sniper."

Adamson broke his granite pock-marked aspect and smiled. "Ahh, that's nothing for you, Nathan. You have a luck bubble around you. You're indestructible."

I scoffed. "Yeah, until that bubble pops, and my luck runs out."

Adamson chuckled. "I'm not too worried. You seem to have a guardian angel. Let's get you inside and talk about the operation. Sand monkeys have been probing our defenses. RPG got through last week. Fortunately, no one was hurt, but I don't want you staying outside too long to challenge my theory about you. Mender, Smith,

Almaraz, Coltrane, come with us. The rest of you fall out. Private Filch will show you to your tents."

The Private stiffened to attention with a crisp salute. "Yes sir, General sir." The uninvited followed the Private.

Travis kept the video rolling as we entered the bunker. A city map was spread on a table in Adamson's command center. Our target was circled with a line drawn from our current location along the path we would take.

"Nathan, you've met Corporal Maynard Coltrane. Corporal, fill them in on the details."

"Yes, sir, General, sir. Mine clearers and bulldozers are working on our path as we speak. Also, night owls continue to soften the pathway. My Marines are cleaning up house by house, but the hospital will require a finer touch. We need your chalk to clear the building without causing any civilian casualties these ragheads can exploit on Aljazeera or the internet. Obviously, we couldn't drop you in," Coltrane said, addressing Ryan. "But once we're close, we'll need you and your men to infiltrate and clear the building. It should be a fairly clean op. My boys haven't detected much activity in the blocks they've cleared. We think the rats went deeper into the city and are massing to unleash hell later. Regardless of how secure everything seems, you'll be part of the forward convoy with two units of my Marines. We'll be riding in three LAV 25s. Your men will be split between three M2 Bradleys. Once the hospital is clear, the rest of the convoy will move in and set up a forward base of operations."

Ryan asked, "General, sir, why don't you use SEALs?"

"We could do that, but we've already lost two AAVs (Amphibian Assault Vehicles) and twelve sailors trying to secure that route.

Overground, block by block, is the only way this city will fall. Then Uncle Sam and everyone else who watched the slaughter last year can sit back and eat popcorn as they witness those raghead bastards getting their payback."

"All right, I'll brief my men," said Ryan.

"Good. We move out at 0600 tomorrow," said the General. "Get some rest. That's an order."

Fourteen

That night, AC-130s continued their nasty work with a *BURRRR, BUMP, BUMP, BUMP, BURRRR, BUMP, BUMP, BUMP,* followed by massive explosions that shook the bunker and my bed. It was the sound of destruction and death for anything above ground or immediately under. With each lethal eruption, I felt better about the next morning, even though none of us slept more than a wink.

We were up at 0500. I ate quickly, but as I got up to clear my tray, I saw my old friend, the Man in Black, sitting with a group of soldiers like he was part of the conversation. He was staring at me with those mystical blues. I rubbed my eyes and he was gone. I needed sleep. I knew I needed sleep. I wasn't about to say anything to Travis who was sitting across from me. I had mentioned some time back that I was still seeing the Man in Black. He thought I was crazy, but that was the day Ryan took a bullet in the arm and the other Ranger took one in the head. Yeah, he didn't think I was so crazy after that and believed my sightings were bad omens. And that was coming from someone who'd never been superstitious or believed in omens. It was also before he reflected on our earlier

46

conversation and previous instances when I confided immediately before more uniformed Americans were sent home in body bags. Of course, I saw my odd Grim Reaper anytime someone was going to die, which was almost a daily occurrence. I studied the varied expressions on the soldiers who'd been sitting next to Death and wondered which of them would die that day.

We piled into our Bradley and the convoy moved out at 0600. I was in the rear vehicle with Travis, Ryan, John, Toby, and Kyle. Jesus, Ricky, Geno "The Demon", Benny, Maynard, and another Marine were in the middle Bradley with Stan, Riley, Thomas, Max, and two other Marines in the lead. Everything moved so quickly that I never got the names of our Bradley's crew, but they were young and tense with no-nonsense and *ready-to-fuck-shit-up* aspects.

It was two miles to the hospital, but the path was tortuous after the AC130 bombing and further block obliteration by MICLICs (Mine Clearing Line Charges) that set off chains of IEDs. Only bulldozers made the way passable.

As we continued, we came to a block that appeared curiously unscathed. I couldn't see anything, but the gunner thought it odd that there was only evidence of small arms skirmishes. The driver told him not to worry since the Marines had cleared the area the day before. His reassurance didn't stop my twisting uncertainty.

Ryan looked at me. He saw through my act, nodded, and gave me a *don't-worry* grin. As the packed Bradley lumbered down the street, Toby told another joke. Other than Toby, everyone was as quiet as the street outside. Too quiet. Toby said something about three hookers and a pimp. I didn't catch the punchline. I was distracted by the thought of the Man in Black's earlier appearance. Was my old companion leading the convoy like the band conductor in a black parade? Or was it someone else? Or was I slipping? No. Who, or whatever it was, was close. And it was never a good sign.

The Bradley was already uncomfortably warm, and the sun had barely risen. This wasn't my first ride inside these steel cans, but it felt more claustrophobic than usual between the heat, the ingrained sweat smell, and the inability to see outside.

I smiled at Travis with eyes that screamed it was fake. My finger tapping gave me away. Travis nodded back. No smile. Just his usual *let's-get-this-done* expression. His camera rolled, catching anything he could edit for this week's episode. Hair poked from my helmet and dripped like a downpour. Sweat poured down Travis's face, like everyone else's, who looked just as uncomfortable in the mobile oven. I wiped my forehead. Something didn't feel right. God, something didn't feel right.

The gunner commented that the next section looked a little less livable. I breathed easier, but my gut told me we weren't in the clear. I wished I could see outside, not that it would do any good. The gunner said the lead Bradley had the bridge and the hospital in sight.

John let out a "Booyah, virgin-fuckers, you'll be seeing yo' muthafuckin' Allah soon."

Toby gave him a hard fist bump.

Ryan and Kyle shot them a deadly smile as the driver and gunner said, "Hell yeah!"

Travis and I cracked a nervous grin. What was I worried about? We were almost there. I chuckled lightly as Travis panned the camera to me. Ryan, Toby, and John glanced my way. I nodded, and they nodded back. It was going smoothly, just as the General

48

promised. He'd assured me it'd be a quick photo op, payback for my access. *What the fuck am I doing?* I thought.

But this wasn't my first rodeo. *Stay calm*, I told myself. I took another breath. *The General has our back*, the voice in my head said. He always did even if he was a *slimy motherfucker* (as Ryan called him), but I couldn't throw stones from the house where I lived then. I told myself that the viewers wouldn't know that Adamson orchestrated everything for maximum ratings. But I knew. I fucking knew and I couldn't stand it. I had become everything I started out not to be and it gnawed at me.

I pushed my anxiety down and reminded myself, *I'm Nathan Miller. What am I worried about?* But oh, I felt sick, like I might vomit. Ryan trusted me. He'd confided in me. I owed Ryan and his family so much, and now I had lied to him. What was I thinking? I *had* lied to him. This wasn't the first time and I knew he would never forgive me if he found out this time. And then I felt the presence again, stronger than before. I knew something wasn't right.

"Hey, what's that up ahead?" the gunner said with a subtle drawl.

"What?" asked the driver.

"Those SUVs. Why're they sitting there? Oh shit! Umph!" the gunner said as AK-47 fire erupted around us and metal clanged off the vehicle's shell.

The gunner slumped, and blood drained into the Bradley from his head above my sight line. I heard the rev of more than one truck engine, felt the impact, then **KA-BOOOOOOMMMMMM-BOOM-BOOM.**

Fifteen

We tumbled in slow motion as our heavily armored tin can left the ground, flipped at least twice, and landed upside down. All I heard was ringing, but the six of us were still alive. Ryan crawled forward to check on the driver and co-pilot. They were dead, and all of us were bleeding. The bubble had popped. My luck had run out.

When the ringing stopped, AK fire rained from all directions. RPGs exploded outside, then another major explosion spun and up-sided the Bradley. Ryan grabbed the M249 SAW (Squad Automatic Weapon) and opened the back door and began firing. Before our eyes adjusted, several insurgents lay dead, and more were falling. Bullets clanged and ricocheted off the Bradley, but none hit Ryan.

"Head for cover in that building through the courtyard. I'll cover," said Ryan, pointing to the left. He stepped from the Bradley as bullets seemed to bend around him and away from us, as insurgents fell like training targets.

We passed through the courtyard and into the building as Ryan followed. Toby, Kyle, and Giant John ran upstairs.

CRACK-CRACK-CRACK, "Clear," said John.

"Clear," said Kyle.

CRACK-CRACK-CRACK, "Clear," said Toby.

From a window, I saw the Demon carrying Benny while Coltrane covered with his M4 carbine as they ran toward the courtyard. Ryan went to assist.

As the Demon neared the courtyard, his head exploded, showering Ryan with gore. What was left of Geno toppled on Benny.

Coltrane must have caught a glint from where the shot came from because he dead-eyed the sniper with his last round. He swung the rifle around to his back, grabbed his Glock, and covered Ryan as he dragged Benny into the courtyard.

Travis put his camera down and sprinted outside with me. We took Benny from Ryan, and pulled him the rest of the way inside. Ryan laid down cover as Coltrane reloaded his rifle behind the block where he was pinned down. Coltrane glanced at Geno, then ran through the courtyard and into the building. Once inside, Ryan checked on Benny. The Navajo's eyes stared through me as I performed chest compressions to keep his dying pump going.

I stopped, slammed my fist into the ground, and looked at the ceiling. "Goddammit. God fucking dammit," I said, addressing the big man himself.

Ryan helped me to my feet. His eyes were steely, terrifying. "Get upstairs, Nathan," he growled. "There's nothing you can do down here except get yourself or Travis killed."

Grenades fell in the courtyard like green hell, exploding and sending showers of concrete and frag into the wall outside. Insurgents poured into the yard as Ryan dropped the empty SAW and lobbed a concussion grenade. Coltrane followed with a frag.

Ryan readied his rifle behind a wall while Coltrane crouched for cover behind a boarded-up window with a firing gap. The grenades exploded, and Ryan flopped prone in the doorway. Travis and I were already at the top of the stairs. Between rifle fire above and below and a few more grenades, bodies piled up and buried the Demon as they sent more of Abdullah al-Janabi's fighters to Allah.

The cries of "Allahu Akbar" died down in the dusty, body-littered yard. Travis stepped halfway down the stairs and captured the flesh barricade that clogged the courtyard entrance. Several insurgents pushed through the corpses and trickled into the kill zone. All were silenced.

Coltrane broke for the second floor as a fighter entered the KZ. Ryan nailed him with a headshot, muzzling his cries to Allah. He fell, firing, hitting Coltrane in his side and leg, sending him down hard on the steps.

Ryan ran to him.

Kyle yelled, "Raghead rats pourin' from the building 'cross the street."

Ryan sprinted to the courtyard entrance, used the bodies as sandbags, and sent more insurgents flailing and reeling to the bloody road.

Travis let his camera fall to his chest, and ran with me downstairs. We grabbed Coltrane's arms and helped him to the second floor as Ryan returned. As Travis and I worked on Coltrane's wounds, Ryan reloaded his M4 and went prone by the steps.

"Coltrane, what the fuck happened?" Ryan asked with bitter ferocity.

"How the fuck should I know? Way was supposed to be clear."

"Where's everybody else?"

"They're all dead, man. They're all fuckin' dead!"

Ryan's eyes blazed. His hands shook. "Let's move," he said.

"Where to? We're pinned," said Coltrane.

"Nathan, go have Kyle make us a door," said Ryan.

"Okay. Travis, hold pressure to this side wound," I said. He did, and I ran to the room where Kyle was single-firing headshots adding to the carnage in the street.

"Ryan needs a door."

Engineer Kyle Wheeler nodded and pulled off his pack. He rummaged until he found a block of C4 wrapped in cheddar-cheese-colored paper. He grabbed detonators. John, Toby, and Ryan picked off the slowing trickle of insurgents while Kyle unwrapped the dirty white clay explosive. He pinched off globs of just the right amount and stuck them at just the right spots on the second floor's back wall to produce no more than the desired effect. He attached the detonators and set the charges.

"Everyone brace. Big boom coming," he said as he ducked into the next room with John, me, and a dead Arab teen laying on his back. The boy's face was partially covered with a checkered black and white scarf. He was wearing a blue and white polo shirt with a spreading ruby center.

Before Kyle hunkered to the ground, I peeked down the hall. Travis was shielding Coltrane with his body. I took cover.

KABOOM. The building shook.

Kyle went to inspect his handiwork through the cloud of aerosolized concrete. The new door led to the roof, protected by ancient-looking ramparts. Kyle trotted down the hall to check on Coltrane, who had part of Travis's shirt crammed in his side and a belt snugly choking blood to his oozing leg. Travis was recording again. Ryan ran upstairs as John and Toby entered the hall.

"Vamanos! Let's get the fuck out of here," hollered Toby.

Another wave of insurgents tumbled over bodies blocking the courtyard entrance, yelling, "Allahu Akbar."

The four Rangers and the wounded Marine fired, obliterating the frontal assault.

"Muthafuckers will be eating virgin pussy tonight," said Coltrane.

One insurgent who made it into the building pushed himself to his knees with a bleeding arm. He held something in the other hand.

"Ryan!" I yelled as the hand revealed an olive orb.

The insurgent pulled the pin, cried "Allahu Akbar," and lobbed the grenade to the second floor as a hail of bullets finished him off. The grenade landed in the middle of us. Kyle dived on the ball. It exploded, and my ears were ringing again.

Ryan grimaced like he'd taken the blast himself. His eyes glared. His nostrils flared. "Coltrane, can you climb down to the alley?" asked Ryan, shaking his head. He looked at Kyle, then Benny's body. It was buried under insurgents, including the one who killed Kyle.

Coltrane answered, "I can do whatever fuckin' needs doing. Let's get the fuck out of here before the next wave comes. We don't have the ammo to hold these fuckers off before the cavalry arrives. Assume they'll be late, so we better start working our way back to camp. If I can't hump it, I'll cover and kill as many of these sand monkeys as I can before they kill me or I pass out."

Travis was still recording, capturing every gruesome detail.

I felt sick. This was my fault. This was all my fault. I deserved to be dead on the floor where blood seeped beneath Kyle's soon-to-be cold body.

Ryan and I helped Coltrane stand.

He stood on his left leg, then tested the right with a squinting scowl. "I got this." He pushed our hands away and limped alongside Ryan to the roof.

Ryan stopped to dig through Kyle's pack for his nylon rope.

John and Toby laid down cover from the top and middle of the stairs until a bird call told them Coltrane was on the ground. Travis and I headed to the roof in front of John and Toby.

Once there, I fast-crouched to the rope secured to a rampart with a tri-hook. Travis went down first. When his feet hit the ground, he resumed recording. I grabbed the rope and began climbing down. Ryan and Coltrane motioned for me to *hurry-the-fuck-up*. I slid into the blind alley, burning my hands. Toby and John were on the ground in a quarter of the time it took me.

We headed down the alley, then followed Ryan toward camp.

Coltrane willed himself to limp and kept up as we moved from building to building, clearing each, letting Coltrane rest before continuing. As we did, he weakened as he bled. Hours passed in slow motion. Coltrane slowed us as his adrenaline tank ran on empty. His eyes closed intermittently, making him appear to be sleep-limping. His blouse and right pant leg were wet crimson. He was pale. The remaining Rangers tried to lend him a hand, but Coltrane pushed away the Army assist until he collapsed.

"Guys… I ain't gonna make it," Coltrane said in a raspy whisper. "Just leave me here."

"Like fuck we will. I ain't losing another man today," said Ryan. "Get your sorry ass moving, Corporal. Semper Fi, motherfucker!"

Coltrane nodded and stretched his eyelids. He bit his lip, then let out a "Grrrrrr" like a demonic Tony the Tiger. Fire filled his eyes, and color returned to his cheeks. He stood, balanced himself, and moved quickly, peg-legging or dragging his right. The others tried to keep up with Coltrane until we saw tan fatigues. We doubled-timed it toward base.

A shot rang out. Toby fell to the ground. Another followed, and Giant John crumpled nearby. Several shots answered, and then there was silence.

Sixteen

I sat for hours in a gray metal folding chair in Adamson's office. I was furious, twisted with unrelenting grief and guilt. I wanted to kill him—let everything be damned. Adamson swore everything was set for a safe, made-for-television operation. Now everything I'd done to keep these men safe had gone to shit, and I was party to a massacre of nine men I'd grown to love, not to mention almost everyone else in the convoy, many of whom had had their last meal with the Man in Black. Coltrane would pull through, but Toby and John's lives hung in the balance. Travis and Ryan were at the hospital with John and Toby, and no one knew if they could be stabilized for transfer to Germany. The way it was looking, neither would see dawn.

I wasn't sure what I would do when Adamson finally graced me with his presence. Murder was not out of the question. I looked around the makeshift office and at the elegant mahogany desk and comfortable matching leather chair. Everything perfectly arranged. I looked on Adamson's desk notepad and saw that same strange symbol he had on his Zippo. It was drawn in blue ink—an ankh with a double-cross. Adamson entered.

I spoke at a private volume. "You sonuvabitch. You told me the route was secure. What the fuck happened?"

"I don't exactly know," he said as if I'd asked him why blood is red. "According to satellite images, four SUV VBIEDs (Vehicle-Borne Improvised Explosives) were hidden in light rubble and trash near the bridge. It seems those rat bastards waited until the right moment to deploy them. Oh, and then there were those two mother-of-all-IEDs buried too deep for our MICLICS to clear. That street is just two big craters now. After that, al-Janabi's fighters poured from their holes. Hey, I don't have to tell you that. You were ringside. Hell, you were in the ring. They probably have a network throughout the city that the Marines missed somehow. Just needed to flush them out. Guess we did that. But I didn't expect them to have such a big surprise waiting for us. How you and those in your Bradley survived—well, I'm just thankful you did."

"We didn't all survive, or haven't you heard?"

"Oh, yes. Yes, I have. Coltrane told me about Kyle Wheeler. I will see that he's posthumously awarded the Medal of Honor for his heroic deed and see if I can throw in a few medals for his friend, Stan, and everyone else who died for our country today."

"I'm sure their mothers, fathers, kids, and significant others won't give a shit about your medals when they find out this shouldn't have happened."

"Is that what you're going to report? I think you know very well our non-disclosure agreement won't allow that. Or maybe you should review the fine print of what you signed when I allowed you this opportunity of a lifetime. The Army will not only sue you, but you will go to jail, and I will see that you don't make it out."

"What? What the fuck? You're insane!"

"No. I just know what I want. And I know how to get it. You need to not be so trusting. Too late for that now. Yesss—you can either ride with me or *burn* alone—your choice. You think Ryan will forgive you when he learns your part in this? No. He will fucking rip your throat out… or some other Marine or Ranger will. Yes. You need to sit back and let this play out. The insurgents are already giving me everything I need to win the information war so I can level this city with one big boom."

I couldn't speak as my mind raced. Did Adamson mean a tactical nuke? He did, and I thought, *How did I get myself into this?* Uncle Frank had warned me that Adamson was a snake. Oh, how he warned me. But I didn't listen. I missed my uncle, but I was glad he didn't live to see the day I was bitten. Adamson was right, though. I had little choice except to let his game play out. This would be *Berets'* last episode, then I swore I'd never make a deal with the devil again.

The General peered into my soul and asked, "Do we have a problem, or do we have an understanding?"

I gritted my teeth and nodded.

"Good. Now, get the fuck out of my office. I need to make a call."

Seventeen

I left and headed straight to the hospital, too angry for tears. Toby was barely lucid, his head wrapped in white bandages covering one eye. I grabbed his hand. He gripped it softly, and then the tears came. Travis put an arm around me as Toby let go of my hand. The monitors flatlined and screamed their unsettling heart-piercing buzz. Doctors and nurses pushed us aside and went to work. A few minutes later, Toby was pronounced dead.

Ryan broke down where he was sitting. I wanted to console him but couldn't even look at him. I wanted to die. Just walk outside and put a hole through my temple. But I had Vanessa, Franklin, Jenna, and Jonathan to think about. I had experienced suicides in my life and knew the hole that they left could never be filled. This was something I'd gotten myself into, and when it was over, I would do everything I could to make it right. But I was fooling myself. This could never be made right, not even if I had the power to move Heaven and Earth.

I willed myself to go to Ryan. I sat by him and put an arm over his shoulder. We cried together. I looked at Travis. He returned the glance—his eyes were reflections of mine. The General owned our souls now, and we would live in our private hells from that day forward—meager punishment for what we'd been party to.

John stabilized later that day, and Travis and I left for New York soon after. I slept the whole way. At least, I thought I did, as nightmares of the previous day looped on the screen on the back of my eyelids. I also had a strange dream where I was walking down a hall with many doors, but that was all I could remember.

Eighteen

Friday, October 29, 2004, WNN Headquarters, Manhattan, New York.

When I arrived at the network, hugs and condolences rained down on Travis and me—each twisting the blade. Making eye contact was hard, and Travis wouldn't look at me at all. There'd be no rest for the wicked. Nate Murphy had suggested an interview (if I was up to it) to let the public know what happened. This was my chance. My chance to lose everything and regain my soul. Instead, I sold it to become everything I hated and everything Uncle Frank despised.

My nerves were still frazzled after sleeping thirteen hours on the flight home and more at a Waldorf Astoria following several shots of Jameson and a few Xanax. I didn't want to face the world, much less the mirror. I went to my office, locked the door, and closed the blinds to the news floor. I collapsed in my chair, cupped my face, and rocked back and forth, sobbing.

I wiped my eyes and opened the bottom desk drawer and grabbed the bottle of Lagavulin and the glass next to it. I poured a shot, downed it, refilled, repeat, then poured a third, and sipped. I leaned back in the chair and stared out the sixtieth-floor window at blue sky, fluffy clouds, and the bird shit caking the outside windowsill.

I set the glass down, replaced the bottle, carried my drink to my office bathroom, and looked in the mirror. I downed the fire and set the glass on the counter. The tingling burn and the flush of the rush cleared my mind for a few seconds while I worked on my game face. I rehearsed what I'd say to draw maximum emotion from the viewing public, which would number in the tens of millions or more. I started to punch the wall, stopped, then went ahead and hit it so hard that my knuckle cracked and bled. No doubt, the crash was loud enough to startle heads outside my office. I didn't give a fuck, but I would have to soon enough.

I wanted to call Vanessa, but didn't want to lie to her—at least not yet. I would have to eventually. Like Ryan, how could I ever tell her the truth? She had always been proud of me, and I loved her as dearly now as the first time I saw her at the frat party. Now every thought took me back to Almawt Lilkifaar and the blood on my hands. I took a deep breath and made the call.

"Hello. Is this Nathan?" said Vanessa, her voice, soft and precious.

"Yeah, it's me."

"Are you okay?"

"No, I'm not."

"I am so sorry. I heard everything on the news. There's already promos for this week's episode of *Berets*, warnings and all."

I wasn't informed. I figured Home Cinema would wait until after the election. That's when it dawned on me what the operation was all about. *How could I have been so blind?*

"Nathan, are you there?"

"Yeah. Sorry. My head is all over the place. Nate wants me to give an interview tonight. I need some time. Hell, I feel like I need a padded cell right now. Only Ryan, John, and Travis survived. Everyone else is dead. It… it was supposed to be a simple op. But then we were ambushed. Most who died didn't even have a chance."

"You don't have to talk about it. Just come home when you can. You know I love you, Nathan."

"I love you, too, Vanessa. I don't deserve you, but thanks for lowering your standards to spend your life with me. I just want to hold you right now. See the kids. I wish we were back in Greenwich Village in our shit apartment, fighting kids, asshole neighbors, and all."

"I'll take a pass on the old apartment and our pet rats."

I laughed. "I guess the not-so-good-ol'-days seem rosy at times like this. I'll come home as soon as I can."

"Okay. Stay strong. You're my rock. My indestructible Nathan. Don't crumble on me now. You can do this."

"Yeah. I can. God, I love you. See you soon."

"Love you too until the end of eternity." Vanessa hung up.

I leaned back and quickly forward, found my bottle, and poured a double. I sniffed the smokey liquid, swirled, and sipped.

There was a knock at the door.

"Come in," I hollered.

The knob rattled. "I can't. It is locked," said Gavrilo "Gavin" Haus in his Balkan accent.

Yes, I know. I haven't mentioned Gavin since Bosnia. Probably should've since he'd been my assistant since Nate Murphy agreed to bring him on shortly before 9/11. I felt sorry for him when he called asking for a job saying he wanted to work with the *great Nathan Miller*. So, I figured, why not? You would think we would've been closer since his family's story launched my writing career, but until Almawt Lilkiifaar our relationship was strictly business and I knew little about his personal life outside work.

"Oh, sorry," I said.

I hopped up and unlocked the door.

"Man, I am so sorry about what happened," said Gavin.

"Why are you sorry? Don't be sorry," I said sharply as alcohol buttered my nerves.

Gavin nodded, spread his arms, gave me a man hug, and released me. He nodded and regarded me with those eyes I'd seen before. He spoke in his deep knowing tone, "You have an interview in thirty. Nate gave me these talking points for you to go over. When you are done, let us scram. There is a party on the Upper East Side that will help clear your head."

"Thanks. I appreciate the offer, but I have to head home to Vanessa."

"Yeah. Right. Vanessa. Sit at home. Go over what happened over and over and over. Have a few nightmares like I still have about Bosnia. Cry." Gavin rolled his eyes. "Give her a call. Make something up. I have seen this look before. You need to get your mind off such things. What is done is done. You cannot change what happened, and there will be plenty of time to torture yourself later."

Everything sounds appealing with alcohol. I would make something up. Vanessa would understand. We would have a nice dinner Sunday night for the twenty-fourth anniversary of the night we met. We would laugh about *Smelly Guy*. I would say, "Yo, Vanessa," and we would watch *Rocky* for old times' sake. But that would make me think about Travis, and Travis would make me think about Almawt Lilkifaar. *Okay, maybe not Rocky*, I thought. We would find something else to watch and talk about anything but shop. Avoid having to lie to her any more than I already had.

"Yeah, sure. Why not?" I said.

Gavin shut the door and said, "You look run down. I have something that will perk you up."

"Hey, I don't do that shit."

"Don't knock it. Just a little won't hurt. I can see it in your eyes, and the public will, too. Something deep down that is hurting you more than the loss of your friends."

"Fine. Just a little."

I followed Gavin into the bathroom. He removed a small vial from his pocket, unscrewed the lid, and tapped a little white powder onto his thumb knuckle. He handed me the vial, raised the thumb, and snorted hard. He rubbed his nose as his eyes widened. He nodded, and I did as he had done. Within seconds, my nose stopped burning and my head cleared. I was less concerned with the world around me and felt less dirty about my deal with the General.

"Better?" asked Gavin.

"Much. Thanks, man."

"Okay. Let us go through the questions."

Nineteen

The interview went well. The public ate it up, then Gavin and I went to the party. The rest was a hazy blur.

I woke up with a splitting headache between two knockout blondes and felt like I'd been run over by a truck loaded with guilt. Both women were passed out, and each had a naked leg wrapped around me. I looked toward the window and saw the bare back of a snoring pasty-white brunette wrapped around Gavin as he slept in the recliner. Gavin's face peeked above the woman's shoulders. His lips were curled in a dreamy smile. I gently lifted the legs and squeezed out from between the two prostitutes (at least, I assumed they were prostitutes and pricey ones with artificial extras).

I dragged myself to the restroom, looked in another mirror, and was repulsed. I had never cheated on Vanessa. Yeah, sure, I looked. Who doesn't? But that was it. Vanessa was my goddess, and I worshiped at her altar every morning that I woke up beside her. What happened? What was I becoming? Whatever it was, it was best to avoid mirrors and maybe take a break from my assistant.

I showered, then sniff-checked my clothes. They smelled sickly of alcohol, smoke, and cheap perfume. My light cream casual shirt had several shades of lipstick stains. I called room service to connect me with someone who could bring me something to wear home where I planned to put on the performance of a lifetime. Then I would have to live with what I'd done. Another person I'd screwed over. At least no one was dead this time.

As I waited, buck naked, sitting in a chair next to Gavin and the brunette, I watched the sleeping beauties, then glared at Gavin. He smacked his gums as he nuzzled closer to his whore. I hated him, but I hated myself more. I picked up the remote, turned on WNN, and left it on mute. There was a repeat of my previous night's interview. Emmy worthy. *Probably will even win*, I thought. Then I would give a bullshit speech. Maybe even thank the General for the opportunity of a lifetime. I shook my head.

The next story showed re-run footage that echoed the previous year's failure. Insurgents paraded every intact body outside the hospital, including Max, Thomas, Geno, Benny, and Kyle. Our snipers picked off a few, sending other AK-wielding jihadists scurrying for cover, only to have them quickly return to goad us. What followed next was a pre-recorded satellite feed of the city. It had run live while I was asleep.

I grabbed my phone from the end table. The mailbox was full, and there were more texts than I cared to dig through as jackhammers pounded my head. I turned up the volume enough to hear WNN reporter Kenneth Prattle say something about General Cornelius Adamson's decision for an immediate pullout of all troops in preparation for a final strike to end the situation in the Wahabi hotbed. The efficiency of the withdrawal told me it was preplanned. Like everything else, I was kept out of the loop as I led Ryan and his men into the ambush. No doubt, Adamson was aware the route wasn't clear. I wondered if he'd set it up, even arranged for our convenient getaway. But even for him, that was too sinister to contemplate.

The streets of Almawt Lilkifaar were alive with insurgents firing into the air, taunting us for their victory over the Great Satan as they continued desecrating the bodies we left behind in ways more horrific than the year before. Then there was a bright flash. A mushroom cloud followed as the ancient city was consumed by radioactive fire. When the dust cleared, nothing remained but foundations and debris surrounding the Euphrates and the Bridge of Death, where the hospital once stood.

Once I was dressed, I left Gavin sleeping and slipped out to call a taxi. When I got home, I performed admirably, which Vanessa applauded as she begged for an encore. We made love as blurry images of the night before made it difficult to focus on the goddess I'd dishonored. When I climaxed, I started sobbing. Vanessa held me and comforted me, making the deception slice deeper as I cried on her shoulder. I loved the way she smelled—like lavender and peaches.

That evening the final episode of *Berets* aired. Travis refused to have anything to do with it beyond submitting the footage to Home

Cinema per his contract. They hurried it into production, and the episode received the most viewers of any program in history. It opened with a rerun of horrors on the Bridge of Death the year before, then moved to an overdramatization of the ambush and stand against impossible odds. The episode ended with the nuclear destruction of the ancient city. Again, the public ate it up. Sure, many felt Adamson's reaction was a bit over the top, but the majority was all that mattered (or at least a majority of the electorates).

On Tuesday, November 2, President Ethan Cranston was re-elected in a landslide equal to Ronald Reagan and Franklin D. Roosevelt's best electoral wins. He also received a record 74.6% of the popular vote. Days later, General Cornelius Adamson was promoted to four-star general and named the president's new Chairman of the Joint Chiefs of Staff. I feared the monster I had created and what that maniac had planned.

Twenty

Five and a half years later.

Every night since 2004, I was haunted by strange dreams about Almawt Lilkifaar. Usually, they started in the hall with many doors. Each door opened to distorted versions of events leading to the ambush or the ambush itself. Some would begin pleasantly enough but would morph into the bizarre and macabre before the Sandman released me. And when I wasn't sleepwalking through my personal Hell, I was pounding away on my old Royal Deluxe typewriter in the Greenwich Village apartment, writing about the Battle of

Almawt Lilkifaar. My upstairs neighbor's music would be blaring while the kids were crying and Vanessa was yelling for me to take out the trash. I had a publishing deadline to meet but I could never finish the story.

When I was awake, I drank like the old Frank I never knew. Before Almawt Lilkifaar, I limited drinking to social occasions and rarely got drunk. And when I did, I felt ashamed. After a drunk driver killed my mother and father, Frank made it clear that alcohol, drugs, and "*druggies*" would never be allowed in his home. That's the reason it wasn't until college I drank my first beer. And yeah, I got drunk—*really* drunk sometimes—but I never felt comfortable letting Frank and Dorothy know that I was drinking. They hated it *that* much. I prayed they couldn't see me now. I would often think how much I wished I could've been the man they wanted me to be before I took another sip or long multi-gulping pull.

On Tuesday, May 18, 2010, I was sitting in my office, wallowing in self-pity at our palatial estate in the elite Golden Triangle community of Greenwich, Connecticut. The mansion was quiet and Vanessa was gone like usual when I was home. Our relationship had deteriorated since 2004. I missed the way things had been but couldn't find my way back through that door I closed that night Gavin and I went out. Why she refused to divorce me and take me to the cleaners, I didn't understand. I mean, I'd given her almost every reason.

So, there I sat trying to write something, anything. I don't know how long I stared at the blank page and lonely typewriter keys that begged to be used for what God and Royal designed them for. I leaned back and took another sip of single malt from a bottle that cost more than three months' rent at the old Greenwich Village rat hole. My mind wandered and the alcohol further fed my guilt, regret, and suicidal aspirations.

"Fuck it," I said and ripped the paper out of the typewriter, balled it, and chunked it over my shoulder to add to the pile behind me. I needed inspiration, so I went to my file cabinet to look through old journals. Each was dated on the front from 1972 to the present. I fingered through the last five. There was a lot of blood on those pages.

I sat the journals on the desk next to the typewriter and took a triple pull from the bottle then refilled the glass to drink like a gentleman. I set the bottle down and opened *2005* and began reviewing the blur of life since my *dreams* came true. I read every entry until I got to March.

March 22, 2005. Vanessa's B-day. In Cancun treating her like the queen she be. How I love those gray eyes. Even after twenty years. Breathtaking, baby. Breathtaking. And as I write this, oh, she looks fucking amazing with her beautiful feet in the sand and the smile and tonight eyes shooting at me. May have to speed up this entry and head back to the room before sunset. Can't believe I ever strayed. Just add it to the mountain of excuses for drinking like a fish that Frank would've called bullshit on. At least, I've kept my distance from the new devil on my shoulder. But then again it's been years since Travis was that devil. I do miss the way things were before... Fuck that, not going there. Not today. It was tough firing Gavin. It was nice that he took it in stride. I offered to help him find a new job, but he said he was good. He's something of a professional gambler and said he does okay for himself. Gavin still sends me invites to join him in AC, but after our last night out I've been battling guilt and treating Vanessa extra special. Well, gotta go Dear

Diary. Vanessa is sending me *let's-go* eyes. God, I don't know how I would've made it through the past months without those gray eyes.

April 20, 2005. Very drunk. Thinking of calling Gavin, but I know I shouldn't. Talk about a shitty day. Haven't talked to Ryan in months, not for lack of trying. But after he didn't call back or return my emails or texts, I figured he needed space to deal with what happened. And anyway, what would we talk about? The truth, maybe. Well, that's not a problem anymore. I guess I'll quote how the conversation went.

"Nathan, how ya doin'?" Ryan asked cordially with a bite.

"Good. Thanks for calling. How's…"

"Just shut up. I'm gonna do the talkin'. I spoke with John Smith. You remember John, don't you? Big black muthafucker that could break you like a twig."

"Uh…"

"I said shut your fuckin' mouth. Well, he's still recovering at Walter Reed after our little adventure in Almawt Lilkifaar. He told me something very interesting. And I gotta say, I would've never thought I coulda been taken in by such a shady white snake."

"What are you talking about?"

"John just got a visit from a friend named Martin Rice. Now I know you know John, but I'm not sure you know Martin. Or maybe you do. Nice guy. Navy SEAL. John tells me Martin and his team cleared the hospital the day before the ambush. Even told me Adamson had them leave a few rats for us to kill for your fuckin' show, your fuckin' ratings, and for Adamson's grand entrance. Well, two out of three ain't bad, and now my brothers are dead because of you. Oh, and Adamson is Chairman of the Joint Chiefs of Staff and their blood paid for that extra star on his helmet. So don't ask about Suzanne… or Alex… or how my Mom or Dad are doing. Just don't. You… you need to just go and die. I hate you, you motherfucker. And if… and if I ever see you again, I'll fuckin' end you. You hear me, Nathan Miller… I will… fucking… END YOU."

Yeah. That's how that went.

May 4, 2005. Jenna Renee's birthday. My oldest baby is 18 today. Big crowd at the new Greenwich Estate. Great way to christen the new place in Connecticut. Absolute dream. Everything I ever wanted for Vanessa. Long road for sure and boy did we have our moments. I have to say, this was a killer day especially after Ryan's call last month.

July 4, 2005. Watched coverage of Ryan's Congressional Medal of Honor ceremony on the White House lawn. The original plan was for President Cranston and Adamson to present the medal to Ryan Mender and John Smith, but John didn't come. Ryan did but looked about as happy as he sounded in April for what I'm sure was the last time we'll ever speak. Yeah, Cranston gave a speech and drew applause. Adamson gave his and got a standing O. Then Ryan stepped up to the plate to receive his medal. As Adamson leaned to pin it on his chest, Ryan swung for the fences and connected with the General's jaw. The blow knocked Adamson off the podium and onto his ass. Ryan lunged and straddled the General and pounded his face, punching him several times before six secret service agents could restrain him.

July 24, 2005. Jonathan Christian hit the one-five today. Typical teenage angst. But hey, it was his party, and he can cry if he wants to. I'll be so glad when this phase is over.

I smiled and sipped.

August 09, 2005. Frank Milton turned 21 today. Frank and Jon. Hard to believe they came from the same place. Couldn't be two more opposite eggs. Anyway, we had another nice get together at the Miller Estate. Just one year and four more months and Frank will be out of the Army. I am so proud of that boy. I just wish his namesake was still around for this special day.

September 13, 2005. Nate told me Ryan was discharged. Nate's been friends with his dad for years and has kept me updated since the July 4 incident. Looks like Adamson didn't press any charges. In fact, he's done everything in his power to keep the case from going to trial. At least, he had the decency to do that. That sonuvabitch had it coming. It was glorious to watch live and I've loved the replays that run almost as often as the planes crashing into the Twin Towers and the Pentagon. Adamson saw to it that the incident didn't stain Ryan's honorable discharge earlier today. The General was even interviewed by KNW's Kettlemeyer. Adamson wrote off the incident as a *"justifiable reaction to what Ryan went through to keep this nation safe."*

October 25, 2005. I am such a fuckin' idiot. What the hell was I thinking? Someone needs to take my goddamn phone away when I'm drunk. In a not so sober moment of irrational nostalgia, I had the brilliant idea to contact Ryan, thinking I could explain away why I did what I did. I was a bottle of rye in when I began thinking about the good times. The times we opened up deep and honest when Travis's camera wasn't rolling. When we spoke about things that would stay between us. The alcohol lied to me and told me our friendship could be raised from the dead. You can't resurrect ashes, but I gave it a go. I knew Ryan meant what he said when we last spoke. He wanted to kill me and had every right. And since our one sided chat, I've given him ample fuel to keep the fire burning. But even before learning the truth, Ryan refused my calls and ignored my emails. So, what was I thinking contacting him so close to the anniversary? How cruel and stupid can I be?

Of course, Ryan wouldn't speak to me and blocked my number immediately after my second attempt. So, I called Suzanne. She took my call. I told her my greatest endeavor was writing about Ryan's family and his ancestors. It had made me richer and poorer at the same time—that, and *Berets*. I wanted to tell her why I did what I did, but I lost my nerve. And what was the point? What was done was done, and what were once good intentions could never bring the dead back to life. Instead, I told her all future royalties were theirs to add to the bundle they'd already received. It's gonna hurt, but it's the right thing to do. I've already contacted my lawyers to make it happen. Every penny from that cremated friendship makes me feel slimy now.

I closed *2005* and set it next to the selected journals. I finished the glass, refilled, and opened *2006*.

73

January 1, 2006. Feel terrible. Travis and I are fighting bad colds in Iraq. According to politicians, things are looking promising for democracy a year after the nuclear devastation of Almawt Lilkifaar. Not holding my breath as more of our boys are sent home in boxes and clueless politicians ignore the obvious. The Iraqis don't want us here and some people will never get along even with Adamson's over the top pacification which has emboldened nuclear powers in other hot spots. Just want to get home to Vanessa. It's our thirty-first anniversary for God sakes, and like usual she's alone. I did call her earlier and we spoke for an hour. Will definitely do something special to make up for it when I get back to the States in February.

May 4, 2006. Called Jenna to wish her happy birthday. The kids' lives are just passing me by. Jenna's boyfriend Simon got on the phone and asked me if he could make my baby girl his wife. He seems like a nice kid, but it'd be nice to meet him sometime before they tie the knot. Hell, I hope I can get away from this hellhole for the wedding. I swear my work and writing schedule is unceasing as I travel the world to every flashpoint in Cranston's War on Terrorism. Alcohol makes stomaching the horrors and keeping my game face a little easier. Got to give the public what the public expects. And it keeps the guilt buried but doesn't help with the depression. Sometimes, I still feel like I need something more. Here in Baghdad, I don't even have that. And god what a place not to be able to get a drink. Some of these people are fuckin' animals. Some kid just yesterday—couldn't have been more than fourteen—blew himself up and took out a dozen of his neighbors and six of our boys. How the blast didn't take out Travis and me... I just don't know. I just don't fuckin' know. Like usual the Man in Black was there and gone

74

right before the carnage. Those boys... I thought I was still seeing things when I looked at their faces and dead eyes. I could've sworn it was Toby, Kyle, Benny, Geno, Max, and Jesus. I rubbed my eyes and it was just six more faces and six more names that had arrived in Baghdad in February. Then everything from the last eighteen months crashed down on me. I asked again, *Why me*? Why did the Man in Black always refuse to take me? I seriously thought of ending it that night and forcing Death's hand. Even had the muzzle in my mouth while I sat on the can. But then I wouldn't have got to wish my baby girl happy birthday and talk to my soon to be son-in-law.

June 24, 2006. Another close call. More dead. But not me or Travis. I'm starting to believe the bullshit my fans are shoveling. I have to be indestructible or have a protective bubble. It's as if Lady Luck is my friend. But I know better, my only guardian angel is a hallucination of a Man in Black that dresses like Johnny Cash. Funny that would be my impression of Death. But hey, if you gotta go, who better to walk off into life's sunset with than Johnny.

August 9, 2006. Frank's birthday. Back in the States. Jon and Vanessa won't let me hear the end of it after forgetting their birthdays. I wanted to do something special to make up for missing our twenty-second anniversary, but now I don't fucking care. I'm not in the mood for this and just need to get shit-faced. I have to get away from this shit or my head's gonna explode. I think I'll call Gavin and see how he's doing. One night on the town won't hurt.

Twenty-One

I closed the journal and set it on the stack with the others. I didn't want to read any more about the hell I put everyone through after my second night with Gavin. But I'm not blaming him. Like Uncle Frank always said, *"You own it when you do it, no excuses. You're responsible for what your hands do and what your mouth says. Don't matter if you're drunk or anything else. And you're responsible for making it right or carrying that burden to your grave."* Yeah, I owned it and knew it would've been much better for everyone if I'd just pulled the trigger.

After that night in August, I started going out with Gavin again and rehired him. I tried to patch things up with Vanessa but all we did was fight. And Jon—he was just dead set on hating me. Rather than deal with Vanessa's shit and face it like a man, I went out with Gavin, who was the release valve that helped me blow off steam. And more and more when I wasn't on assignment or editing (write drunk, edit sober, thank you very much, Ernest), I found every excuse to stay clear of the Miller Manor.

Gavin never went out on assignment with Travis and me. My old college buddy didn't care much for my newer bestie. It was always uncomfortable since Travis ignored Gavin and acted like he wasn't there. Of course, other than doing his job as my cameraman, Travis and I didn't speak much anymore—other than business, that is. He was the man when it came to the cam, but the unspoken became harder to bear. I thought about replacing my wingman, but we had history—twenty five years of it. We were like estranged brothers. I couldn't fire him.

Concerning Gavin, he was like Travis when we were at Penn State before Vanessa's friend, Candy Thomas, pussy-whipped him. And boy, did Gavin like to gamble. During my breaks, we spent a lot of time in Atlantic City. I tell you, the guy just couldn't lose. Those gambling at the tables loved him and the casinos hated him. We were even banned from a few. In those that didn't have his face posted at the door, we were greeted with fanfare. And it wasn't for me. In fact, one might've been confused who was the bigger star. People even started calling him the *God of Luck* and *He-Who-Cannot-Lose*. Funny. And ironic. I really was best friends with Lady Luck after her sex change.

Gavin and I sometimes stayed in Jersey for days, where waking up with different women became easier and easier, just like the hangovers and dealing with the guilt. Gavin always had something to perk me up—to keep the wear and tear from showing. After all, I had an image to maintain. I was the modern-day Ernest Hemingway. That's when I started writing *Among the Dead*. Yeah, the guilt. I didn't say it was gone. And the book—it was about where I wished I was and deserved to be. But no, I continued to survive. It was my punishment, and alcohol and coke numbed the pain.

In time, Vanessa cared less and less about my all-nighters and multiday binges. She wasn't stupid, though I fooled myself early on. I guess Vanessa wanted to believe there was still something left of the shy boy from the Halloween party that fame hadn't poisoned. That boy was gone, consumed by the fame monster.

As we drifted apart, she took up my liquid diet minus the nose candy. By then, it wasn't just Jon who hated me. Frank and Jenna kept their distance as well, and I rarely saw my new grandkids except in photos.

Gavin saw me suffering in December 2006 and introduced me to something new. He said it would help my creative juices flow and keep my demons buried. It shimmered, varying in shade from aquamarine to deeper aquarium blue. It glittered and was cold as snow. It was beautiful. Otherworldly. He wouldn't say what it was. He just said, "trust me," and I did. And after a bump, my head cleared, my focus returned, and all was right in the world again—until it wore off.

The events of 2007 that sent me spiraling are covered in future volumes. As immortals know who lived during this period from the reality in focus, the effect of that year's aftermath on the future of existence cannot be understated. It was a dividing line in mortal history. Before that year, we believed in a fixed reality where the world beyond required faith. But after, superstition became reality and reality became increasingly nothing more than a dream in what became known as the Age of Ethereal. It was also the year Ryan Mender was killed.

That November, after Ryan's funeral, I returned to the Miller Manor and tried to write, but everything that came out was shit. Vanessa withdrew more and spoke little. At least we didn't fight anymore. How could we? She was passed out most days, and most nights I was out with Gavin. Party after party. Woman after woman. Sometimes only two, often more. Sometimes we shared. I didn't care.

In early 2008, a deep-water blue or cobalt designer version of Gavin's lighter, aquarium-colored dream hit the streets. It was called *Dead Blow*. By summer, the light blue version called *Light Ethereal* (or LE) was just about everywhere and had become a morning staple added to coffee. It's hard to believe that when Starbucks opened, people balked at paying a couple of bucks for a cup of Joe. Now, no one batted an eye at forking out fifteen to twenty dollars for what people called *Charlotte Lees*.

After Gavin introduced me to LE (before it was cool, no pun intended), I used it to cut my coke. By the time it hit the international coffee market, LE wasn't cutting it anymore (again, no pun intended). So, Gavin turned me on to Dead Blow. The uncut cobalt version was different from LE. It froze the sinuses and drilled the skull like sipping a 7-Eleven Slurpee too fast. Unpleasant at first, crystal clear clarity followed. I felt like I could fly (figuratively speaking, of course). Gavin made sure I didn't take too much. A little was enough to smother the demons, and soon I was on a roll, writing something that seemed decent. That's the curious thing about writing when you're high. It might be great, or it might be absolute shit. This was shit.

The only reason my publisher agreed to consider the new manuscript was the name that would be on the cover. Regardless, sales were terrible, and reviews were worse. The publisher wasn't happy and insisted I do a book tour even though I hated doing them. But I needed this book to sell since my habits sucked up most of my cheddar. I regretted signing over future royalties to the Mender Estate. Norine Jones had used the money to set up a scholarship fund. It was a good cause, but I didn't give a fuck. I needed the money bad. I was tempted to use more dark stuff, but Gavin warned me that its side effects shouldn't be taken lightly. That it would open doors I wasn't prepared to deal with.

That was about all I could remember without opening the journals that I couldn't remember writing. Probably would give Aleister Crowley's *Diary of a Dope Fiend* a run for its money. Yeah, don't ask me about the rest of 2008... or 2009... or the first half of 2010. It's just one purply blur. How I pulled off the act for Nate

Murphy and the public... I got nothing. But no matter how much I tried to destroy myself, my legend grew. That's why I kept a journal that maybe one day I might find the courage to open up and read.

I do remember one thing, though. It was after releasing the book *that shall not be named.* I took a break from writing. Truth is, it wasn't really a break. I was just tired of the starts and stops, as nothing measured up to my previous efforts. But that was a lie, too. The real truth was my fingers screamed to reveal something too terrible to tell.

Like usual, I was staring at the typewriter and a blank sheet of paper. Eventually, I got up and stretched, did a line of coke, wiped a trickle of blood from my nostril, then filled my empty glass with something dry. As I brought the glass to my lips, I spied with my wired, tipsy eyes an old box labeled *Mementos.* I opened it.

Sitting on top of crayon artwork, report cards, and awards was an old, tattered children's book and soiled white teddy bear. Vanessa had often read the book to the kids between changing diapers and breaking up fights between Franklin and Jonathan as Jenna played in a corner by herself. Oh, the memories of those shitty-wonderful years in Greenwich Village.

I smiled and read the cover as my fingers brushed along the worn edges—*The Adventures of Toivo the Bear* by Kaisa Jännök. Kaisa's black and white photo was on the inside cover. She was beautiful, but the memories of her stories were more so. They made me think of Vanessa, what we were, and what I'd become. In my haze, it was a sober, lucid moment. I hated it.

Twenty-Two

I slammed the drink and went to the bathroom. In the mirror, I could see myself now, and I wanted to die. I set the glass down and went to find something to hang myself with. Vanessa would be out for a while with her group of lonely housewives and househusbands. When she came home, she would be free of me.

A linen sheet was the first thing I found. I made a noose and tied it over the pull-up bar in the house gym next to our indoor Olympic-size pool. I slid a bench under the bar, stepped up, and put the noose around my neck. Then I started crying—just sobbing—and I closed my eyes. I breathed in and out quickly, nearly hyperventilating. I removed the necktie, sat on the bench, and rocked back and forth. I screamed, *"Fucking coward,"* in my head as not to alarm the manor staff. The world thought I was so brave, but my so-called courage was an act of someone who believed he couldn't be killed. Well, except by my hand, but I wasn't even brave enough to do that and rescue Vanessa from the hell I'd created for her.

I took down the noose and went back to the writing room. I took the vial of white powder from my desk and grabbed the cold vial next to it. I bumped a line of white with a dash of dark blue, and my suicidal thoughts dissolved into a blissful snowstorm.

Twenty-Three

Vanessa was blitzed when she staggered through the front door that evening. I clearly saw what I'd done to her. Again, why she wouldn't leave me, I couldn't understand. She glared at me briefly, then brushed past on her way to the kitchen. She grabbed a wide-bottom wine glass, a bottle opener, and a fresh liter of Chardonnay. She popped the cork, filled the glass to the rim, then took a large swallow from the bottle. She glowered at me, her lips pursed with eager bitterness. She swayed and balanced herself with a hand on the island counter.

I looked away.

"Yo, Nathan. Just like old times, sweetie. Just like fucking old times," Vanessa said as she precariously held the bottle. She took another swallow.

I still couldn't look at her.

"Why can't... why can't you look at me? Ain't I beautiful? Don't you think I'm sexy? Do you even still love me? You sonuvabitch. You can't even look at me, can you? Well, I loved you, you fuckin' asshole. I didn't want to believe it was true, but I knew it was. You really need to be more careful. People talk, and what they say might hurt your image with your *adoring* fans, Mr. Indestructible Nathan Miller," she said with a nasty whip, slurring every other word. "Fuckin' look at me. Look at me, Goddamnit!"

I raised my eyes, lips quivering as bottomless black revulsion poured from ghostly gray eyes. A flat hand sliced the air and caught my cheek with a *POP*, leaving a red imprint.

"Nathan, I want a divorce, and, and I want you out of this house. I want you gone... now. GO! GO NOW! GET THE FUCK OUT!" she screamed.

Vanessa grabbed the full glass with her free hand and gulped enough to keep it from spilling and stormed around the corner of the island and into a living room. She set the glass and bottle on the end table and collapsed into the pillowy chair facing the palatial gardens around the pond where Hispanic groundkeepers were trimming the hedges.

I packed a few things, then called Gavin to pick me up. This wasn't the first time she'd kicked me out. When Vanessa sobered, she would call and apologize and beg me to come home again. She always did. I knew this time wouldn't be any different. I also knew Gavin was the last person in the world I needed to go out with.

As we drove away in Gavin's cobalt Lamborghini, I saw Vanessa through the window. She flipped a bird my way.

Twenty-Four

We stayed at the Ritz Carlton in Westchester. Gavin invited a few girls. We had a typical night, woke up the next morning, and forgot the girls' fake names once they'd been paid and left.

I arrived thirty minutes late to a book signing at the *Buckley and Nolan's Books-N-More* in Times Square, a block from the WNN building. I waved at the long line of fans, shook hands, posed for a few pictures, then rushed inside to the table stacked high with that hardback waste of trees I won't name. But the line was still long. The book could've been about paint drying, and people would've bought it to have *"N Miller"* written on it.

I smiled and said nice words. Listened to the endless droning about how great I was and how much everyone loved me. How I changed their lives. I'm sure if the news had reported, *"Nathan Miller found hanging in his home gym,"* these same people would've thought their lives were ending before starting endless vigils for the *"great* man" I was. *Schmucks—every one of them*, I thought. But I smiled and said more nice words. Nodded appreciatively as my minions worshipped their god. I wondered what real gods were like. Were they just as vile as us? Just as fallible? Just as worthy of hanging from the end of a rope? Yeah, that was definitely a *be-careful-what-knowledge-you-wish-for* moment.

I smiled, signed, smiled, signed until the most exquisite female specimen I'd ever laid my eyes on stepped up with a copy of my book. Her skin was Scandinavian white and looked soft as silk. Her hypnotic blue eyes connected with mine like a hook tearing into a marlin's mouth, with Hemingway pulling at the other end. She smiled, licked her lips, then reached into her purse and took out a small piece of paper. She opened the cover to use the title page as a writing surface, grabbed the gold Sharpie from my hand, and wrote her name, phone number, and "Call me." She closed the book with note concealed.

I opened the cover, read the message, and looked up.

Her eyes dug deeper.

I nodded, took the note, and wrote on the title page:

To my adoring fan, Delores Destiny
-N Miller-

When the last book was signed, I called the number. Ms. Destiny told me to meet her at the Waldorf Astoria, Room Three-Thirteen. After donning a black fedora and mirrored sunglasses, I took a taxi to Park and Forty-Ninth. I went to the front desk in the massive but quaint lobby and asked the clerk to ring Ms. Destiny's room. He did, then handed me a key card.

84

I knocked on the door, and the same fully clothed goddess now stood naked. Every feature perfectly sculpted. Light chocolate areolas with nipples erect. Long legs that started at flawless toes, feet, and ankles, and continued to the inviting arch between them that led to the promised land. Her abs were chiseled. Her breasts natural, ample, proportioned. Her arms muscular, but feminine.

She licked her lips, then ran her hand from her chin, caressing her breasts as it slid down until it cupped her labia. She smiled and said, "Come inside, Nathan Miller."

Twenty-Five

Sex with Delores was like nothing I'd ever experienced. It was like making love to a goddess. A real one. I thought I was hallucinating as she slowly drained me, only to raise me up for another round. Over and over. Pulsating, vibrating. Time would slow and stretch, then speed up. I thought I was losing my mind as she pounded against me, and I pounded against her, and she screamed with no thought of the two floors below or the forty-four above. Sweat poured off us like a river and soaked the sheets.

We finally stopped as dawn's first light seeped around the window blinds. Delores regarded me, grinned, and lit a cigarette under the no-smoking sign. She inhaled, her face glowing orange in the dim light, and exhaled rings, which rose in distorted shapes. She snapped her fingers as the swirling mist twisted upward, enveloping the smoke detector which refused to scream its shrill warning.

"That's some magic trick," I said.

"Yes. Magic. Well, that was fun," she said, her tone sultry as a naughty angel.

"Yeah. It... it was amazing."

"Hmmm. I hope you won't be upset that I turned your phone off last night. I hate being disturbed when I'm in the groove if you know what I mean," she said with a delectable smile. "Probably should check if you have any messages from the wifey."

I chuckled, got up, and grabbed my phone. I pressed the power button and headed to the bathroom. I looked back.

Delores blew me a kiss, then took another drag.

I flipped the phone open, set it on the counter, and took a leak. I glanced over and saw several missed calls, voice, and text messages.

After shaking the drips and washing my hands, I started with texts.

Travis: *Where are u?*

Next message.

Nate: *We've been trying to reach you. Just wanted to tell you how sorry I am to hear about Vanessa.*

My stomach fell. I stepped from the bathroom. "Delores, I..."

The room looked like it hadn't been touched. The bed was made, and Delores was gone. I shook my head and checked the first voice message. It was from Vanessa.

"I'm sorry for the things I said. I just don't know what's happened to us. I've loved you from the first time I saw you, and life without you isn't worth living. Call me. Let's work this out. BEEP.

The next message was also from Vanessa, sent several hours later. Her voice was tearful. *"I just wanted to say goodbye and that I will always love you, even if you don't love me anymore. Tell the kids and grandkids... tell them that I'm sorry. That I'll miss them. When you get to the otherside, come by and say hi. BEEP.*

Next message.

I shook as a deep raspy voice came on. *"Mr. Miller, this is Inspector Chip Colson of the Greenwich PD. Please call me as soon as you get this message."* He left a number.

I called.

"Greenwich PD, how may I direct your call?" came a pleasant female voice.

"This is Nathan Miller. A Detective Colson called me."

"I'll patch you right through."

Several long seconds followed as I rubbed my mouth and stroked my beard.

"Detective Rich Colson speaking."

"This is Nathan Miller. You called last night."

"Mr. Miller, is there any way you could come down to the station? Or maybe I can meet you somewhere? There's a matter I prefer to speak with you about in person."

"What is this about?"

"Umm. It's concerning a matter I don't feel comfortable discussing over the phone."

"Just tell me. Is it my wife? Did something happen to my wife?"

Silence.

"Just fuckin' tell me. Tell me now! Is Vanessa okay?"

"Alright. I'll tell you." Detective Colson paused. "This is the worst part of my job. I'm very sorry, but your wife was found dead last night by one of your maids. She, uh, she apparently hung herself in your master bathroom sometime yesterday evening."

I couldn't speak as the room collapsed around me. I stood there naked, staring at the made bed. The odor of Delores's cigarette still hung in the air.

"You still there, Mr. Miller?"

My reply came from a ghostly shell. "Yeah. Yeah. I'm still here. But I have to go. What do you need from me now?"

"I need you to come down to the morgue and identify your wife's body and answer a couple of questions. Is that okay?"

"Yeah. Yeah. I'm in Manhattan. It'll take me a while to get there, but I'll leave as soon as... as soon as I'm dressed. Do my kids know yet?"

"No, not yet. I figured it best coming from you. And if you or anyone in your family needs to speak with one of our grief counselors, let me know."

"Okay. I will. Thank you. I... I'll be there soon."

I hung up and stood shaking, then sat on the bed and wept.

Twenty-Six

Saturday, May 22, 2010. St. Marks Methodist Cathedral, Greenwich, Connecticut.

It was a rainy spring day, and the masses were mourning on television and around the world for the death of Nathan Miller's wife. A tragic suicide. Condolences for poor Nathan Miller poured in from every corner. Never for Vanessa. Never for the kids. Always for me and the Miller name. She would've been better off with any other last name. She would still be alive with any other name.

During the service, I sat by Jenna, her husband, Simon, Franklin, his wife, Kimberly, and their four children. Jonathan asked to be seated anywhere but near me and wouldn't look at me or let his twin boys near their grandfather.

Thunder rumbling made it difficult to hear the pastor. I stared on. My eyes were dry. My soul was broken, ripped to shreds, and ached to be made whole again.

Images coursed through my mind of Delores Destiny, riding me with devilish blue eyes devouring my soul as she let out a sinister laugh and slapped my ass as I bucked harder. My stomach twisted. I gagged, covered my mouth, and ran down the center aisle to the restroom. I dropped to my knees at the porcelain altar and left an offering.

When I finished vomiting, I leaned against the toilet. Franklin entered. He knelt and put an arm around me and we found our tears together. I didn't deserve his touch or his love, but I took it anyway.

Franklin helped me back to my seat as the preacher finished his eulogy. I didn't want to see Vanessa's body, but I needed to see what I'd done. I walked gingerly as Jenna and Franklin supported me in case my legs failed. I wanted to stand firm since the media would raise me up as a saint if I fell. But if I stood firm and showed no emotion, they would report my shock of losing my wife, the emotional numbness of losing the love of my life.

I peered into the casket and looked at someone caked in makeup. Cold skin covering nothing but a mortal shell. It wasn't Vanessa. It was no more than a mannequin. But it was *her*, and I had put her there. Jonathan stood some distance away. Our eyes met. His darted away with a twinge of disgust before slipping on the proper public mask.

I stared at Vanessa's corpse as the clouds crackled and lightning flashed outside. My legs gave out, and Jenna and Franklin struggled to keep me standing as I convulsively wept. I didn't care what was said. The fucking public would love me no matter what, and I would hate myself more with every kind word. Travis, Nate, Julie Florid, and Gavin were all there. They tried to ease my pain, but only Gavin had what I needed.

The rain stopped in time for the graveside. Even a little sun peeked through the clouds after the wake, which Jonathan skipped to avoid me. Travis was cordial, but outside work and tragedy, he was done with me. After a limp man-hug and Candy's polite kiss on the cheek, they headed back to Queens. When Frank and Jenna were gone, I endured the final round of condolences and left with Gavin.

Twenty-Seven

For once, Gavin didn't offer to take me out to make things better the old-fashioned way. Instead, we headed to a small park on Long Island Sound and sat on a bench near the water. He acted like a real friend. I talked. He listened. And when he spoke, I listened. With Travis's friendship dashed on the rocks, Gavin was now my best friend—probably my only one—even if he was leading me further into Hell.

As we sat, seagulls sang their pitchy lullabies while time moved in fast forward. We avoided painful topics, and he made me laugh about old times. Somehow, even in my darkest hours, he could always make me laugh. Gavin told me some better memories of his childhood in Bosnia when Yugoslavia was still under Tito's thumb. I revealed happy memories about my parents, Frank and Dorothy, my grandfather, and Ryan Mender and his family. He kept my mind focused on pleasant things, temporarily erasing the horrors of the past few days. We continued our chit-chat for hours until the sun sank in the west and the street lamps came alive.

Gavin turned sullen as the moon rose, as if exhaling after holding his breath all day. My joy evaporated, and the full weight of my life crashed down.

"I am very sorry about Vanessa," said Gavin. "I do not know what to say."

"There's nothing you or anyone can say. She's gone. My one good thing. She killed herself because of me. How can that ever be made right? I wanna die. I swear I just wanna blow my fuckin' brains out. End it all, but the public would eat it up. Probably make me the poster geezer for suicide prevention and grief counseling—no word on the real bastard these idiots worshiped. And I wish my guardian angel would go fuck himself. Let a bullet or blast find me. Maim me or kill me slowly. Painfully. But no, I'm cursed with life."

"Do not talk like that," said Gavin.

"Why the fuck not? It's how I feel. There's shit you don't know about me. Shit I've done. What happened in Almawt Lilkifaar. What happened to Ryan, his family, everything else in 2007 that fucked up our world worse than it was already fucked. Vanessa… she was just one of my many sins. I played a part in all of it. Whether I meant to or not, I played a part. I have so much blood on my hands, even if I haven't taken a single life with them."

91

Gavin gazed into the darkened sound. Twinkling lights dotted the far shore. I knew there were things he kept from me, things too horrible to put into words. Maybe stuff he'd done and things he'd seen. I knew much of it, but there was more. No doubt there were doors he wanted to keep closed and locked up tight.

Gavin sighed. "Remember when we met in Bosnia?"

"Yeah. You showed me what was done to your family and your village. Told me what they tried to do to you. Crushed me. Writing *Ghosts of Bosnia* was like slicing my wrist open with a dull blade every time I sat down at the typewriter. I was so glad when I finished the final draft. I haven't opened the book since... except to sign autographs. Look, we don't have to talk about this unless you need to."

"It is more than that. We have both done things we are not proud of. Things we wish we could change. Be something we are not. But some beings are just hardwired a certain way—programmed to be bad. Like a celestial joke that a master creator played on us all."

"It always weirds me out when you talk like you're something more than human. Like you've been around for a thousand years."

"Nathan, I have been around for a lot longer than that." Gavin faced me. Light from the streetlamp hit his eyes just right, and I swore I saw a flicker of blue beyond his pupils.

I smiled and snickered through my nose. "You're a funny guy. I'll give you that. Hey, you got any of that dark stuff? I could use some right about now."

Gavin nodded with a wistful, faraway grin and said, "Yes. I will always be here to fix you up, my brother."

He nabbed a frosted vial from his pocket along with an octagon-shaped mirror. He unscrewed the lid and tapped a small amount of the sparkling blue on his reflection. Before he could tilt the vial upright, I tapped the back, doubling the size of the micro-mound.

"Man, I… I told you—be careful with this stuff."

"Why? Why does it matter anymore? I can handle it. *I'm the Goddamn Indestructible Nathan Miller*," I added with comical bravado.

Gavin shook his head with a wry grin. "Suit yourself."

There was twice the amount on the mirror than I'd ever done before. Gavin took a credit card from his wallet and fashioned the half-centimeter pile into two lines. He closed his palm around the card, opened it, and the card was gone. In its place was a short plastic straw.

"Still don't know how you do that," I said.

Gavin gave me a *my-little-secret* smile, handed me the straw, and held the mirror. I snorted a line, then the next. A cold sledgehammer fell from the sky and hit me between the eyes. I doubled over as a frigid bullet smashed through my skull. I wanted to yell as my brain froze and icicles formed inside my eyeballs. I hit my forehead with the heel of a hand several times. Slowly, the pain dissolved into purest ecstasy. I felt like I could fly.

"I think I can fly," I said.

"You can. All you have to do is believe."

"You're a crazy fuckin' Bosniak."

"No, I am serious. Try it. Imagine you are a bird, but do not stay up too long."

I stood and did as he said, feeling silly as I flapped my arms. Gavin looked at me and made me believe he wasn't kidding. So, I flapped my arms again. Suddenly, I left the ground. I thought I was just really stoned, but as I waved my arms faster, Gavin shrunk below me, becoming smaller and smaller, until he was ant-sized, sitting under a model-train-size streetlamp.

In a distant muted holler, Gavin said, "NATHAN, COME DOWN! THAT IS A LONG WAY TO FALL. PLUS, YOU DO NOT WANT ANYONE TO SEE YOU."

I gave him a curious look he couldn't see, then flapped down and gently landed in the grass.

"Holy shit!" I exclaimed. "That was amazing. What is this stuff? I mean, what is it—*really*?"

"It is called *Dark Ethereal*, but it is nothing like the light stuff mined in Colorado or what everyone is spiking their coffee with."

"No shit."

"Yes. Both substances are the building blocks of the world beyond—a world created from belief and faith. Few in the mortal worlds have a true concept of what it is like after they lose their fleshy shells and cross over," Gavin said as he pinched my arm. "Light and Dark Ethereal are but a taste of the place known as the Afterworld."

"Okay, whatever," I said, tiring of his humorless joke. "I'm laughing inside. Ho, ho, ho. Whatever it is—it's amazing. But seriously, what is this shit?"

"As I said, Dark Ethereal, and as you know, it is also called *Dead Blow*. But where it comes from… uhh, you do not want to know that. And what it is… well, let me tell you what it is not. It is not a drug, though it seems like one to a mortal shell. It is the substance of dreams and imagination."

"Damn. Everything is so clear around me—like I can see through spaces in front of my eyes I never knew were there."

"Yes, that. Be careful. Dead Blow can show you things you may not want to see."

"Like what?"

"The world beyond that I spoke of—the one you think I am joking about. It is the best and worst thing about Dead Blow."

"This stuff's amazing. Like sex with..." I stopped as reality's icy fingers crept down my spine at the thought of the demon Delores. Who was she? What was she? I hated myself for thinking about her, but I couldn't stop. She'd ruined me for any other woman. And what I was feeling was greater than the sex we had, if that was possible, and I'd just learned it was.

"You okay?" asked Gavin.

"Yeah. Sure. Hunky-dory."

"It is good stuff, but do not do too much. Addicts call it *riding the blue dragon*, but the more you do, the more you will need the next time. And the side effects—worse than meth, but you get to keep your teeth. Ages the human body with every dose, though. And once you are hooked, you can be in your thirties and a few months later, look like you are ninety. Mortal shells were not meant for this stuff. I tell you this because I care for you and want us to be friends for a long time."

"Then why'd you give me this shit?" I asked. I had tasted a new world, and that irresistible taste made me want more.

"You were sad, and I hated to see you down. You are my brother—my best friend. Hell, you are my only friend in Heaven and on this Earth."

I put an arm around Gavin. "Thanks, man, but you know you're gonna have to fix me up with more."

"I will. Just promise me you will not take more than you did tonight. What you experienced might have been out of this world, but I will say it again—the knowledge Dark Ethereal can reveal—well, there are some things mortals should not know or see."

"Gavin, you keep talking like you're not even human."

"Nathan, I will level with you—I am not. This mortal shell I wear *might* be, but I have never told you who I am. And I do not think you would like me much if I did. So, let us leave things the way they are—Please."

"Yeah, sure, you Balkan Mad Hatter. Someday you gotta come clean with me."

Gavin sighed. "Maybe one day I will show you who I really am. I dread that day since it will be the day our friendship dies."

I left it hanging there. I wasn't sure what to think but knew my best friend was out of his mind. Had Gavin done something so unconscionable that he had designed this alter-ego? Could I be sitting next to an angel of death? At least he was honest about having a past he wished to hide even from his best friend. Regardless, I was in no position to judge. Gavin merely wanted a new life. To walk away from the old one and not look back. Whether he deserved it or not, I didn't plan to pry deeper because I loved him. Not in a sexual way, but as strongly as one could otherwise.

Twenty-Eight

We left the park, and Gavin dropped me off at the mansion. I offered to let him stay the night, but he said he had things to do.

I walked through the bedroom where I wouldn't be sleeping and into the bathroom where Vanessa was found. I looked at the sturdy showerhead and didn't cry. Images of her struggling for breath filled my mind. Her eyes bulging. Her face red. It morphed into the demon Delores's moaning face, stricken with pleasure. I closed my eyes and shook my head. I opened them and the image was gone.

I rubbed my lips, then went to the kitchen. I took the cold glass vial from my coat pocket, unscrewed the lid, and tapped a little cobalt powder on the kitchen island's white ceramic. I fashioned a sparkling line with a knife and a hungry nostril made it disappear. The excruciating sweet freeze sent icicles into my brain. I closed my eyes, and thoughts of the demon melted as I imagined another time and place.

"Hey, what do you think about the one over there?" said Travis.

I opened my eyes. My old friend's younger version was dressed as Dr. Groucho Marx in a white lab coat with a fake mustache, round rimmed glasses, a stethoscope, and a fat cigar. I was at the Halloween frat party with Blondie's *Call Me* blaring in the background. Across the room in black and white was the most beautiful prisoner I'd ever seen. Her magnetic gray eyes captured me. I didn't look away this time.

"Be right back. There's someone I want to meet," I said.

Travis laughed and said, "Get you some, big boy."

I didn't respond and made a bee-line to the brunette between the two blonde flower children.

"Hi," she said. "Who are you?"

I grinned wide and laughed. "Nathan Miller. And who might you be?"

"Vanessa Richardson. I saw you staring at me and was hoping you'd come over."

"Hey, why don't we go upstairs, where it's a little quieter?"

"Frisky one, huh?"

"Sorry... the alcohol. Kind of a lightweight. If you don't..."

She pressed a finger to my lips. "Shhh. Hope you didn't drink too much, and everything works okay, 'cause what the hell, I'm feeling adventurous tonight. Let's go."

We headed upstairs, pushing past another couple who'd been sitting on a couch smoking a joint. We found an empty room, locked the door, did a little talking, then got down to business. Images of Delores swirled in my mind, and my manhood refused to cooperate. Vanessa was kind and understanding. She stroked and kissed me as I pleasured her until she withered in my arms after disturbing the neighboring rooms. I peered into her eyes as sweat dripped, and our warm, wet bodies slid gently against each other in the afterglow.

Vanessa smiled, then faded until only her eyes remained, illuminating the darkness around me. Then they were gone, and I was alone in the mansion, sitting in the same chair Vanessa sat in when I drove away with Gavin the day she killed herself.

I stared out the window into the yard, darkened except for flood lamps and the few brighter stars peeking around the faint impressions of clouds. I bit my lips, rubbed them, then came the downpour. I screamed. I wailed.

Twenty-Nine

I tormented myself one more night before putting the mansion on the market—priced to sell at six million—a steal for what we paid for it. Before leaving Vanessa's palace forever, I thanked the help and gave each a bonus that would keep them comfortable for a year or two. As my limo drove away, I didn't look back. It was too painful.

I headed straight to WNN for a meeting with Nate Murphy. He had called me earlier that morning, opening with comforting words concerning Vanessa's death, but his tone told me I wasn't coming in for a pat on the back. He said there was a *situation* and that the WNN executive board needed to see me immediately.

When I arrived, I opened Nate's door without knocking. I nodded at everyone in the ruling council and started to speak, but Nate raised a hand and silenced me.

"Nathan, have a seat," he said, pointing to the empty chair at the opposite end of the oak conference table.

"Okay. What's wrong?" I asked as I sat.

"I want to ask you about something before we run with it. God knows every other network will soon."

"What? What is it, Nate? Spit it out."

"We got several emails from women who say you raped them. One claims she's pregnant. A few even claim they have children of yours. Several said they were afraid to come forward until now because you threatened them. And they all say you gave them some kind of drug to make them do whatever you wanted."

"Nate, that's bullshit!"

"I'd like to believe you. God knows, I want to believe you. But there's more than one. And they're not asking for anything except for the world to know what kind of *bastard* you are. Their words—not mine."

My face contorted with confusion. I thought about everything and anything I could've done to make these women say such things. But then, my extracurricular activities weren't something I wanted going public, especially in the wake of Vanessa's suicide. I thought about Gavin. *You bastard—you Goddamn bastard*, I thought and asked, "Have you spoken with Gavin?"

"Gavin? Who's Gavin?" asked one of the executives.

Nate shrugged. "Yes, Nathan, who's Gavin?"

My face dropped. My head swam. Pictures of a friend I had known since Bosnia flashed through my head. "Gavin, my assistant. Gavrilo Haus. You know, the guy and the family from *Ghosts of Bosnia*."

"Nathan, I know who Gavrilo is. Last I heard, he was working for our WNN affiliate in Moscow but he left that job before 9/11. I haven't seen or talked to him since. I know you've been drinking a lot, and I hear rumors that's not all. You've never disappointed me before, so, right or wrong, I chose not to get involved in your business unless it impacted mine. Now, it has. I hate to do this, but we have to get ahead of this. For the best of everyone involved, I'm releasing you from your contract. I also suggest—speaking as a friend—that you get some help," he said sincerely with barely contained grief. "You were one of the greats, and you were like a son to me. It breaks my heart to see you fall so hard, but I fear you haven't hit rock bottom yet. So, get that help before you do."

My mouth was dry. I couldn't speak. I felt like I was going crazy. What was I saying? I was going crazy. Did I imagine Gavin all these years? I stood blank-faced as I shook each hand. Each talking head moved their lips, but I didn't hear a word they said.

As I left Nate's office, I walked past the desks of once adoring eyes that now looked away. I called Gavin's number on the elevator ride down. There was no answer.

I thought back. Five years passed after finishing *Ghosts of Bosnia* before I heard from Gavin again. I knew about the Moscow job since that's where he was when he called me, wanting a transfer to Manhattan to work with me. I didn't think it would be a problem. Come to think of it—when I asked Nate, he was distracted. He only said, "*Sounds good. Make it happen,*" then he took an urgent call about a deadline. He never asked about Gavin again, and my new assistant never came up in conversation. And Travis—I couldn't understand why he ignored Gavin the few times the three of us were together after Gavin moved to New York. They had seemed to get along in Bosnia in '95, so all I could figure was that Travis was jealous, but I never confronted him about being an asshole. The truth is, Travis and I had been growing apart long before Almawt Lilkifaar. Even at Vanessa's funeral, Travis, and everyone else, ignored Gavin as if he were a cathedral fixture.

I often felt terrible about how people treated him, but I never said a thing since Gavin didn't seem bothered by it. He appeared content, knowing he was my assistant and later my friend. Had this *Gavin* I knew been a figment of my imagination? I wondered. If so, I really was a bat shit looney.

I reached into my coat pocket and felt the cold vial. *Definitely, not my imagination,* I thought. Gavin had given me the Dead Blow, or someone had. I needed to talk to him and find out what the fuck was going on. Then my phone rang. It was him.

"Hey, Nathan, just checking to see how you are doing."

"I can't talk now, but we need to talk. Come to my apartment. Just you."

"Okay, I will be right over."

"Good. If I'm not there, let yourself in. You have a key."

Thirty

Manhattan traffic was its typical terrible mess—yelling, honking, middle fingers galore. I walked to Hamilton Tower instead of taking a taxi or the subway. I needed to think, and the long trek alone in the crowd would give me plenty of time, maybe even do me some good. It didn't. My thoughts were a merciless merry-go-round rehashing the past fifteen years. Then I bumped into a man in black.

The man turned, but he wasn't my blue-eyed guardian devil, yet, he was dressed the same down to his Stetson, trench coat, shirt, pants, and boots. And rather than his usual grim aspect or a New York *"fuck you buddy, watch where you're goin'"* greeting, the man's features were as pleasant as a follower of Hare Krishna. He tipped his hat.

"Excuse me," I said.

"No problem, buddy. Here—take one of these." He extended his hand. Between his fingers was a religious tract, the likes of which terrified me as a child.

I rolled my eyes, but rather than play the part of unapproachable mega-star, I nodded, said, "Thanks," and took the tract. Why not? I was curious what was up with a guy dressing like Death—my Death.

The tract had the curious title, *Death is Love*, and below the inviting typography was my protector—the Man in Black that I first saw at the Harrisburg County Summer Fair. His hands were palm out with straight arms forward, like Christ without the nail holes calling his children to follow with a smile to match. His hair was silver and frazzled. His dark blue eyes sparkled like Dead Blow. That made me itch. I flipped the tract over. On the back was a picture of the founder of the *Church of Death's Enlightenment*, Rajesh Batra, an Indian immigrant from Delhi. I shook my head, crumpled the tract, and littered the pavement. I walked on.

At Hamilton Tower in Greenwich Village, I punched my personal code and "2519". The door lock disengaged. I entered and went to the office. I asked the manager if anyone had used my passcode. The manager inquired why. I told him someone might have stolen it and that I needed it changed. The manager checked and told me the last entry was Friday around noon.

The elevator was out of order, so I trudged up twenty-five flights. I was panting and sweating by the time I reached my floor. I continued down the hall to my apartment and opened the door as Gavin bumped a fat Hollywood rail off my glass coffee table. A quarter-full bourbon snifter sat next to an additional white mound.

"Nathan, you need some?" Gavin asked as he rubbed his nose and sniffed.

"No. I'll pass," I said coldly, wanting some like lungs want air.

"Suit yourself," he said and proceeded to mold and clear another robust white stripe.

"Who the fuck are you?" I asked. "No, no, no—What the fuck are you?"

"Oh—yeah, that. I saw the news. Umm. How do I say this? Uhh. I am not of this world. I have tried to tell you before, but you always think I am kidding around."

"What? Are you some kind of alien? Or are you like Brad Pitt in *Fight Club*, a figment of my deranged imagination?"

"No, no, nothing like that. I am from the world beyond—a place you and almost every other soul trapped inside mortal shells will go one day. It is the place I have told you about more than once—the one called the Afterworld. I am your guardian angel. Your good luck charm."

I have two? I thought, and asked, "So, no one can see you but me?"

"Some can, maybe, but only if I want them to. Look, I know you are upset. Those women cannot prove anything. It was not your semen that got them pregnant. It was mine. I wanted to have some kids. Some little baby mortals to spread my magic around. The paternity tests will not show up with your DNA. In fact, I would love to see the doctor's faces when they read the results. Let us say the results will be *out of this world*."

I shook my head and glared into Gavin's glossy, dull blue eyes. "Wish that was the way the world worked, but perception is reality. And there's nothing the public loves more than to see the mighty fall—the harder, the better. I'd be better off putting a bullet in my head or swan-diving from the top of this building. Give them a storybook ending—like a Stephen King novel."

"Brother, I hate to hear you talk like that. That will not do anyone any good."

"I'm not your brother. I don't even know who you are. I mean, I know who you look like. And I know Gavin is or was a real person because Travis was there with me in Rajza Vjernika."

Gavin (or whoever or whatever it was in my apartment) said nothing, held the glass of bourbon, swirled it, and watched the amber liquid spin before gulping the crystal dry.

I plopped onto the couch next to him. "What am I gonna do? Vanessa's gone, and I've fucked up everything else in my life. My kids. Only Franklin will talk to me and only out of obligation. Jenna barely acknowledges me. And John wishes I was in that grave instead of his mother. I want to blame you for everything, but I'm still not convinced you aren't me. That evil little spider. That spark of chaos and mischief buried deep inside me born after Almawt Lilkifaar—manifestations of guilt for so many deaths. But you were already with me, so I must have started losing my mind long before I imagined your call in 2000."

"Nathan, you are not crazy, and I am not a figment of your imagination. I am sorry for getting you into this situation. You know, I am not good with mortals. I mean, I have only recently started liking them. I guess I do not understand what it is like to be one, but I am learning. You do not understand that I would give anything not to be what I am. How I wish I were mortal. To live and die. To love and be loved. To answer in the end for all the evil that I have done—but... but I cannot. I am what I am to the end of eternity.

I once hated your kind. Thought you were a plague destroying every good thing the Original Three created."

I curiously narrowed my eyes.

"Yes, long story about those three. But let us take things slow, lest your mortal brain explode."

"Are you a god?"

"You could say that. A really shitty one."

"I think I'll go ahead and have a fat rail."

Gavin smiled, chopped one, and handed me the straw.

I bumped hard. Nothing. Absolutely nothing. "That's weird. I don't feel a thing."

"Oh, man. Sorry, that sometimes happens after you ride the blue dragon. Nothing compares. Here, let me add a little." Gavin sprinkled a little dark blue to the white, then formed another, more conservative line.

I did the second bump and felt something akin to a light chill tickling my nose.

"Nothing?" he asked with surprise.

"Gavin, I don't feel shit. And damn, I *really* need something right now."

He looked worried as he tapped more Dead Blow onto the table. It sparkled like blue diamonds. He formed a pure blue line as the glass frosted around it. I grabbed the straw, snorted hard, and slammed my head into the table, cracking the glass. I raised my head and smacked the heel of my hand against my forehead several times, and yelled, "OHHH YESSS, GODDAMNIT!"

Icicles formed around the room, and fluffy, dark-blue snowflakes fell like ash inside the apartment.

"Better?"

"Oh yes, Gavin. Oh, yes, I love you, my friend. Thank you so much."

"No problem. Just be careful and do not mainline this stuff. No matter how desperate you get—do not do it. Do heroin. Whatever you have to. But do not ever mainline this stuff. It will kill you, and if it does not kill you the first time, it will the next, or if you are lucky, the time after that. And there will always be a next time until it kills you, or else you go insane when you can no longer feel the *Hand of God*."

I looked at Gavin. He looked different—beautiful—the most handsome man I had ever seen. His short brown hair was now flowing blond under a white Stetson hat. His dull blue eyes were now fiery dark-blue shimmering baubles. I thought he might sprout golden wings and fly away. He reminded me of the Man in Black, only much younger. He even dressed the same, except he wore white. I wanted to ask again who this apparition haunting me was, but questions faded as I basked in the frigid radiance.

"I'm going to leave you now," said the Man in White without any discernable accent. "I have things to attend to."

"Oh, okay," I said, admiring him as he glistened like morning sunlight sparkling over crystalline snow.

The Man in White set a frosty vial on the cracked coffee table, then dissolved into blue mist. When the mist vanished, the light around me brightened until there was only white.

Thirty-One

Whiteness took form, and I found myself in a Gothically decorated waiting room with stone benches facing a window. I went to the window and looked outside at a world with a swirling psychedelic sky. Strangely, I felt as if I were thousands of feet above the surface but saw everything in intricate detail. My vision moved through structures littering several continents, allowing me to explore fantastical architectural wonders milling with every sort of being. There were humans, anthropomorphized animals, and aliens beyond my reality. Besides massive, marvelous cities, there were mountains, valleys, open plains, lakes, rivers, seas, oceans, and islands—every place teeming with life and joy with more than enough space to comfortably exist. I thought of Dorothy.

Suddenly, she was in front of me in a rocking chair on the porch of a magnificent mansion on a green, grassy hill. She was alone. I wondered where Frank was. *He must be inside*, I thought with a peaceful grin. Dorothy was knitting a blanket. She always loved handcrafts. But I didn't sense joy as melancholy etched her face, which was smooth—a younger version of herself before Frank left for Vietnam. I was far away but felt like I could reach out and touch her, yet when I tried, my hand hit a thin sheet of glass. It vibrated but didn't break.

Dorothy looked up. "Is that you, Nathan?" she said, hopefully, her spirit rising in anticipation.

She'd never seen me with a beard. "Yeah, it's me."

"But… how? You didn't die, did you?" she asked, facing me on the other side of the glass.

"No, I'm still alive."

"Well then, come here and sit with me, and we can talk like we used to on the porch back in Williamsport."

"I can't. There's something in the way."

Her lips pursed glumly, and her eyes drooped as her head shook. "Hmmm. A Reality Window. That's too bad. Would you like to see your mom and dad?"

"Yes. Yes, I'd love to."

"Jonathan, Jenna. We have a guest. It's Nathan."

My mother and father ran out the mansion's palatial gilded double doors, smiling with corners that could've touched the surreal sky.

"Oh, Nathan, we've missed you so much," my mother said. "Your Aunt Dorothy tells us you got along well after we died."

Dorothy sat and went back to her knitting.

"Yeah, I did okay."

That's all I had to say. *Seriously?* I thought. I'd waited for this moment. Dreamed of it. Cried about it. And put it to rest when I sank into irredeemable depravity. But here they were, as I remembered when they left me with Uncle Frank and Aunt Dorothy, never to return. I wanted to hug them. Oh, *how I wanted to hug them*, but that Goddamn glass was in the way. At least we could talk.

"Modest are we?" asked my mother. "Dorothy says you did a lot better than just *okay*. But modesty is good. I guess we raised you right. Well, partly. Dorothy and Frank obviously did a good job where we left off."

Dorothy's eyes rose and her lips curled.

"Son, we are both so proud of you," my father said. "I just wish we could keep tabs on your progress as a mortal. We have this dang Reality Window. It's supposed to let us watch over you, but it never seems to work when we check on you. Well, not recently—I mean, not since... well not since sometime before 9/11. That was terrible to behold, but that sort of thing happens all over the Realities. I miss you, Son, but it's nice being up here away from all that heartache. I still wish we could see you, but it's like there's some kind of bubble around you. Weird."

Yeah. *Weird*, as if this wasn't weird enough. It was a relief, though, and gave me a morsel of peace that they hadn't seen what I'd become.

"You know, Jenna, we never have this problem when I look up anyone else," my father said.

"Jon, it's probably for the best. He's not a little boy anymore and deserves his privacy. Mortals have enough to worry about without dead loved ones looking over their shoulders. I'm just happy you're here, but I wish I could hug you and pinch your fuzzy little cheeks. You look so handsome and manly. You really do look like a modern-day Hemingway. Oh, how I wish I could break this silly window, but it's the way things work in the Afterworld. We did see you get married. I cried like a baby. About as much as Dorothy did. So jealous she got to be there in mortal flesh. Such a beautiful ceremony for such a gorgeous bride. I really like that Vanessa. She's a real sweetheart. And boy, does she love you."

I felt the knife go through my heart, but smiled with trembling lips, trying to keep my eyes dry and not throw up.

"You picked a good one," my mother continued. "And those grandbabies. Cute as three buttons. It was nice to see them grow. Jon

110

and I watched you become a writer, and Dorothy has told us all about your Home Cinema show you did to honor Frank. That was sweet."

I couldn't speak. I hoped Frank would join the reunion soon. That would at least help soothe the wound my mother ripped open.

My mother raised her hand and pressed it against the glass.

I raised my hand to match. It was much larger than hers now. I remembered the warmth as she held it in my first memory. The window was cold.

Her smile turned to a melancholy lip curl. "I miss you so much, Nathan. I'm sorry we couldn't be there to watch you grow up."

Like it was her fault. Typical of this wonderful woman. I matched her longing smile.

My father raised his hand to the glass with a proud smile and doting eyes. I raised the other hand to match his. Our outlines were equal.

My father finished my mother's thought. "But my brother and Dorothy sure did a good job picking up where we left off. It was nice when Dorothy finally showed up."

Again, I wondered, *Where is Uncle Frank?* "Dad, where is Uncle Frank?"

Dorothy's eyes rose from her knitting. She looked like I'd stabbed her with the same knife my mother used on me when she mentioned Vanessa. Behind those blue eyes, a soul soldiered through immeasurable pain.

My mother looked away, and my father's smile vanished.

"Dad, where is Uncle Frank?" I asked insistently, my words tinged with panic.

His lips parted, closed, then opened again. "He's not here," he said bitterly.

"Where is he?" I asked, my words no longer masking my alarm.

Before my father could answer, the paradise beyond the window darkened and faded, dissolving into the reality of my lonely apartment. I stood with both palms pressed against the window gazing at the building across the alley. A neighbor was curiously observing me from the other building.

I dropped my hands and closed the blinds. I wondered how long I'd been standing there. I knew at least day and night had passed. It felt like the next morning. I looked at my watch. It'd been three days since I was fired.

Thirty-Two

Late July 2010.

Time dragged, and I was rarely sober after returning from Paradise. I quickly discovered that when I wasn't flying on the blue dragon express, my hypothalamus didn't function properly. My temperature regulation was jacked. I felt like I was roasting. I thought I had the flu at first, but whenever I checked my temp, it was subnormal. Actually, shockingly low. In fact, the ear unit typically read *LOW*. I even checked an old-school mercury rectal, and it said, "You're dead, buddy."

Besides having a basal temperature like a rattlesnake or tortoise, every minute, every second, every millisecond, I wasn't high, my body ached to giddy up on the icy blue dragon. And, when I gave

112

in a little, the question, *"Where is Frank?"* echoed in my head along with my father's answer, *"He's not here. He's not here. He's not here…"*

Had Uncle Frank done something so horrible in Heaven's Paradise that Dorothy kicked him out? I couldn't imagine it. They were like mashed potatoes and gravy and would be for eternity. No. It had to be something else. But what?

Part of me wanted to know. That part made me want to snort all the Dead Blow that Gavin left me in one massive bump. But the other part is why I endured withdrawal as much as my sanity allowed. Plus, I had no idea when Gavin would return. The cobalt snow wasn't like Jesus's magic loaves and fishes, and I was already getting down to crust and bones.

Where was he? Gavin had been nowhere to be found since my glimpse of Heaven. He also wasn't answering calls, texts, or emails. I finally got my answer during the KNW news report concerning the false accusations that cost me my reputation and job—accusations that set a team of lawyers in motion to keep me out of court and jail. The report stated that paternity tests proved that none of the children were mine. Doctors had no further comment concerning the results, and all but two women recanted their statements.

The segment clipped to tear-filled apologies from over a dozen women. These women (several of whom I recognized) said they'd never slept with me. They went on to say (convincingly) that, to their knowledge, I'd always been a faithful, loving husband and for God to rest Vanessa's soul.

Each woman now faced criminal charges for false allegations and asked for the maximum penalty for smearing my name. Only two were unable to retract their accusations. Rumors swirled that they had overdosed on something, but the medical examiner wouldn't speculate what that something was. I knew this was Gavin's work to clean up his mess to protect me. No doubt, he murdered those two women.

I flipped off the TV and licked the last sparkling crumbs from a frosty vial (not without a little panic since I'd need more *very* soon). Yes, I feared withdrawal, but I needed to return to Dorothy and my parent's window. I needed the answer to the *Frank* question. And now that I knew how, I wanted to find Vanessa and say I'm sorry—sorry for everything. But for whatever reason, I could never find my way back to the window. I always found myself in never-ending halls filled with people I didn't know. Unlike my recurrent dreams, there were no doors—only one way to wherever the hall led. Some of those around me were smiling. Some were downcast. Others were terrified or angry. There was always a light at the end of the tunnel, goading me on but never letting me get near. I needed to know what happened to Frank. I had to know.

I licked the vial again and turned frantic and irate. What the hell was going on in the world beyond? And who the hell was this Man in White I used to think was Gavrilo Haus? My inebriated vision could've been a hallucination, but in my heart, I knew the blond, blue-eyed, pale-skinned cowboy was real. Was Gavin a ghost? Had the Man in White done something to him or taken his body? If so, how was he related to the Man in Black, who looked like his frizzy silver-haired grandfather? Like an older yin to a younger yang?

Whoever or whatever he was, the Man in White had the answers, and he wasn't telling me everything he knew. That's why, among a million other questions besides '*Where is Frank?*', I wanted to ask my parents and Dorothy if they knew anything about my constant companion and whether or not guardian angels were real. If they did, I believed I had two. One was Death. And the other? I wasn't sure but knew which one enveloped me in a bubble, protecting me from heavenly shame and earthly infamy while cheating me of the natural death I desired and the violent one I deserved.

Thirty-Three

August 2010.

One muggy Manhattan day, the Man in White returned as Gavin's mortal shell. I continued calling him Gavin for lack of knowing what else to call him, or *it*. Rather than entering through the door, he just appeared in my small living room. I looked up from the recliner, and wanted to ask what he did to those two women. That was one of many questions that sloshed around in my head, but all were smothered by one nagging concern. "Do you have any more Dead Blow? I *really* need it," I pleaded as if my sanity depended on it.

"You used that whole vial? I warned you. Once the dragon's claws are in you, there's no turning back." Again, Gavin had lost his Bosnian accent.

I rattled desperately, "I know, but I have questions I need answered. I saw my parents. I saw Dorothy. But Frank wasn't there. I didn't see Vanessa, either. Maybe you know where they are."

Gavin shook his head. "You shouldn't have gone there. It'll drive you mad. Go fly like a bird again. Run faster than a speeding bullet. Bench press a train. Do anything, but don't go there. Don't go to the window. You can never crossover in life, and the things you'll learn—they're things I told you no mortal should know."

"Fuck you. You got me hooked on this shit, and now you're fuckin' holding out on me. If you don't fix me up, I'll fuckin' kill you if you can be killed, God-man. It fuckin' hurts. I'm on fire. I need it. I need to know, man. You opened the door, and now… and now I can't close it until I know."

Gavin bit his lip and exhaled through his nose. "Damn. Whatever. Mortal shells are so puny." He reached into his pocket and pulled out a doeskin pouch many times larger than the vial. "Here, take it. Go kill yourself. It's what you wanna do. I wasn't supposed to let it happen, but fuck you, and fuck it. I don't give a shit anymore. You're the last mortal I'll ever waste my time on. Marduk, be damned."

He tossed me the pouch.

I caught it with a greedy smile. "Thanks, brother. But who's Marduk?" I asked as I untied the pouch and dumped a small but sufficient bunny hill on the table for another trip. I waited, but Gavin didn't answer. I didn't care enough to ask again or wait any longer to return to the Afterworld. I made three stout lines and ravenously hoovered the icy dust. Icicles extended from my nose and chin as my skin turned cobalt blue.

The Man in White appeared. He scrunched his lips, glared at me, and shook his head. "Have fun, Nathan," he said bitterly. "Call me when you get back if you're not dead. You've chosen your path, and I have no choice but to guide you to its end."

Gavin's voice faded as I was sucked down a rabbit hole.

Thirty-Four

I found myself in front of another impenetrable Reality Window, separating me from the ones Death had taken from me. I thought about Frank and feared where my thoughts would lead. Too late. Swirling darkness wrapped around me.

Darkness became an inviting light, and I found myself hovering in a massive glass-bubbled chamber with a gray stone floor. Above and all around, I saw the Afterworld (or was it below me?). My parents and Dorothy's mansion were far away, but I could still see Dorothy on the porch, knitting.

I watched an endless stream of shimmering essences enter from a hallway to the left through a Gothic arch. There was an identical arch to my right and each had menacing wooden double doors, intricately carved with magnificently gruesome designs. The doors on the right were closed. Something was written above that arch, but it was blurred out.

The entering specters stepped through each other as if unaware of any other presence. They gawked in awe at the vast world above (or below?) like children in a toy or candy store with everything out of reach. More and more souls entered, crowding the gray stone floor. Many had joy in their eyes as they looked up (or down?). Whatever they saw made them want to cry, but no tears formed.

When the new arrivals reached the height of visual ecstasy, the bubble blackened to reflective obsidian, and the inviting light turned ruby-red. All smiles faded as deafening pounding shook the floor beneath. The obsidian bubble quaked as the gray stone floor turned to ice, and the temperature plummeted to sub-zero. A macabre mosaic of flesh-eaten souls spanned below, packed like sardines, pounding their fists, mouths gaping and gasping.

A terror-stricken soul tsunami raced for the entryway as the doors slammed shut. The doors to my right burst open. A horde of grotesque creatures poured out onto the ice. Some appeared humanoid, but all looked as if they'd been ripped from the deepest, darkest pits of lunacy. They could only be described as demons and all were paired like ravens. They tackled their targets, wrapped each spirit in heavy chains, and dragged them kicking and screaming toward the open doors. As the Damned were hauled into an obsidian hall beyond, the words above the archway became clear.

Abandon All Hope
Ye Who Enter Here

A verse from Dante's imagination. Or was it? *Will I see Virgil soon? I* wondered. *Will he be my guide through this cold inferno?*

I continued drifting like a wraith as the steady stream of convicted souls was yanked like stubborn dogs into the freezing, wide, black-mirrored hall with crimson marble floors (which might have been white if not for the lighting). In the devilish redness, it looked as if the Damned were being dragged through blood. Innumerable elevator doors lined the seemingly endless hall. Ruby Roman numerals were etched above each. When demon pairs arrived at the assigned elevator, the doors opened, and the frightened spirit was pitched inside with malice.

I floated along until I stopped at elevator CCCXIII where a demon pair held a soul dressed as a Green Beret. A black hood covered his head, like a POW in Vietnam. He was dressed like Uncle Frank when I last saw him in his coffin. One of the spirit's tormentors looked like a corpulent monster clown with spiraling ram horns. In its chest was carved, *Abomination*. Its partner wore steampunk goggles, had a bone spike mohawk, and its mouth was barb-wired shut. On its chest was *Cruelty*.

Before viciously throwing the soul into the elevator, they removed the hood. *Holy fuck!* I said in my head. It *was* Frank. I wanted to cover my eyes, but I had no hands, and my eyes were fixed like saucers. I tried to wake up, but the blue dragon gripped me and pulled me into Frank's consciousness. I was now him, and we were both in Hell.

"Who the fuck are you? And what am I doing here?" Frank barked from the elevator corner as he got to his knees. He struggled to stand under the weight of the chains.

Abomination laughed, glanced at Cruelty, and rolled his eyes. "What am I doing here?" it repeated in a clown voice, then slammed a purulent hand on Frank's shoulder. My uncle's knees buckled like putty. A dirty fingernail zipped across Frank's lips, and the lips vanished leaving a smooth patch below his nose.

Cruelty belly laughed. When the demon caught its breath, it replied through barb-wire, "Oh, did you tink you were going to da udder place—the Paradise of your beliefsh. Sho shad, you didn't get da memo, but you are guilty of breaking da Black and White Rule. We didn't get da memo either when we died, but we both knew which way we were headed. I take it your beliefsh gave you shum hope. I can tell you from experience—there ish none here."

Both demons chuckled as they stepped inside. The doors clanged shut. Abomination pressed a button on a silver panel. The elevator lurched, then dropped like an amusement park ride. I watched through Frank's eyes as he fell helplessly—his thoughts filled with rage, hate, and feelings of betrayal... and love and sorrow for Dorothy, who he'd never see again.

After falling like lightning for what seemed like forever, the elevator stopped abruptly, slamming Frank to the floor. I felt his bones snap and a scream rise in his throat, which couldn't escape from sealed lips as he contained the pain with gritted teeth.

The demons regarded the puddle of Frank, giggling, as they cocked their heads from side to side, unphased by the sudden halt.

Frank's shattered soul quickly healed and regained form as if it was never broken.

The doors opened to another long, much narrower, black-mirrored hall lined with gray steel doors. Each door was numbered above with Roman numerals like the elevators. The floor was white marble as above, but there was no blood-flood lamping. The hall's meager light was like dusk's last gasp before a full-dark night.

Frank's pointless chains dissolved into black mist, and his clothing melted away, turning to light blue dust, leaving him barefoot, naked, and shivering. The demons grabbed him. He thought to struggle but had no strength and limply floated along as his bare feet dragged the ground. I felt blunt, slicing, ripping pain. I looked down. The white marble was now jagged glass and upturned nails. Frank's feet and legs were shredded meat and exposed bone, but the wounds didn't bleed, and healed as fast as the skin and underlying structures could be mangled and torn again and again. The demon clown and the skeletal steampunk dragged us past hundreds or thousands of doors, maybe more. Frank's sanity slipped with my own. He thought to laugh—to cry without tears. He tried to scream, but it came out as a muffled rattle.

The demons stopped at cell number MCMLXX (1970) the year Frank returned from Vietnam. Abomination waved a decaying hand across a silver panel, and the steel door groaned open.

Inside was a dark, dingy, grey-stone cell with black slime-coated walls. It was cold enough to pass as a walk-in freezer. The floor was covered with a thick black film that looked like oil but smelled like a mix of tomcat urine and rotting bodies under a desert sun. The smell was as unforgettable as Rajza Vjernika's killing field. Frank gagged.

Cruelty spoke. "Thish ish your lash stop until the Curator comsh for you. Ohhh, and he willl. He alwaysh doesh, and he eshpecially likesh da good onesh like you. Let'sh just shay light doeshn't belong down here. And it ish our job and thosh here at the Prishon of Homicide, to make sure dat we shmother dat light and turn you into one of ush."

The demons shoved Frank into the cell. His lips unsealed right before he landed face down in the fetid oily mixture and swallowed an unhealthy mouthful. Frank rose to his knees and violently retched.

Abomination slammed the door.

Frank tried to get up, but night-colored tendrils burst from the blackness and wrapped around his arms, legs, and face. Micro-tendrils sprouted from the larger ones and sliced through skin, muscle, and bone. I felt it all and wanted to cry, but again Frank had no tears. The pain and assault on his senses were like nothing I had endured. Frank wanted to pass out but couldn't. His soul was bare and bleeding.

The tendrils wrapped tighter and tighter as micro-tendrils danced on every nerve ending like a sound check for a bigger show.

Frank's eyes darted around the dismal room until two more tendrils erupted from the coal-colored mire. The first slid into his mouth and down his throat, making him gag. The second split and sliced into Frank's eyes. Everything went black as an unrelenting cacophony of anguish and torment washed over him. And then there was light.

It was hot and humid. I was in the jungle. Around me, several short, skinny Vietnamese men were dressed in army-green fatigues, sandals, and green flare-rimmed helmets typical of the North Vietnamese Army. Everyone around me held an M1 carbine, a tommy gun, or a standard rifle. I whispered in Vietnamese and understood every word, even though I'd never learned the language. I felt a ringing concussion, a deafening bang, and everything went black.

I peered through another set of eyes as all hell broke loose. I felt a sharp burn, then another and another. I looked up and saw a younger version of Frank as he released the killing burst. Everything went black again.

I looked down at a baby wrapped in my arms, nursing one of my breasts. I could hear gunfire and explosions outside the bamboo hut. I wondered if my husband was still alive. I realized this wasn't me as I felt the sharp burn in my back and looked down as blood mixed with milk from my breast and my baby's skull. The door flew open. I saw Frank and another Green Beret. I felt hatred for the face I loved. Frank's face crumbled, and tears erupted as he ran to help me. Everything dissolved.

I was back in my apartment. My sense of time, space, and reality returned seconds later. I shrieked. I ran to the bathroom, washed my face, then sat on the toilet, rocking back and forth, sobbing. *It was just a nightmare. It was just a nightmare. It's not real. It's not real*, I told myself but I knew better. I wished I'd listened to Gavin, or *whoever*.

There were things we shouldn't know, but I'd opened Pandora's box. Already it was calling me to peek inside again, nagging me to know Vanessa's fate. I swore I'd never do Dark Ethereal again. But the call of the Afterworld was more seductive than ever, and I knew the blue dragon would never let me rest until there were no unanswered questions.

Thirty-Five

I left New York in late August in the middle of an unrelenting heatwave. I didn't call Gavin to let him know I was leaving. By then, it'd been several days since I flushed the remaining contents of the doeskin pouch. As those beautiful dark blue crystals swirled away, I frantically dropped to my knees and dunked my head like I was bobbing for apples, lapping up what I could before licking the pouch clean. I had to get away from the devil on my shoulder. I had to break the dragon's grip even if questions remained unanswered until I joined my parents and Dorothy on the other side. Experiencing my uncle's cruel, unjust fate was too much to bear. It'd broken me, and I feared the truth I would learn about Vanessa. Again, I was a coward, but I couldn't go on living this way. As I said, I had to get away. I had to get clean. I figured someplace cold in the middle of nowhere would at least help with my reptilian thermostat while I suffered going cold turkey. I thought, *Why not Barrow, Alaska*?

Known as Utqiagvik to the Iñupiaq locals, Barrow was the northernmost point in Alaska, with average temperatures ranging from negative five to negative eighteen degrees Fahrenheit. True, New York's winter was coming, but I knew I'd blow my brains out

123

long before then. Definitely would've been the easier option. But just like the noose, I was too cowardly to follow Vanessa's example that would've saved her, our kids and grandkids, and many others a lot of sorrow.

Before I boarded my flight at JFK, the grip hit me hard. I had second thoughts. I pulled out my phone and began dialing Gavin's number, but went to the bathroom instead. I set the phone on the floor and stomped it, and stomped it again and again, which anywhere else would've gotten odd looks from restroom goers. But this was New York City.

I arrived in Barrow on September 1 after a long connecting flight from Anchorage. Once there, I was greeted by massive whale bones and a direction sign that reminded me I was three-thousand three-hundred-eighty miles from home. The natives were very kind. Many were starstruck and brought me their copies of *The Menders: A First American Story* to autograph. Every *N. Miller* was bittersweet, but mostly bitter, and full of self-loathing. At least every penny was going to Norine's scholarship rather than my habit I was there to break. Many were impressed that I dressed so light for an Anglo, yet anything heavier than a t-shirt and shorts had me sweating like I was in a sauna with someone who didn't know when to stop pouring water on the rocks.

I was invited to different homes every night for local fare, including whale, seal, polar bear, walrus, caribou, and various waterfowl and fish. Locals told me stories hoping to inspire another bestseller, and I entertained my hosts with tales of adventure and close calls. Several invited me to return next summer for the bowhead whale hunt. I said I would consider it, and I meant it.

I spent my days running, fishing in the Arctic Ocean with locals, and finding my Zen meditating in the barren tundra with one eye

124

open for polar bears. I even swam with the seals when most visitors only dipped their toes in the icy water.

It was nice to feel normal again, high on sobriety, without all the bullshit of excess fame. Weeks passed and soon I felt a chill. My shakes and headaches lessened. By mid-October, I was cold enough to wear a parka and long johns under snow pants. It seemed so easy (relatively speaking) and I believed Gavin had been wrong. I'd licked my addiction even if nagging questions gave me nightmares and sleepless nights. My skin was now alligator tough over the warm-blooded mortal I was re-becoming.

I left Utqiagvik on October 26. The days were already getting shorter, and soon night would fall for months. Most of the town was there to see me off. It was no longer Barrow to me, and I considered more than just returning next summer. Maybe I would come back sooner to enjoy the endless night and northern light show. I felt inspired. There was nothing like living through hell to get the creative juices going. I was brimming with ideas for future projects for the new, improved, sober, and still indestructible Nathan Miller.

Thirty-Six

Thursday, October 28, 2010.

Yeah. That didn't last. The grip had returned by the time I stepped off the plane in New York. I was sweating and my stomach was twisting when I opened the door to my apartment on that chilly day. Every nerve was frazzled. Every muscle ablaze. I had tried. Oh, how I tried. Even made it to day sixty-nine, but it hurt so bad I wanted to sob. I thought some time away from New York—away from Gavin—would help. But I was wrong.

Gavin was waiting in the recliner, uninvited. I regarded him like a man near death crawling toward a desert oasis. He acted like he didn't see me as he pulled from a whiskey bottle and continued reading a fat novel. It was the new Stephen King—something about a dome.

Sweat poured off me like rain. I glared and pursed my lips but didn't say anything. I went to the bathroom and looked in the mirror. My eyes were bloodshot. I thought this was over. But nooo. I splashed water in my face to cool off. I screamed as it scalded the skin. Steam rose as a voice inside promised that ice in my veins would do the trick and take me to where all my questions would be answered. Not back to the hell where I left Frank. Sweet serenity. A twinkle of fear surfaced, only to be squashed by a repetitive refrain sung by a cannibal corpse. *"Feed the Dragon, Feed the Dragon, Feed the Dragon…"* I gripped my forehead as the chant blazed through my brain with a rapid beat that could've driven anyone mad. Well, anyone, except maybe my old neighbors in Greenwich Village.

My hands trembled. I couldn't wait any longer. I needed my medicine. I needed Dead Blow. I stormed into the living room. "Gavin, I need it now. I need it bad. Fix me up."

"Sixty-nine days. No joke. Not bad for a mortal," Gavin said without his accent. "I told you that you can't stop once the dragon has you. But if you keep up your previous pace, I'll have to teach you a trick to keep you from becoming a bag of bones. It's not pretty, but it'll save your life."

"Sure, fine, whatever! Just hand the shit over, you motherfucker. Hand it over, now!"

Gavin smirked, reached into his coat, and tossed me another doeskin pouch. I dumped the contents on a coffee table and formed a line massive enough to make my eyes bleed ice cubes.

"Stop! Don't use that much," he yelled and pulled out a baggy filled with brown powder. "Here, cut it with this. You won't need much."

"Oh, okay. Thanks, man," I said like a shaky, desperate junkie.

It was dope. I had avoided it up until now, but I figured *what the hell, giddy-up, I'll ride two dragons at once. What's the worst it could do, kill me?*

I dusted most of the Blow back into the pouch, left a small amount on the table, and added some brown sugar.

"That's enough," said Gavin. "This shit packs a punch, but if you do it right, it helps with tolerance. It's like Methadone when the Ice Dragon has its claws in you."

I formed a new sparkling blue and brown rail and imagined brown spines erupting from a snake-like cobalt dragon. I bumped the line and looked into its shimmering blue eyes. *Sooo pretty*, I thought. Its head swayed side to side as its body undulated with the rhythm of a better song—one I couldn't place but pleasant all the same. The beast opened its jaws. Icy flame poured out and consumed me.

Thirty-Seven

I found myself hiking a narrow mountain trail. I believed I was somewhere in northwestern Pakistan since I was approaching a pyramid mountain that looked like K2. A ring of churning gray clouds obscured its summit. The trail steepened as I slowly approached, and then I climbed and climbed, one foot after the other, as I spiraled around the mountain. Always out of breath and near collapse, I moved higher and higher as I went on and on until I disappeared into the gray clouds. Above the clouds, I saw a stone platform at the summit. In the center were spiraling stepping stones floating in the air, which vanished into the eye of another layer of twisting grayness.

I continued on, step by step, round and round, until I emerged and stepped into a vast courtyard filling most of a gravity-defying rock. Thirteen rows of thirteen columns spaced equidistant filled the titanic square. Each column told a story, and upon each monument sat a single monk. Each monk was dressed in a different colored robe giving the tops a rainbow appearance. All eyes were shut. In the distance was a massive monastery. The structure reminded me of central Java's nine-story Borobudur, only many times larger.

I approached the monastery's thirteen stacked platforms. As I passed the sixth column row, I could see the porches around each level in better detail. Between each, monks sat on thousands of platforms-for-one. Past the third row, I could see that all eyes were closed, like the monks atop the columns.

On the porches, monks of varying ages played a variety of instruments: bamboo and human thighbone flutes, oboe-like flageolets, conch shells, trumpets, long tonqin horns, finger and larger bells and cymbals, and hand, paired half-skull, and dama drums. It was an unmelodious cacophony broken only by melancholy chants from the platforms.

At the entrance, there were formidable, vermillion wooden double doors interlaced with dragon carvings. The door frame and arched exterior were painted in brilliant colors and images of many gods, goddesses, animals, plants, symbols, and shapes. Monks not praying or meditating at the entrance walked with arms folded and hands hidden in their sleeves.

Two mouthless monks nodded at the steps that led to the entrance. They moved up the steps, opened the doors, and bowed as I entered. The disjointed orchestra and chanting ceased. Not even the closing doors made a sound. I would've thought I'd gone deaf if not for my heart's thunderous pounding. I looked around the hall. Like the monks at the entrance, none had mouths, but these spirits had no ears. It was as if the senses had lost relevance inside this strange place.

At the opposite end of the titanic foyer was a colossal golden statue that nearly touched the ceiling. While it appeared Hindu in origin, I didn't recognize the golden woman with prayer hands that towered over me. Around the statue was a mix of discordant religious symbolism. On the wall behind the statue was a mammoth yin-yang filling much of the space. The rest of the walls were covered with a mix of religious symbols and a cornucopia of various representations of deities from every continent. It was as if every imaginable mythology from every culture and religion in existence and extinct was on display.

I passed the statue and entered a wide passageway. Somehow, my feet knew where to go.

My feet stopped and my eyes peered up at many flights of steps that rose with no end in sight. I started climbing, flight after flight, never tiring, never short of breath. I knew my answer was near.

When my feet came to the right floor, I continued down a long doorless hall that turned several times. It should've returned me to

129

where I started but always led to another corridor. I continued on and on. I felt like I was in a dream where you never reach your destination.

As I began to despair, I came upon a gray door bordered by one-way mirrors. The room inside was snow-white. A woman in a strait jacket sat in the middle. Her head was shaved cue-ball smooth. She sniffed the air and slowly turned her head. It was Vanessa. Disturbed gray eyes met mine, and I was pulled into her silent nightmare.

The one-way windows became white walls of countless squares that flashed black-and-white images or showed videos before turning white again. Visions of things that never happened. All the could've beens. I saw them simultaneously in every direction as if her head was made of eyes. Tears streamed as vision after vision led to repetitive suicides. In some, we divorced and went our separate ways. In those her life was better without me but never as happy as we once were. In others, we stayed together but I never changed and became more wretched with each passing year. In a few, our youngest, Jon Christian, murdered me to save his mother which further fractured Vanessa's heart. In only one vision did I do what needed to be done—I ate a bullet. She found the mess, but carried on. She passed when she was old but never remarried and died in bitter discontent. Unlike the others, this vision continued on. Like a blooming flower, she was reborn as someone else for one more revolution. She had a wonderful life without me and a pleasant forever in the Paradise thereafter.

Thirty-Eight

The white cell dissolved. I awoke on the floor hyperventilating. My heart pounded. I shivered and sweated like a broken fever.

Gavin stood over me. "Damn you! You scared me. I thought I'd lost you."

I sat up and tried to focus. "You almost killed me with that shit!"

"I know. I'm sorry. I thought your shell could handle it. I sometimes forget what fragile creatures mortals are."

"I can't do that shit again. You gotta help me get these icy claws out of me. I can't go back to that place, or I swear I'll kill myself. Hell, why does it matter? I should be dead. I saw what became of Vanessa."

"Saw what?"

"Don't act like you don't know what's going on. What was that place? The place where Vanessa was being tortured?"

Gavin paused and rubbed his face. "It's called the Asylum of Silence. It's a place reserved for mortals who end their lives. Once there, condemned spirits witness what would've been had they not ended things before Fate's appointment with Death. What you saw are potential outcomes, an endless chain of what-ifs to punish your wife for breaking the Black and White Rule. It is the same rule that governs the Prison of Homicide where you witnessed your Uncle Frank's torments. There, the Curator punishes those who take mortal lives of other shells before Fate's predestination. It's why your uncle is there now. He doesn't belong there, like countless others who don't belong there or…" Gavin shook his head and acted like he was about to continue.

"What?"

"Nothing." Gavin pulled hard on the whiskey bottle.

I didn't pry further. I sensed that he too had lost someone he cared for to my vision of Hell. "Look, you can't let me do that blue shit again. You can't give me any more, no matter how much I beg."

"No problemo. This is the last of my stash. You're welcome to flush it down the toilet."

I looked at the pouch on the cracked coffee table and licked my lips.

"That is unless you're not sure."

I looked at the pouch again, picked it up, and felt the frosty glow. I opened the pouch. Inside, starlight twinkled back and swirled like a miniature Milky Way. "No. I'm sure, but you'll have to do it. I can't." I set the pouch down.

Gavin nodded and reached for the bag.

I grabbed his wrist.

He glowered into my desperate, quivering eyes.

I let go.

Gavin went to the bathroom. A flush and running water followed. He returned with an inverted wet leather bag that didn't sparkle.

I started crying. My head raced with images of the Reality Window and Dorothy alone on the other side. She called out, pleading for me to come back and visit. My mother and father stood beside her. There were no visions of Hell or Purgatory—only the most pleasant of pleasant thoughts as the remaining Dead Blow swirled away.

Gavin sat on the couch and removed a small leather case from his jacket. Inside was a spoon, lighter, a few tuberculin syringes, a rubber tourniquet, and a baggy filled with brown powder. He set the contents on the table like a place setting for a feast. He tapped a small amount of powder into the spoon and heated it with the lighter. I watched sugar melt into an opaque liquid. He put the lighter down, grabbed a syringe, and sucked up the spoon's contents.

I sat by Gavin.

"You'll need this if you want to survive withdrawal."

It's funny. When heroin was brought to market by Bayer, that's what it was marketed for: to save Civil War veterans from morphine addiction. Kind of like Oxy before the Age of Ethereal. The more things change… well you know how it goes.

As the blue dragon swam downstream, I licked my lips. My mind and body screamed. One almost escaped my mouth.

Gavin tapped the syringe, held it between his teeth, and knelt.

I hungrily extended my arm.

He wrapped and tightened the tourniquet above the elbow and slapped the vein. The eager vessel rose to attention. Gavin tapped the stainless steel fang's plastic holder once more and slid the needle in. He released the tourniquet and injected the venom.

Rockets went off, and visions of Heaven returned. The Doors played *Break on Through* as a heavenly host of angels danced and sang along. Frank was kissing Dorothy. Grandpa Milton and Grandma Dorine were chatting with my mother and father. Ryan and Suzanne Mender were there. Ryan was smiling as he swung Alex around in a circle. And Alex was laughing. Oh, was he laughing. Then I saw Vanessa. She was dressed in her prison black-and-whites. She was beautiful. She smiled as her twinkling grays beckoned for me to join her. Dance with her. I did, and she whispered that she forgave me and that she still loved me. Yeah. Yeah. Yeah. Franklin, Jenna, and Jonathan got the invite. Jonathan hugged me and told me he loved me and that he forgave me. We all ran with crowds of dearly departed and rushed a massive stage in the middle of a beautiful garden where two Men in Black sang *Folsom Prison Blues*. One was Johnny Cash, and the other was the man who'd been following me since my thirteenth birthday. The Reaper of Souls tipped his hat and nodded at me. Johnny walked to the edge of the stage and motioned for me to join them for *Ring Of Fire*. The crowd went wild and chanted, "NATHAN, NATHAN, NATHAN."

Halfway through the song, my stomach rumbled.

I opened my eyes, popped from my chair, and ran to the bathroom. I vomited several times, then dry heaved several more. When I finished, I leaned against the toilet. Everything I'd seen was a lie, and the heroin haze couldn't fool me otherwise. I started weeping as I rocked forward and back. I slammed my fists against the ground, got up, and... and started throwing anything that wasn't nailed down in the bathroom. I moved into the living room and proceeded to destroy everything that could be broken before moving onto the kitchen.

Gavin watched bemused as he took another pull from his bottle. I wanted to smash his face in but I still had more to destroy.

When I saw nothing left to break, I glared at Gavin. "Get the fuck out. I want you gone, you Goddamn devil. This is your fault. I want you out of here and I want you out of my fucking life."

"Okay, okay. I will let you cool off. Call me later," Gavin calmly said and headed for the door.

"There won't be a later," I said, hurling a heavy paperweight at his head.

He lifted his hand lightning-quick and made a backhand catch. He set the paperweight on an end table my rampage had neglected. He faced me. "Like I said, I'll see you later. You don't have a choice. You'll need me soon."

I seethed as Gavin shook his head, left my apartment, and closed the door. I knew he was right. I was fucked from the moment Gavin gave me the Dark Blue. But he was also wrong. There wouldn't be a *soon* because I planned to join Vanessa in her silent hell. I only wished I'd done it sooner while she was still alive so her happy ending in the next life would've come true.

I went to the bedroom and pulled my pistol from under the mattress. I glanced at the phone on the chest of drawers and thought about calling Franklin and Jenna... and Jonathan if he would even take the call. I knew he wouldn't and would probably dance on my grave after I did what should've been done long ago.

I sat on the bed, checked the magazine, racked the slide, and placed the business end in my mouth. I thought about Vanessa in her white cell. I thought of everyone I had loved, disappointed, hurt, and irreparably damaged. I thought of those who didn't know me, who would lament my passing with candlelight vigils. A somber laugh escaped. I said, "Enough. Let's do this." I flexed a finger. And... realized I'd forgotten to flip off the safety.

My phone buzzed.

Really? I thought. I set the gun on the bed and grabbed my Blackberry. The text was from an unlisted number and read:

*Let's not meet this way. Come
down to Charlotte's so we can
talk. Coffee's on me.
Your friend, Morton Death
AKA The Man in Black*

Thirty-Nine

I set the Blackberry next to the deadly Pez dispenser. I studied the gun, and thought about how close I came this time. I removed the magazine and unchambered the round. I rubbed my mouth and stroked my beard. I was at a loss. Why didn't I finish the job? It wasn't fear. Okay, maybe a little. No, not really. If not fear, then what? Journalistic curiosity? Yeah, whatever. Okay, it must have been. After all, the Man in Black had been following me my whole life. Well, most of it, and I'd been waiting for this moment since the Harrisburg County Fair. Then there was that creative writing paper about a war correspondent who gets a once in a lifetime opportunity to interview the Grim Reaper. I still had Mr. Brand's *A+/Wow* rated paper in a folder mixed with a scrambled mess of long untouched manuscripts that testified to the state of my disheveled mind. Everything was heaped next to a dusty Deluxe Royal typewriter which now lay in pieces.

Well, here was my chance. But why did the Reaper stop me? It was like he was cheating at his own game. We would've met either way, but the Man in Black wanted to chat while I was still breathing.

I even had a name to go with the hat and coat now. Once I was dead, I doubted this *Morton* would've been in a talking mood since he was a very busy man in this world.

I reinserted the mag and replaced the pistol under the mattress. I could always finish the job later once I had the scoop of a lifetime no one but I would ever know about.

I slid my jacket on and used the restroom. As I pissed, I regarded sunken, dead eyes behind dark rings. Even with the heroin buzz, my nerves and muscles burned. Gavin was an evil idiot. The smack would only kill me slightly slower than the Dead Blow. I looked at the yellowing water and wanted to cry as I thought of the cobalt dream swirling away. I thought about the pistol again.

I neurotically scrubbed my hands until they bled and did the same to my face. Before I left, I rummaged through files for my *Interview with Death*, found the yellowing paper-clipped essay, and regarded the *A+/Wow* in red ink at the top. "If Mr. Brands could see me now," I said and found the strength to chuckle. I slipped the essay into a folder and grabbed my handheld recorder. I donned dark sunglasses and headed to the coffee shop.

When the sun scorched my eyes, I realized it was mid-afternoon. Of what day, I hadn't a clue. I checked my watch. It was October 29. It was cold and I'd forgotten my jacket. I was wearing jeans and a Johnny Cash t-shirt with the country legend flipping the camera a defiant middle finger. I felt like a fanboy and I didn't smell so good, either. I thought about running back upstairs but my hazy head said, "Fuck it."

Food carts lined the streets as people packed the sidewalk. Honking vehicles of every sort clogged the thoroughfare. I pushed forward to the café where Death awaited me. It was strange since it would be a friendly visit, not the one-time business call he made to everyone else.

The café had been a Starbucks until a few months ago. Like everything else, Charlotte Lee's Cafes were taking over the coffee world. I stepped inside the crowded café. Behind the counter and menu was a large image of the smiling buxom belle from Alabama herself, Charlotte Lee, with arms outstretched, welcoming everyone to her humble establishment. I glanced around and saw a man in black wearing a Stetson. He sat alone, reading a newspaper. I couldn't see his face but knew he wasn't the same man from the Church of Death's Enlightenment who I bumped into five months earlier.

"Are you Morton?" I asked.

His cobalt eyes rose. He smiled and said. "Yes. Have a seat."

Death's hand motioned to the chair in front of me, and I sat.

"We have a lot to talk about," he continued with the grainy but charming voice of a gentleman that would've been pleasant to listen to even if he were reading a dictionary from A to Z.

I laid the folder on the table.

"What would you like?" Morton asked, scratching his neck. "As I texted you, coffee's on me. And may I suggest the blueberry kolaches? Quite amazing if I do say so myself. Almost as good as my sister's cookies."

"That sounds good. Thanks," I said.

The Man in Black went to the counter. The male barista addressed him with a thick Jersey accent, took his money, and gave him change. A moment later, the young man handed Death two coffees and a pair of kolaches. The Man in Black returned to the table and handed me my coffee.

I sipped. *Cream and sugar. Just like I like it... as if he knew. Well, almost,* I thought. Something was missing.

"You're probably wondering—do they see me? Of course, they do. Why would I hide? They just see me as another face in the crowd. Sure, I tone down my eternal blues, but not for you. Without that, I'm just another person they pass without another thought while tangled up with their daily worries. If they do notice me, they just think I'm one of those religious kooks that took what I revealed to Mr. Batra a little further than I intended. Ahhh, but they're harmless enough. Yes, Raj was among the few like you that I have allowed to see me as I am. He was a pet project of mine after 2007 and was about where you were when I asked him to join me for a cup of Joe at Charlotte's #1 in Packer City."

"Yeah, I met him there once with the Menders."

"I know," replied Death.

"Yeah, of course you do. So, if you're here—what's happening with, well, you know?"

"The dying—the ones Fate so kindly schedules for me to meet. That's the problem when I spend time here or in another there—mortals go on dying and can't be ushered through the White Room until I attend to them. It's kind of like a waiting room—a waystation. But sometimes, I need a good cup of coffee. And there's none better than Charlotte's."

I sipped. Again, something was missing.

"Yes, I made yours De-Ethereal. I see it in your eyes through your glasses. Someone's been hitting the dark stuff. Just curious where you've been getting it."

"From a friend of mine."

"Yes. Some friend. We'll talk about this *friend* of yours later. For now, drink up and enjoy the kolache. It's to die for. Pardon the expression," Morton said with a grin.

"Thanks... thanks for saving me," I said in a humbled tone.

"No problem. You're a good man, deep down. Deep, deep down. You've just lost your way, and I am determined to help you find it. Then perhaps you can help me, but I'll get to that later. Much later. So, what's in the folder?"

"I, I feel a little embarrassed," I said as shyness, thought long extinct, made me feel like the awkward teen who wrote the essay for Mr. Brands. I slid the folder across the table to Death.

Morton opened it and slid out the essay.

I took out my recorder. "Do you mind?"

"An Interview with Death, huh?" he said, looking at the first page. He glanced up and saw the recorder. "Oh, not at all. But, we won't be here long. I have a much better place for us to have our more lengthy and overdue question and answer session."

I slid the recorder back in my jeans pocket.

Morton read my paper as I took my time nibbling the kolache and sipping the very hot coffee. His expressions changed as he perused the pages. He grinned. He chuckled. He nodded. He turned pensive. When he finished, he slid the paper back in the folder and looked away, his eyes heavy with thought.

I let him process my words as I watched people mill about, oblivious of their close brush with Death. When the last of my kolache disappeared, I emptied the coffee that was now warm.

"You ready?" asked Morton.

"Sure. Where're we going?"

"For a walk."

Morton tucked my folder in his trench coat. We stood, and he brushed past several people on the way outside. I saw two men in black.

Death tipped his hat to the pair.

They tipped theirs and replied, "Peace in Death, my brother," and bowed with prayer hands.

Morton smiled and responded in kind, "Peace in Death, my brothers."

We stopped at the corner down from the café. I saw a young girl holding her mother's hand. Death's head turned to me with a grim aspect I knew well. He nodded and laid a hand on my shoulder.

The world turned sepia black and white, empty of everything living except for me and Morton (but I wasn't sure I counted him among the living). Seconds later, the mother and girl entered the alternate reality.

"Who are you?" asked the little girl.

"My name is Morton."

"And who are you, mister?" the girl asked me.

"Uh, uh… My name is… my name is Nathan Reaper." I had no idea why I said that. It just came out and sounded natural—like it was my given name.

"Where are we?" asked the woman.

"This is the White Room," said Morton. "I'm here because you both just died." He pursed his lips thin. "That might have been a little harsh. I'm, I'm sorry." Three doors appeared. The door on the

141

right creaked open. "And sorry about those hinges. They need some oil."

"What do you *mean* we died?" asked the woman.

Morton pointed at a bus. "You really should look both ways before you cross the street."

The woman covered her mouth. "Damn. Oh damn. Oh damn. I'm… so sorry, Victoria."

"Don't be, Mama. We're together. When's Daddy coming?"

"Not for a while," said Morton. "But you get to wait for him in a *really* nice place. And don't you worry, your daddy will be here in a blink of an eye, or maybe a little longer."

Little Victoria smiled.

The woman lipped, "*Thank you*."

Morton extended his right arm and pointed toward the open door.

The woman and little Victoria started to skip through but stopped at the threshold. The woman looked back, suddenly unsure.

Morton waved his hand forward and said, "Just keep walking, and you'll find yourself at your destination when you get there. And when you do, make sure to leave a review of your experience and anything else I could've done better to make your dying more pleasant."

"I definitely will," said the woman, clearly pleased with her first and only death experience.

"Bye, Mr. Morton," said Victoria. She smiled and waved as they crossed the threshold.

The door closed and I found myself walking the crowded street with Death as sirens screamed and onlookers gawked at the two bloody shells that once contained the woman and Victoria's immortal souls.

"Nathan, I have been doing this since the first mortal death. I'd like to say it gets easier, but something in me—something in my programming doesn't let it get any easier. And I remember every death that has ever been. Every mortal life ever lived. It is a burden that gets heavier with every soul I reap, but there's no one else who can do my job. But certain deaths weigh heavier than others—ones that still haunt my existence. I couldn't let you take your life. Like Mr. Batra, I sense there is a plan for you that not even I fully understand. Let's head to my office. We can talk when we get there. That way, the Dying won't continue to pile up while we get to know each other."

We turned from the carnage and stepped around the corner. Morton placed a hand on my shoulder, and we weren't in New York anymore. I looked at my watch. It had stopped at 3:13:13 p.m.

Forty

I stood by Death facing what looked like a cross between a fancy law office and a church. It was painted gray with stained glass windows. The front door was black with a white doorbell to the right. Upon the door was a platinum plaque that read:

Soul Reaping Offices of
Gladys Fate
&
Morton Death
Ushering in the Afterlife
since the dawn of Mortalkind

We walked up the steps. Morton opened and held the door. I entered, but before the door closed, a shrill voice sliced the silence.

"Dang it, Morton. We are so far behind. What have you been doing?" She paused and looked at me, "Oh, hello, Nathan Miller," she said, then returned to ripping the Reaper. "Do you know how many souls have piled up since you decided to take your little coffee break? You know our responsibilities. You can rest when you're not Death."

Morton sighed, shook his head, and looked at me. "If you could take a seat, I'll be back in a little bit."

The woman handed Death a thick stack of papers. He quickly perused them and impossibly slid them inside his trench coat. He lowered his head and stepped outside. Morton sighed, closed the door, and left me alone with the elegant older woman.

The woman had the timeless beauty, fair complexion, and curves of someone much younger. She wore a black long-sleeve dress that extended below the knees and low-heeled loafers with bow tassels. Around her neck was a pearl necklace with a platinum Scythe pendant. Above it, a warm smile, and soft eyes hiding behind a pair of white-framed horned-rimmed glasses. A single red rose was drawn on each horn. Her dark-graying hair was shoulder-length and pulled over her ears, curled and voluminous in back with two large curls on top. She reminded me of a model on the cover of a 1950's glamour magazine.

"Nathan, would you like some coffee, or are you more of a milk and cookies guy?" she said with a seductive wink. "Fresh chocolate chip?"

"Uhh. Yeah. Cookies sound great."

The woman looked familiar but much older than the one tickling my brain. Her face was pleasant, but the memory wasn't. Why I couldn't place the face, I didn't know. She returned minutes later with a plate of steaming sweets and warm milk.

The woman sat across from me in a black leather chair with her legs crossed. She leaned forward and rested her elbows on the crossed leg and rested her chin on interlaced fingers.

"Nathan, it is so nice to finally meet you," the woman said with a pleasant smile. "Morton has really taken a liking to you in this reality and revolution you find yourself in. No offense, but some of the other versions of you are, umm, much less interesting." She dropped her hands, sat back, uncrossed her legs, and huffed a sigh. She pointed at me and said, "But this one… I can't help but wonder how everything will work out. Usually, I know, but you're something of an enigma. Oh, I'm sorry, I haven't introduced myself. My name is Gladys Fate." She leaned over, held my hand, and patted it gently. "Morton's my brother, by the way." Her voice softened to a tender tone. "I know you're going through a rough patch right now, but hang in there. It'll get better, but don't ask me how it ends. That's for me to know and for you to find out. Of course, how you end up there, only my sister knows."

That's when I recognized her and thought, *Delores Destiny. Gladys looks like an older version of Delores Destiny—that evil bitch!*

"Is something wrong?" asked Gladys.

"Your sister—I think we've met," I said, with barely contained disgust. I casually withdrew my hand as not to blow off the lid.

"Really? When? Where?"

"I don't remember, exactly," I lied.

"Hmmm. You know, it amazes me to this Age in every mortal reality that Delores and I were created together. Twins, can you believe it? Like my brother Morton Death and Frederick Chance. The Man in Black and the Man in White. But there couldn't be a kinder creation than Morton or a viler creature than Frederick. And don't get me started about Delores. Well, enough talk for now. Here, let me turn on the idiot box you mortals like so much. You can watch my brother catch up on the backlog his little coffee break caused."

Fate waved her hand. The widescreen lit up, filled with thousands of picture-in-pictures. It was like a dragonfly eye, except every facet had a picture split between the colored, grisly world of reality and the sepia room where Morton ushered souls through one of three doors. Each video box was virtually microscopic, but somehow, I could make out every facet. I observed the aspects of every spirit as they passed through the door open to them. Those stepping through the left had emotions ranging from terror to anger. Those passing through the middle, melancholy to anguish. But the faces of those striding through the right door were pleasant and joyous, like the woman and little Victoria.

Gladys left me alone in this waiting room.

I watched the screen for a few more minutes. Slowly the pictures-in-picture became less numerous and larger until only one remained, then none. Morton stepped through the door.

146

"Well, all the souls that needed reaping are reaped... at least for now," Death said as he hung his hat on a hook by the door and exposed his Einstein frizz. "Nathan, why don't you and I head to my library where we can talk. Nice thing about this realm is that your world is paused when we're here. So, we can take as long as we need to answer questions I should have answered long ago."

Forty-One

Death's library was multi-story with black spiral staircases connected to a roomy open area with floors and columns of mirrored obsidian. Breaking the lonely openness was a black leather couch and recliner with a contrasting deep water blue coffee table between them. Its top swirled with slow eddies of aquamarine, aqua, and darker shades. Everything around me was coal-colored but the library was well lit from no obvious source.

Morton sat in the recliner and motioned for me to make myself comfortable on the sofa.

"I see you like to read," I said, stating the obvious as I gawked in awe at the mind boggling collection of volumes in the near distance.

"Yes. But I don't have many opportunities to sit long enough to enjoy a good book. So, I collect. Fortunately, along with remembering everyone's death, I have an elaborate memory of each and every life..." Death said, tapping his forehead. He pointed at me, "...including all the great authors who ever walked the Realities. I know their works and every detail that went into creating them. But there is still something to be said about sitting back with a good book, smelling the pages, feeling a former tree between one's

147

fingers, and creating new worlds from mortal imaginations. I've always been fascinated with your kind. How they can create such marvelous things but destroy just as marvelously. Some of us thought it would be best to do away with mortals shortly after their creation. Nothing against you, personally. And I'm not saying I agreed. But I'm getting ahead of myself since I doubt you have a grasp on any of this or who or what we are. And after saving you from yourself, this may not be a good time."

"It's okay. I've been waiting a lifetime to meet you."

Morton chuckled. "Doesn't everyone? Alright, then I'll continue." He retrieved my folder from his trench coat and removed my essay. "You had several good questions in this marvelous essay of yours. And yes, I agree with your teacher. That was *A+/Wow* and the first taste of great things to come. So, are you sure you're up for that interview with Death you've been pining for since you were sixteen?"

So much went through my head at that moment. Every instant Death visited me. Every close call where his hand passed over me. Every time I asked the question, *Why me*? Why did he choose to take the hazel-eyed girl and not me? So many lives would've been far better if she'd lived instead of me.

"Well, yes or no? Are you ready?" Death asked insistently.

"Yes. Yes, I am," I said, taking off my sunglasses having just realized I was still wearing them. I set them on the coffee table as my eyes quickly adjusted to the library's strange illumination.

"Well, here's your paper," he said, extending the arm holding the pages.

"I don't need it. I know the questions by heart. It's yours now. A gift if you want it," I said and unconsciously raised a hand and

148

stroked my beard. There was nothing there but smooth skin. I leaned forward, regarded my dark reflection on the floor, and saw my sixteen-year-old face. Death didn't seem to notice the change. I figured I was losing my mind in my heroin haze, but I didn't feel hazy. My mind felt crisp and crystal clear as if I'd always been clean and sober.

"Really? Well, thank you," said Morton. "Nathan Miller's first literary work of any acclaim. I will cherish it for an eternity. I know just where I'll put it."

I pulled out my recorder and pressed record.

"I guess I'll start with my first question. Why do you dress like you do?"

"Oh, and would you like to know my favorite color, too? I'll keep you hanging," Death said with a grin. "But seriously, why do I dress the way I do? Or better yet, why do I choose this appearance? Your answer was close. I once tried to keep up with all the different versions of myself people came up with. I finally said, 'screw it.' It is true I once masqueraded around as the Grim Reaper when the Bubonic plague was having its way, but it didn't fit my personality. Scared people like all these other yahoos mortals came up with. Again, it just wasn't me. I mean, I'm a nice guy, but I was given a shitty job. So, I decided on my current uniform and haven't regretted it since. And for the most part, the newly dead seem to get a kick out of it. I mean, seriously, why do I need to be scary? Souls are scared enough when the wind of life leaves their mortal lungs, and their fleshy shells cease their usefulness." He smiled and chuckled with a thought and asked, "Did you know your Johnny Cash stole his look from me?"

"Really?"

149

"Sure enough. He was in a bad way back in *your reality's* 1966. He had overdosed in Toronto on enough pills and booze to kill an elephant. Yes, reports said he was found *'virtually dead.'* But I can tell you, he was dead as a doornail—pardon the cliché—when we spoke in the White Room. I knew he still had things to do so I gave him a second chance to clean up his shit. And he did. After that, he started dressing like me, and a few years later, he wrote *Man in Black*. Since your Uncle Frank was a big Johnny Cash fan, I'm sure you know he arrived in Paradise on your reality's September 12, 2003. Well, at a concert in the Heavens of Christ, he thanked me for the second chance and said I'd inspired the song right before he asked me to come up and sing *'Men in Black'* with him."

"Wow," was all I said as I nodded and jotted a mental reminder to ask about these other realities he kept referring to, as if there were several more than the one I knew. I paused a little longer to make sure Death had nothing to add.

"Okay. Next question. Where did you come from? I mean, how did you come into existence?"

"Yes. Quite an imagination you had back in '76. I loved the skeletal stork bringing baby Death to his skull-faced parents who dressed in Black Plague robes." Death laughed. "And then my rebellious teen angst when I wanted to be a country legend like Johnny Cash rather than to carry on the family business. Funny stuff. Absolutely love it. But let me tell you the truth of how and why my brother, sisters, and I came into existence. When I'm done, much will be clear about a whole lot of things."

Morton leaned forward. "I find answers are better with visuals." He waved his hand over the aquamarine coffee table. It rippled like water and transformed into a beautiful tropical garden with every imaginable fruit and vegetable. There were flowers, bushes, and trees of every variety. Creeks snaked through the lushness creating ponds and waterfalls. Animals of every shape and size interacted with each other and spoke a language understood by all. In the middle walked a man carrying a toddler and a woman holding a young boy's hand. The man doted on his youngest but refused to look at the oldest.

"The four of us came into being around the time the Eternals Gaia and Marduk created the original nine mortal couples."

"Wait, who's Marduk?"

"Oh, I'm sorry, I'm getting ahead of myself. He is who you call the Devil, Satan. He has many other names, but, he also played certain roles in various pantheons but only used his real name in Mesopotamia. He used to have a thing with the mother of all creation, Mother Earth, Gaia, before they had a falling out. But I'll get to that."

From there, it just got stranger for this stranger in this strange everafter. And as my impressions of the Afterworld Frank and Dorothy had raised me to believe in were systemically shattered, I relaxed, listened, and decided to discard several of my childish questions and go with the flow of this unlikely interview.

Death continued. "As far as anyone knows, Gaia, Marduk, and their son Timethy—or Time as mortals call him—were the first Eternals. That's what me and my siblings are. Of course, there were also Eternal Guardians, or big *A* angels, who inhabited what was known as Old Paradise. They were programmed for service, and I have no idea if they played a part in creating the world we were dropped into called New Paradise. This place is now called Earth or Terra or the Mortal World, and was designed for the mortal creature. That would be you. Both Gaia and Marduk had high hopes for their creation, and each couple was given their own garden paradise like the one you see on the table. This one was Eden.

"The couple before you is Adam and Eve. The older child is Cain, and the younger one is Abel. This mating pair was Marduk's personal creation, and he was quite proud of them. But something wasn't right between Adam and Cain. I had observed Adam and Eve's other children and the children of the other eight couples. All of them, except Adam, nurtured and showered their offspring with love. But Adam hated Cain. I never understood why. As the years passed, Adam's loathing of Cain grew as his love for Abel blossomed. And Adam... well, he never spared the stick for Cain while spoiling Abel. Cain came to despise Abel, who wanted nothing more than to be loved by his older brother.

"One day, they got into a fight. What happened next was an accident, but the story passed down was that Cain slew his brother. The truth is, they were wrestling. It got out of hand. You know, mortal kids will be mortal kids. Cain got angry and pushed Abel to the ground. Abel hit his head on a rock. It busted open, and he died. Simple as that.

"I watched tears fall from the young man's eyes as Abel stared sightlessly at the blue sky that day as the ground beneath him turned red. Cain picked up the cursed rock and threw it to the ground to punish the object that never knew life. Then he ran to his father and mother, crying, and told them what'd happened. When they returned to Abel's body, Adam saw the rock with Cain's bloody handprint. Adam didn't believe Cain's story and beat him within an inch of his mortal shell's usefulness. Eve tried to stop him and covered Cain's broken body with her own to block the killing blow. Adam grabbed Eve's arm and pulled her off. By then, his fury had cooled. So, he just dragged Eve back to their cave by her hair and left Cain to die in the field. But Cain didn't die, and when he came to, he ran from Eden, and never returned. Yes, Abel was the first Mortal I led through the White Room. I guess I've accidentally answered your next question."

"It's okay. So, why do you call it the White Room?"

"Yes, I know it's more sepia, but White Room sounds better."

"Oh. So, who created the White Room?" I asked.

"Same Master Creator who created us all. No one has ever seen him, or any Eternal who has, isn't saying. We sometimes wonder if he or she or whatever it is even exists. Maybe we just *are*. That's why we're called Eternals. We are different from Immortals. Immortals are *Overspirits* that sleeping *Underspirits* in mortal shells are destined to become.

"But let me continue with the previous question concerning Abel. That boy knew it was an accident and was worried about his brother. I mean, even though he was dead, he still loved Cain. I still like that kid though his Overspirit is many thousands of years old. Anyway, Abel blamed his father for Cain's anger management issues and hoped I'd show mercy and let them be together wherever the hall beyond the door led."

"Door? I thought there were three."

"Yes, there are... now. Back then, there was only one door because that's all the White Room's creator believed was needed."

"So, how did the other two doors come into existence?" I asked. "And... what are they? I watched the monitor. I saw you usher people through all three."

"Yeah, those. You can thank my sister Delores for that. Well, her and Marduk. My younger sister—well, younger-looking, that is—

has the gift of seeing the future and when there was a future, the present, and the past. She's a Farseer, but not an Allseer. A fine distinction but an important one. But within the Realities, she sees the past, presents, and futures of every mortal who has ever lived and died, is now living, or will come into existence."

Death waved his hand over the table again. "As your mortal world grew older, Delores saw all pasts and presents and how they interacted, leading to the outcomes my other sister, Gladys, is charged with, that is, each mortal's fate. Only she has the power to open the White Room that I alone control. But, back to *sweet* sister Delores.

"When Abel died, Delores saw all that would follow the first murder, even if that was *not* exactly true. She saw more killing as mortals organized into civilized groups and began committing organized murder and called it war. Delores saw the tools of death that started with hands, sticks, and stones. From there, the tools and the tactics mushroomed until mass murder became art. Eventually, a single atom was split with the potential to destroy the beautiful creation provided to the mortal creature.

"Delores was terrified by her visions and went to Marduk and Gaia. I was there, along with my younger-appearing brother, Frederick Chance, and Gladys. We tried to console her. And Marduk... well he was in shock and refused to believe that Cain murdered Abel since Adam and Eve were his *perfect* design. But Delores convinced him of Adam's *truth*. I told him it wasn't as it appeared, but Marduk wouldn't listen. Delores had his ear and recommended that Adam and Eve's line be terminated to see if the other eight couples' futures had been tainted by their defective influence. Marduk agreed but felt it best to terminate the entire *Grand Experiment*—also known as the *Mortal Project*—for the good of all creation. They would start over with another creature like they had done before the four of us existed. Gaia was furious that Marduk would even suggest such a thing. She believed all mortal lines should be allowed to live and that with the proper nurturing, Delores's visions could be changed.

"That's when the eighth ruling Eternal appeared. Her name was Karma. Like the Original Three, she was never given a last name. She was different from the four of us and the Original Three. She had free will and a terrible temper. We learned fast she was not to be trifled with. As the gulf widened between the Eternal couple, Karma refused to take sides, and her will was unpredictable. And if you made her angry, she could be—as you mortals say—*a real bitch*. Word to the wise, if you ever meet her, don't ever call her that or even think it. I'll be honest with you, she scares even me.

"When it came to a vote concerning the mortal creature's fate, Timethy recused himself because he didn't want to side against his mother or father. So sad. Good kid, crappy dad."

He paused and his piercing eyes fell on me as if accusing me of the same, or maybe, it was the guilt for all my failings as one of the flawed creatures these gods despised.

Death continued. "Anyway, without the supreme will of the Original Three, it was up to Karma to decide the creature's fate. Of course, Marduk pissed her off, and she voted with Gaia to spite him even though she hated mortals. Yes, to this epoch, she has no qualms calling the mortal creation an *idiot's conception*."

Death waved his hand over the table. It rippled flat then rose into animations of seven gods furiously arguing on golden thrones arranged in a circle. Four had a female appearance and the others looked male. I recognized four of them, but Fate and Death were

155

wearing black togas and Destiny and Gavin's alter ego wore white. All four had mystical deep water blue eyes. None looked as if they'd aged a day since Abel's death. One of the other two female forms sat on an elevated throne. She was full-bodied, well-proportioned, with long hair that was half blue and half green. Her skin was creamy cappuccino and her eyes two-toned aqua and emerald. She wore a loose-fit, low-cut emerald peplos with a blue aquamarine belt. Her bosoms were barely concealed. It wasn't hard to guess her name. Across from Gaia was the shortest of the seven—a female form with dark brown skin and coffee-colored eyes, wearing a colorful, flowery sari. I recognized her as well. Her face was the same as that on the massive statue inside the silent entrance hall in Vanessa's asylum. To Karma's left was the tallest of the Eternals. He had angry, mocha-colored eyes, and a mustache that flowed into a beard. Like his hair, the beard was squared-off, collar-bone-length, and braided. His arms were crossed over a broad chest. I'd seen him before on Mesopotamian stone reliefs, often standing next to a strange beast that looked like a unicorn dragon with the hindlegs of an eagle and forelegs of a lion. This was Marduk and I wondered if his beast Sirrush was more than mythological legend. At this point, anything was possible.

Death looked at me to make sure I was following his graphic display. I refocused and he continued. "With the future of mortalkind secured, the next question was, how do we prevent Delores's visions? Marduk proposed a compromise known as the *Black and White Rule*. So, rather than terminate the Mortal Project, he recommended an absolute punishment for any mortal who willfully took the life of another by any means for whatever reason. Based on the visions, he thought ahead to when hands would no longer be needed, and stone, metal, disease, fire, and even other mortals would be used to take lives. He even thought about those who used their hands to take their own lives. Delores and Frederick were impressed with Marduk's skill as a lawmaker, but Gaia didn't like the idea of revenge masquerading around as justice. She believed mortals who had gone astray could be brought back to the right path. She believed in finding ways to restore their peace, harmony, and balance. Gladys and I agreed because we saw too many gray areas where Marduk's proposal would be unfair. We both pushed for moderation and something we called the *Gray Rule*.

"Karma was unimpressed with everyone's arguments, but her vote leaned toward the Gray because she hated Marduk. Marduk knew this, so he made Karma a proposal. Since Karma had a mindheart of her own, Marduk thought it best to let her punish those who ended their lives as she saw fit. She liked the idea and agreed to vote for Marduk's rule if he would sweeten the deal and let her deal with those who didn't break the rule but weren't quite ready for Paradise. Gaia worried what Karma had in her mindheart."

I quizzically narrowed my eyes.

"Oh, mindheart. Of course, you don't know what that is. It's just the way Eternals and Immortals are made. The heart and the mind are one and can't be separated from the other as in mortal shells. Same is true of Underspirits, or Pre-Immortals, and Imaginaries. Anyway, as I was saying—those who enter the White Room with their peace and harmony out of whack, it would be Karma's job to assign them a new *Revolution*—recycle, um, reincarnation, a new life, that is—but not always as a mortal or even an animal. But not a rock. Has to be a living thing. Scratch that, there are a few rare exceptions, but we won't get into that. But anyway, each Revolution would be connected to the essence of the original Wholespirit, which is the amalgamation of all versions of the Underspirit. That's how Samara Station came into being. Are you still following me?"

I was just barely as I furrowed my eyebrows. *Realities? Imaginaries? What the hell else? Oy vey. Focus, focus, focus,* I thought.

"Well, are you? Do you have any questions?" Death asked with a palm out and his head tilted.

"Yes. And… No, not yet," I replied, waving a hand.

"Good. Alright then. Knowing that Marduk's Rule would pass, I proposed there be three doors in my White Room. The Right Door would lead to Old Paradise, now known as just *Paradise*. The Middle would lead down a hall that imperceptibly split. The fork to the right would lead to Samara Station and the one to the left would lead to what Karma would call the *Asylum of Silence*. The Asylum would be built on a cloud over the Afterworld's highest peak. There, those who took their own life would be damned to suffer visions of futures that would've been had they waited for Gladys's appointment. Gaia, Gladys, and I knew Karma was an unstable creation and knew she could change her mind on a whim and possibly side with Marduk's original extermination plan. So, we didn't argue against her controlling both realms."

I gave Morton a curious glance.

"Yes?" asked Death.

"Realities. You keep talking like there's more than one."

Death chuckled. "Oh, yes. Quite a few more than one. But that is something I'll show you later. Seeing will help your mortal brain comprehend the incomprehensible. But back to the White Room's three doors. The last was the Left Door that led to Marduk's realm, which would be called the Prison of Homicide. The single criterion for entry was taking another mortal life by any means for whatever reason. An absolute Black and White Rule that saw no extenuating circumstances, and for the offender, an eternity of unimaginable torment without the possibility of parole."

"So, you know about my Uncle Frank and Vanessa."

Morton sighed. "Yes, I do. And the weight of their good souls is heavier than most I've ushered through the Left and Middle Doors. I have no choice but to do the Council's will and follow the Laws agreed upon, which cannot be changed without a majority vote of the Original Three. Timethy still refuses to get involved, and as long as Marduk exists, the Rule will never be changed or abolished. Marduk was once removed from the Council after a major incident in your Americas. And then there was the Fall of 2007 in your reality. That broke me."

Death went on to tell me of the behind-the-scene details and machinations of a celestial council that led to the tragedy, but as previously stated that will be covered in future volumes.

Morton paused. His eyes were heavy and I thought for a moment he would cry like he did over me in my dream—the dream where I died instead of the hazel-eyed girl and woke up to write about an interview with Death. The Reaper's lips quivered. He swallowed hard and let out a sigh. He composed himself and said in a thirsty tone, "I guess I gave you more than the question asked for. I do have a tendency for tangents."

"No, no. Thank you. I'm just trying to process everything."

"Don't worry, it'll get easier. You've just taken your first step into the rest of existence outside the brief dream you call reality. So, ask me the next question."

159

"Okay. How do you do what you do? Especially with so many realities and mortal creatures, as you call us, that are dying all the time?"

"Yes. I enjoyed what you wrote. Interesting answer and you weren't far off with your Santa Claus theory."

"What? Fate gives you a list and you check it twice to see who's naughty and nice?"

"No, not that part. The splitting part. Most mortals think I just move super-fast. I do, but they also think their reality is the only one there is. And it's even more complex than that. Like the Realities, it's something you have to see and experience to fully understand, but you did get a taste when you watched me work earlier. But about the naughty and nice part—I can only review a life after the Underspirit steps into the White Room. I could be a creeper and spy on everyone from the outside looking in before then, but I don't have the luxury to waste my existence like that. You are a special case, but I'll get to that when you ask me the last question of your marvelous essay. No, what I'll address now is how I do what I do and why the Death Family in your paper was given the job."

Morton lifted the silver chain tucked in his shirt and exposed a circular squash blossom-like talisman. The background was arrayed with repeating black, cobalt, and aqua cobblestones. Centered was a platinum skull over a silver scythe. The skull's eye sockets were filled with dark blue and white, swirling like hurricanes.

"What is it?" I asked.

Death reverently admired the talisman and said, "It is what gives me the power to do what I do. It is the *Burden of the Scythe*. It is a curse no creation should've ever been tasked with, much less an old softy like me. But I realize that's why I was given the job. If it'd been any other Eternal, there's no telling what they would've done with the power invested in the Burden. As such, I'm cursed to wear this for eternity because no one else with a good mindheart is *crazy* enough to wear it."

"It's stunning," I said.

Morton released a humorless snicker. "Yes, at least it is that. You want to try it on?" he asked, meeting my eyes.

I paused, then chuckled. "Yeah. Sure."

Death lifted the chain from his neck. "Now sit."

I sat on the couch. Morton gently placed the chain around my neck and tucked the talisman under my shirt. I flinched. It was ice cold against my skin. The chill radiated through my heart, slowing it, freezing the blood passing through.

"Now, try to stand."

I tried but felt like heavy weights had been placed on my shoulders. "I... I... I can't."

"What you feel is the weight of all the souls I have sent through those cursed three doors and the injustices I have been a party to since my creation," Morton said as anger seeped through.

Death effortlessly lifted the Burden from me, slid it over his neck, and tucked the talisman under his shirt. Morton sat by me.

I opened my lips to speak, then closed them.

"What?" asked Death.

I sighed. "I know what you said about not wanting to talk about it, but what *really* happened in 2007? You told me what happened on your side. But what happened in my reality. I... I still blame myself."

161

"Nathan, I know you struggle with what you were a party to, but you're not the first mortal fooled by the gods. What happened in your reality's 2007…" Death blew out a sigh. "What's done is done. It can't be undone, and you'll find no peace knowing that *truth*, just like I know you found no peace before my intervention with that bullet you tried to eat. Let's talk about something else. 2007 takes me to a place I don't wish to return. But there is the matter of my brother who had a hand in that mess. I'm curious—how often do you see the Man in White?"

"Only when I was flying on Dark Ethereal."

"That he gave you?"

"Yes. Well, Gavin did, but I don't think my friend is the same Gavrilo I met in Bosnia."

"No, he's not. He's my brother, Frederick. I haven't seen Loki in ages. And I never will unless he wants me to. Same goes for him. Eternals don't have the ability to spy on one another. I tell you—I hate that sonuvabitch. *Sonuvabitch*. What a silly curse for creations without bitches to birth them but fitting all the same for Frederick. Yeah, your friend Gavin isn't who he appears to be. Materializing into solid or spectral forms is something Eternals can do. But I don't care to wear mortal shells or play fleshy dress up. Gladys is the same way. But the same cannot be said of Frederick and Delores. Eternals can sport a mortal shell, morph into any living thing they please, make themselves small or any size up to titanic, or simply appear in their pure form. And they can be seen by whoever they wish. Concerning my brother—I called him *Loki* for a reason. Other than being the Man in White, he is the God of Chaos, Mischief, and Luck. He is your guardian angel, or should I say, guardian devil."

"But why did he choose me?" I asked.

"Yes, indeed. Why did he choose you? I guess I'll address your essay's last question at the same time about why *I* chose you. You got it wrong. Truth is, I didn't. Let me tell you something. You're not special. You've had heartache. All mortals have heartache. And sure, you're a good writer. Some say better than good. But as a mortal, you're weak. Materially successful, at least for now. But you've fucked that up. Just one of the many things you've fucked up. I can give you a pass for what happened in Kirkuk with those massacred boys and you playing along with General Cornelius Adamson to cover it up. I saw what you saw through the eyes of the fallen before I ushered them through the Left Door. Something was amiss. There was evil magic at work and I recognized the fingerprints of the one responsible. Adamson won your trust, I understand that, so, I won't fault you for what transpired in Almawt Lilkifaar since your intentions were pure. Still, they paved the road to Hell in your reality. But then you let my brother lead you astray by allowing him to feed your self-pity. But that's nothing new. You've been blown like a feather throughout your life. And when you were given something good you squandered it. You were entrusted with a beautiful, gray-eyed bird and you let her fly away and now she's lost forever…"

My lips trembled. Everything he said was true.

"…I thought long and hard at Charlotte's how I should say this to you. But sometimes you just have to say what needs to be said, and *you* have to take it like a man—not the phony, destructible, self-loathing excuse for a mortal shell that you are right now."

"I… I thought you liked me."

"Oh, I do. I'm something of a big fan. But I also need you to be the man I know you can be because someone is waiting in the wings with big plans for you if you can't. There's a bigger game being played here and there's every reason to believe it is the reason my brother is protecting you. Yes, it all makes sense now. I suspect Frederick was at the fair all those years ago. I think you know the girl who died was a work in. My appointment that night was with you."

I bit my lip. I saw the dead girl's face, staring hazel eyes, and the candy apple in the crimson puddle. "Yes. I've always known," I said in a hollow tone. "Somehow, I've always known. You still haven't answered the last question. Why me? What do you want from me? Why am I here?" I croaked out.

Before he could answer, Gladys entered the library with more milk and cookies.

I looked at my reflection on the floor. I was middle-aged again with my wannabe Hemingway beard, which I stroked.

"How are you boys getting along?" asked Fate. "I figured you might want some more cookies. The few mortals who've tried them have told me they're to die for."

"Yeah, sure. Thanks. I'll have another," I said with a desert-parched throat. I grabbed a warm glass and a chocolate chip cookie. I took a bite and swallowed. I shook my head as it soothed the sting of Death's honesty. "Wow. These are good. So good."

"Why, thank you," said Gladys with a thankful smile. She set the tray on the table. The blue eddies scattered around the tray.

Morton grinned. "I'll have a few." He took three. "Better than that kolache, huh?"

I nodded as I finished the first and grabbed another.

164

"Something I should tell you about my sister's cookies. They aren't your run-of-the-mill Tollhouse. Take another bite. Savor it and tell me how you *really* feel."

I did and chased the gooey goodness with more warm milk. The dragon's burn and itch went away the instant the mixture rolled into my stomach.

"I know there are a few questions I didn't answer but I think I covered the important ones. That's enough for now," said Morton. "You should stay with us for a while. The clocks are stopped in your world until you return. I need you well before we start your training. Withdrawal from Dark Ethereal isn't as pretty as it is for heroin, and you'll have to do both. I know I don't need to warn you—it's why you're here."

"Training? What do you mean, *training*?"

Morton smiled. "Oh, I didn't tell you, did I? This is an interview with Death. Look, I'm tired, and I'm looking for a relief Reaper to fill in every once in a while. I haven't had a day off… like, ever. Oh wait, there were a few weeks after Cain killed Abel, but that's pretty much it. And you looked so good wearing the Burden. You even introduced yourself as Nathan Reaper to that girl, Victoria, and her mother, Valeria. It rolled off your tongue so… naturally. Made her smile before she walked through the Right Door. I tell you, you were made for this job. Look, I know there's a good man inside you, and this is a responsibility like no other. I've been around long enough to be a good judge of character, though you have challenged my faith in that judgment. Your uncle Frank was a good man who doesn't deserve the eternity he received, but he raised you right and that will be your saving grace. He will always be the compass who will guide you back to port even if you occasionally get lost in stormy seas."

I leaned forward, rubbed my lips with prayer hands, and regarded my dark reflection. I pressed stop on the recorder.

"Eat your cookies," said Gladys. "I can take that for you and keep it safe."

I handed her the recorder.

"Look, I have a room made up for you to stay in while my brother is out doing his thing. You won't be able to leave until you're well, but if the pain is too great or you need a shoulder to sob on, just call my name, and I'll be there," she said with a tender Aunt Dorothy smile.

Forty-Two

Morton left the library. I finished the last cookie then followed Gladys to where I'd be staying. It was a simple room with a mattress, a thin pillow, and no sheets. That was okay since the Home of Fate and Death was perfectly warm, not cold and drafty as one might expect.

Inside was a barren desk with padded, rounded edges and a simple stool. There was a single open window too high to reach. I could smell the aroma of roses outside.

On the walls were photos of me, but none I'd ever seen. Morton was in each, but we were never side by side, except in one. It was of us standing at Ryan Mender's grave. Funeral attendants were shoveling dirt to fill a hole that could never be filled. I remembered a breeze on my shoulder on that breezeless day. It was Morton.

"I figured you would want a desk in case you felt like writing," said Gladys.

"But, there's no paper or anything to write with."

"Oh, that. Can't give you anything sharp. You're apt to slit your wrists open when things get rough. And I'm sorry to break it to you—they will, and you will want to die. As weird as it sounds in this interdimensional realm, you won't age, but if you die, you're still dead. It just won't mess up Morton's schedule like other work-ins do. Look, you don't need paper, a pen, or even a typewriter. Just use your finger, and the sheets of paper will appear, and ink will flow from your veins. That Hemingway said it best. Or at least he was credited for saying it best. Writing's easy. You just open your wrist and bleed on the page. Or something like that. Fortunately, I don't mean it literally, but you'll want to open your wrists for real before you're well. Anyway, sit down. Give it a try."

I sat at the desk and moved a finger in a circular motion. A sheet of paper appeared with a crimson spiral.

"See. Simple," said Fate. "And don't worry, the blood you let will be filled with all the humors and demons feasting on your soul. But don't get me wrong, I'm not advocating bloodletting. That was just plain silly. I can't tell you how many appointments I had to set up for Morton because of that foolishness."

"Thanks, Gladys."

"My pleasure, sweetheart. Remember, when it gets bad, you don't have to go it alone."

I nodded with tears welling.

Fate smiled, nodded, and closed the door. A lock engaged.

I began to write. And it helped. Not as much as Gladys's milk and cookies, but it helped. I wrote about everything going back to Almawt Lilkifaar, then went even further to the death of my parents. I stopped and studied a black and white photo of me looking at Morton before he disappeared into the crowd at the fair. I wondered who'd taken the photo. Gladys, maybe?

I wrote and wrote, letting more and more blood as page after page materialized, and the stack on the desk grew taller and taller. Surely, I had no more blood to give. But I didn't feel weak. Actually, I felt light as a feather—as if a soft breeze could blow me away and send me spinning out the window into the sky above the Realm of Fate and Death.

I continued to write until I reached the part where I sat in the Reaper's home writing my memoir, locked in a room waiting for withdrawal to hit me like a train. It was coming. I heard the whistle. And I was chained to the track.

I tried to keep writing, but suddenly there was no more blood. My finger was dry, and no more pages appeared. The pages I'd written dissolved into a pile of cobalt snow. It sparkled and called me and showed me the faces of those I'd lost and a mirage of Heaven where everything was perfect and everyone was there. I heard music playing outside. It was The Stones' *Sympathy for the Devil*. I looked at the mound of chilly powder as the room turned into an oven that made a summer in Iraq feel like a dip in the Arctic Ocean. Sweat poured from me in rivers as I gazed at the mound of glittering dark blue relief. It took the form of a cookie monster on meth. It started singing, "Feed the Dragon, Feed the Dragon, Feed the Dragon, Feed the Dragon," then crumbled back into a snow hill as The Stones resumed. There was more than enough to send me wherever I wanted to go in the Afterworld. Hell, enough to give me the strength to break through that Goddamn Realty Window and stay there forever with my parents and Dorothy. Hell, fuck the Devil, Marduk, or whatever the fuck. I would bend him over and make him my bitch, free Frank, then take care of Karma and break Vanessa out of that asylum. Then… then everything would be right again. I looked at all the Dead Blow calling me. I licked my lips. I tried to resist but couldn't stand it any longer.

"Ahh, fuck it," I said and plowed my head into the mound as the desk reappeared. My face slammed hard, busting my nose as real blood spilled. To my right, the manuscript was neatly stacked as it had been.

"GODDAMNIT!" I yelled and swung my arms through the neatly stacked pages.

I grabbed the desk and threw it against the wall. It shattered into shards of dark blue glass. I wanted to end it and reached for a shard to slice my arm from wrist to elbow, but the broken glass was gone. I looked to where the desk had been. There it was with my manuscript neatly stacked.

I tried again. I scattered the papers, broke the desk, turned over the mattress and bed. The Dead Blow and shards reappeared, only to disappear as the room and its contents returned to its original arrangement.

After continuing this futile exercise for a maddening while longer, I collapsed to the floor, curled up, and wept. My insides twisted and felt as if dull, rusty razor blades were shredding them. I got to my knees and vomited crimson like water from a fire hydrant. When it hit the floor, it froze, cracked, crystallized, and formed into perfectly sculpted rails of Dead Blow. I fell face forward and hoovered up a rail of bloody vomit filled with creamy chocolate chip cookies, rancid milk, and bile. I leaned back to my knees with putrid cream dripping from my beard. I pulled myself onto the mattress and sobbed as I rocked back and forth.

I whimpered like a child, "Gladys, Gladys, Gladys. Help me, help me, help me, please. Please, help me."

The door unlocked, and Fate ran in, wrapped me up in her arms, and held me like my mother did when I was a child. As she embraced me, I felt her warm tears wash over me, cleansing the pain away. My head cleared, and soon I was asleep in the arms of Fate.

Forty-Three

I awoke sometime later. I don't know if time was even the proper term, but something had passed. I sat up and looked around the room. It was pristine clean again, as was my beard. My original manuscript for much of what you're reading now was neatly stacked on the desk next to more milk and cookies. Strangely, the sight didn't make me want to hurl.

I ravenously ate and drank like a man at an oasis after crawling through a desert. I figured I needed something more, but I wasn't hungry. I felt stronger, as if Fate's cookies and milk were everything my body needed. I smelled the scent of roses. I heard birds chirping and singing the most delightful tune. I decided to exercise and did some push-ups and sit-ups.

After an hour or sixty seconds or six months, I called for Gladys, but not in the desperate tone as before. It was more the tone a small child would use when calling their mother to come give them a goodnight kiss.

The door unlocked, opened, and Gladys and Morton stood with shadowed faces.

"How you doing today, Nathan?" asked Death.

"Much better. Much better, thanks to Gladys. I swear there's something in your tears. I haven't felt the pain, the burn, or the itch since you held me."

Fate smiled. "Dear, those tears are like my cookies. They're infused with love, and nothing's stronger than love—not really—even if your world seems to have forgotten. I'd like to say you're out of the woods, but you don't get free of Dark Ethereal that easy. Let's just call this the first good day of many to come."

Morton stepped to the desk, picked up the manuscript, and started reading. "Now, this is good," he said, his lips curling with pleasure as he shook an approving finger. "You've been slipping lately, but this is good. Can't wait to see how it ends. Well, there are spirits that need reaping. I'll check on you later."

I nodded with a serene grin and eyes that were windows to a peaceful soul.

Gladys put a hand on my shoulder. "And remember, when it gets bad again—call my name."

I have no idea how long I stayed in that room. And yes, there were more bad days (or whatever) to come. And when the bad came, Gladys soothed my pain with love-infused tears and cookies. Morton checked on me every day before and after work. Eventually, there were more good days than bad.

After what my mind told me was three months without a bad lunar cycle, Morton came to me.

"I think you're ready. Let's go back to your reality. No time has passed, and the mess you made is still there for you to clean up. I'll check in on you as always. I probably don't need to say this—stay away from my brother. He'll tempt you because what he has to offer is how he controls you. And when I believe you're ready, we'll begin your training to be my relief Reaper."

"You know, you've never asked me if I want the job."

"Well, do you want the job?" asked Morton.

"After what you and Gladys did for me, you've got yourself a Reaper."

Forty-Four

Fourteen months had passed since my visit with Fate and Death. To say they were difficult would be a monumental understatement. I regretted not contacting the kids but felt their lives were better without me—at least for now. So, I kept to myself, and spoke to almost no one except my sponsor and those at my Wednesday AA meetings. And I wrote. Mostly shit. But I wrote. And I shaved off that damn beard.

Death's brother tried to contact me several times, but I ignored his calls. I'm not saying I wasn't tempted to answer. There were many times I craved what the Man in White could provide, but the road back was much harder than I'd imagined. I was clean and meant to keep it that way.

It was a rainy April night when my mind truly cleared, and I found my stride amongst the short stories and dead ends that lay in a drawer of drafts to be. While perusing these old manuscripts, I found a dusty one about the Ackerman Massacre. Of course, the story had been told so often that books on the subject were cliché, like writing about Abraham Lincoln and his assassination. Still, they sold, but there wasn't much left to say.

I read through the draft and cringed a little, but overall, it wasn't *that* bad, even if it didn't measure up to the standard the public expected from me (which I failed to deliver with the rubbish I published two years earlier). After my time with Gladys and Morton, I felt there was more to the story than anyone had scratched in the past five years.

Before I started the rewrite, I called James Mender. As usual, he was gracious but didn't say much until our second call on burner phones. He told his part of the story which was nothing short of miraculous and gave me contact information for other survivors of the events of 2007.

When I finished the manuscript, I contacted my agent, who'd fired me after my last book. He still believed in me enough to find a smaller publisher that would give me a second chance. But he said I'd have to be happy with a meager advance that would barely pay my monthly expenses. Just like old times.

I thought about leaving Manhattan. My former lifestyle had sapped my fortune during my downward spiral. I could hardly afford rent and ate like a starving artist. But I couldn't bring myself to leave Greenwich Village, where I lived a block from where my dreams took me every night. It was like starting over, but unlike last time, I was alone. I missed Vanessa and could hear the ghosts of the kids playing, yelling, fighting, and the spirit of Vanessa's kiss on my neck as she encouraged me as I wrote *Ghosts of Bosnia*. And when she whispered I would look at the wedding ring that never left my finger, reminding me of the bird I let fly away.

On that rainy April night, I found the courage to call Franklin. It'd been two years since we'd spoken and, God, I missed him. And Jenna. And I missed Jonathan, who hated me. I was sure they all did now.

The phone felt like a cinderblock in my hand as I dialed Franklin's number. Even though we were always the closest, I was surprised he didn't hang up on me. I told him the longer I'd waited, the harder it was to pick up the phone. Franklin apologized for not calling me himself, then unloaded constrained venom that stung worse than Morton's verbal lashing before detoxing in another dimension. I absorbed the righteous poison and ended the call on the road back to where we'd been when Vanessa was still with us.

Before I hung up, I asked him to call Jenna and Jonathan to let them know I would be calling and to ask them to please not hang up on me. I spoke to Jenna the next day. She was much less cordial but agreed to meet for dinner with Franklin, but she told me Jonathan had a message for me. Just seven words she delivered verbatim: 'Tell him to fuck off and die.' It was the response I expected and about what I deserved.

Forty-Five

Ackerman's Curse was a smashing success and eclipsed my first-month sales for *The Menders: A First American Story*. Quickly, I was on the talk show circuit promoting the new book. It was about this time the Dead Blow crisis reached epidemic proportions and made my continued sobriety that much more miraculous. I was the only former Dead Blow addict in my support group with a one year and handful of one month sobriety tokens. Most who were less successful wanted to know my secret. I wasn't ready to reveal my story, so I lied with a smile and gave them a cookie. Still, knowing someone who had kicked the habit gave them hope. And the cookies I brought every week certainly didn't hurt. I never saw Fate when she made her deliveries, but she always left plenty for everyone.

The supply of Dead Blow came from several places in Central and South America and was controlled by a violent cartel based in Sinaloa, Mexico and Saõ João, Brazil. While the Brazil branch was controlled by a shadowy figure known as the Blood Queen, the Sinaloa franchise was ruthlessly commanded by Emelio Azrael, a homicidal maniac that many believed was certifiably insane. He made Pedro Escobar, El Chapo el Diablo, and Santiago Gomez look like pious priests. He was personally responsible for triggering the ongoing War on Ethereal after a massacre in Seattle in 2010. The war and the unrest in South America was already responsible for several million lives including forty-five thousand U.S. servicemen and several hundred federal agents.

When Dead Blow hit the streets in mid-2008, few people knew what is was. Many called it Dark Ethereal since its appearance was similar to Light Ethereal. Earlier that year, Charlotte's World Famous Ethereal-infused Frespressos took the planet by storm. Soon Charlotte's Coffee knocked Starbucks off the market's top spot. Not long after, CEO Francis T. Pickens successfully negotiated a buyout of the mermaid-logoed juggernaut and made its company name disappear.

By 2009, rival coffee shops and chains began serving Dark Ethereal-infused drinks to compete with the unstoppable *Charlotte's*

Coffee. The new cobalt powder packed more punch and began to cut into Charlotte's profits, but Pickens refused to allow it in his cafés. The FRES ticker plummeted. No one on Wall Street understood Pickens' resistance, but he was vindicated when the Dead Heads (as Dead Blow addicts came to be called) reared their fluorescent cobalt eyes.

The first victim was a sixteen-year-old boy in Cincinnati. He was flying like a bird when the drug wore off and he became a blood smear on the PNC Tower. Then it got worse. People who'd never smoked a joint were being arrested for theft, murder, selling DE, or prostituting themselves or their kids for eight balls of the glistening substance. The effects were similar to PCP, but much more refined. It gave many users temporary super strength, lightning quick speed, and hyper focus. However, it also aged users exponentially. I never experienced any of these effects on my trips since my focus was on the Afterworld and finding answers. It was rumored that the military was considering applications to improve soldier performance once the aging side effects could be controlled.

President Harvey Rollins shut down any consideration of that on February 13, 2011, when he signed an executive order, banning all Ethereal products, dark or otherwise. He was assassinated the next day by his press secretary.

She was unhappy when she got to work and didn't find her Light Ethereal next to the creamer. She stormed into the oval office and stabbed Rollins thirty-nine times with two letter openers (the first broke before she was done). Then she killed two Secret Service agents with their own pistols before she was gunned down. Reports stated she was shot fourteen times. Tox reports confirmed she had Dark Ethereal in her blood stream.

Vice President Patricia Cochran took the oath of office immediately after Rollins was pronounced dead on the presidential eagle. She instituted martial law to bring the situation under control, but once restored, President Cochran retained absolute power. Thereafter, she used everything at her disposal to crush dissent. She suspended habeas corpus and other protections under the Constitution. Cochran's draconian methods stemmed Dark Ethereal's flow from Mexico but didn't stop it, and many coffee shops became Dead Blow speakeasies.

As the M.A.D.E. (Mothers Against Dark Ethereal) movement gathered steam, Charlotte's Cafés were commended for their integrity. While the FRES ticker never hit its former highs, many people drank only Charlotte's Ethereal-free Frespressos, which were basically pre-Ethereal Starbucks Frappuccinos.

By Summer 2012, the country Uncle Frank fought and still suffered in eternity for had become a fascist state in everything but name, yet things weren't much better worldwide. In 2010, Iranian President Akbar Banisadr called for the re-conquest of all lands that once belonged to Persia. Some called him a modern-day Cyrus the Great, while many more called him Cyrus the Terrible. Once in power, he cracked down on all forms of Islam and mercilessly purged the old government. Ayatollah Muhammad al-Mahdi (the self-proclaimed embodiment of the Twelfth Imam) barely escaped alive. Surprisingly, the Saudi royal family and clerics who once would've called for his head granted him sanctuary in a rare act of Muslim solidarity between Sunnis and Shias.

Banisadr publicly and personally executed the remaining Shia clergy with an ancient Persian straight sword from the National Museum of Iran. It was said to have belonged to King Cyrus, and was returned to the exhibit without being cleaned or repaired. Since then, several assassination attempts had been thwarted, and retaliation by his secret police was swift and ruthless to the third generation. Nothing that was said or happened in New Persia escaped Banisadr's knowledge.

After killing the Shia leaders, he called for the destruction of all mosques. He simultaneously rebuilt temples to the old gods, particularly Marduk, the patron god of Babylon and Hammurabi. Few people had heard of Marduk, but the ancient gods of Mesopotamia soon became household names when Banisadr declared war on Iraq in 2011. It was a scene reminiscent of the blitzkrieg. Banisadr's forces swept through the country with savage brutality, retaking Babylon's ancient ruins, where reconstruction of the ancient capital was underway before the blood of millions dried.

In Saudi Arabia, the Ayatollah Mohammad al-Mahdi was not a grateful guest and began sowing dissent against the Royal family. He publicly called them false believers and defilers of Mecca and Medina and the sacred Kaaba. Before the Royal family could act, their servants rebelled and slaughtered them. Immediately after, Muhammed al-Mahdi called for the Caliphate's return, the death of the Nation of Israel and all unbelievers, and the return of Jerusalem to a unified Islamic State.

At the Vatican, Pope Romanus II only made things worse by preaching for a new Crusade. He warned the world to prepare for the coming of the Four Horsemen of the Apocalypse. He even dredged up Pope Urban II's old saying, *Deus le volt!* God wills it!

In London, the tide of fascism continued as Prime Minister Lord Byron Smythe, facing the Dark Ethereal plague and Islamic extremism, called for similar measures taken by NATO colleague U.S. President Patricia Cochran.

To make matters worse, Russian Federation President Vladimir Vasily christened himself the new Czar and signed a pact with New Persia (which the United Nations has yet to recognize). Vasily and Banisadr's intentions were clear. When the predicted Apocalypse came, Russia would take Europe, Africa, and keep northern Asia, while New Persia would take the southern half (including China), India, Australia, and all islands around and in between.

Only China seemed to be doing okay. Over the previous two years the first Emperor of the new Republic of Black Dragon China (RBDC) had instituted massive humanitarian projects. The Chinese people adored him, and he had the respect of much of the world. That's not to say his road to power wasn't without bloodletting.

When the Black Dragon Emperor came to power, there were purges and mass executions that rivaled Mao Zedong. Since then, Emperor Lee had tempered his methods and created a nation that was the beacon for truth, justice, and liberty in a world growing dark. His democratic reforms had given a voice to the voiceless. In short order, independent review by legal and human rights experts attested that Emperor Lee's transparent system of checks and balances was fair and seemingly flawless. Even Hong Kong, who had long fought Chinese domination, welcomed the new Emperor. It was as if the entire world had been turned upside down, inside out, and sat on a powder keg, ready to explode. And as the world burned, I released a new book.

Forty-Six

Saturday, June 15, 2012, Buckley and Nolan's Westfield World Trade Center, Manhattan, New York.

A massive crowd greeted me for my first book signing in a few years. I was running late, and several fans caught me outside. I graciously shook their hands, thanked them for their kind words, and told them I'd see them inside. I stepped past several heavily armed mall guards. They were screening one woman's eyes with a retinal scanner for the tell-tale retinal sparkles of Dead Blow. I hoped she was clean. She was, and the guards allowed her to pass and get in line. Those around her avoided eye contact with security officers.

Near the bookstore entrance were two Death-Love Krishnas (as they were being called). One was a blonde woman and the other was a skinny brown-haired man. Both wore Deathly smiles and were dressed like the Man in Black. Adherents were becoming a regular sight as worldwide hopelessness turned many to the new faith. As mentioned, the cult leader was former Packer City motel owner Raj Batra. He was originally from Delhi. I met him once at Charlotte's #1. Nice guy, and a peaceful religion that couldn't have been based on a nicer god.

The woman tipped her Stetson and handed me a tract. I liked her. No pressure. Just read and believe, but they were preaching to the choir. As usual, I tossed the tract in the first trash receptacle I found. Heaven forbid, I litter New Singapore on steroids.

Inside the bookstore, there was a display easel next to mine. It announced, *"Storytime with renowned children's book author, Kaisa Jännök."* There was a photo of her new book, *Toivo goes to New York,* and a color photo of the author. I had only seen a black and white of Ms. Jännök since she rarely allowed photographs.

Her rare appearance was scheduled after mine. I had always wanted to meet her, as had Franklin, Jenna, Jonathan, and my grandkids who'd been brought up with Vanessa's bedtime tradition that began with a ragged old copy of Jännök's first book. It was Saturday, and I had no idea what anyone had planned. So, I called Franklin and Jenna and texted Jonathan, starting with *"Kaisa Jännök and Toivo the Bear,"* so he'd read the message. I asked that they come quickly to Manhattan and bring the grandkids. I wasn't holding my breath that Jonathan would come but held out hope that he'd at least think about it out of respect for his mother's memory. Emotional blackmail. Okay, guilty as charged, but damnit, I wanted my kids back.

When it was time, I signed and smiled, smiled and signed, posed for a picture, signed and smiled, smiled and signed, and repeated that a few thousand times. Then I saw *her* walk in—Kaisa Jännök. She was far more beautiful than her photo. She didn't look my way and went straight to the children's section arranged like a fairy tale courtyard with store workers dressed as princes and princesses. There was also a grizzly-sized Toivo the Bear, Mikko the Moose, Pietari Little Bear, and Markus the Puffin. The line of children and parents was almost as long as mine had been.

After I had signed the last book and posed for the last photo, I bought a copy of the new *Toivo the Bear* and got in line to meet Kaisa and listen to her reading. My agent asked if I wanted to meet her after she signed the book. He said he could speed things along with a mega-celebrity express pass. I said, "No." I would wait in line like everyone else.

Most in line recognized me. Several people stopped to tell me how great I was. I was humbled as I took more photos and signed more autographs.

Finally, Franklin, Kimberly, their four kids, Jenna, and her boyfriend, Roger, arrived. Jenna had divorced Simon two years earlier. I politely asked if anyone would mind if my son, daughter, and grandkids cut in line. No one minded. Of course they didn't. I was Nathan Miller—the indestructible Nathan Miller, who had destroyed himself and was trying to become a decent human again.

Then *he* walked into the store—Jonathan, with his wife, Rebecca, and their three kids, the youngest, a granddaughter I'd never seen. I smiled as tears overtook me, but sort of held it together. In Jonathan's hand was the old, ragged book. He smiled back and approached. He stood in front of me and glanced at Rebecca. She nodded. Jonathan turned to me with his eyes welling. I extended my arms, and he fell into them and sobbed. I did too, and we made a spectacle of ourselves as people snapped photos of a memory that would be plastered everywhere. I didn't care. At that moment, there was no one else around. It was only me, my baby boy, and that old, ragged book. Jonathan let go.

I held him by the shoulders. "I love you so much, Jonathan. And I am… I am so sorry for what I became and what happened to your mother. I will never ask you to forgive me or forget what I did. I only ask that you give me another chance to be the father and man I once was." I glanced around—not a dry eye. I wiped my nose as cameras clicked.

Jonathan nodded but couldn't form words that didn't start with tears falling and his nose sniffling.

I put my arm over his shoulder, and we stood in line.

Kaisa took a break from signing, and moved to a comfortable chair in the fairy tale section. She leaned back, crossed her legs, and opened her new book while oversized characters from her imagination sat behind her on the grass-green and aquamarine carpet. Everyone stood or sat spellbound as she read with her sweet Finnish accent. I closed my eyes.

I saw Vanessa's lips moving, and Kaisa's voice became hers. Franklin and Jenna were sitting on the ground in front of her with Jonathan on her lap.

I opened my eyes. Fresh tears wet my cheeks. I loved Vanessa's voice, her eyes, her mouth. I felt guilty, feeling the same for Kaisa at that moment. I didn't deserve to be loved or to love anyone, but I truly loved Kaisa though we'd never met. I loved her for a simple story that had given me back my family—given me back my son, Jonathan. I knew we had a long way to go, but it was galaxies closer than *Fuck off and die.*

When we arrived at the signing table, Jonathan handed me the ragged old book. Kaisa looked up with emerald eyes. "Nathan Miller? You know I would have allowed you to cut in line."

"I know, but we're big fans just like the rest of these folks."

"Well, that was very considerate. What is that you have in your hands?"

"Oh, this. It's a copy of your first book. My wife used to read it my kids when they were babies. Let me introduce them. This is Jon Christian, my youngest, his wife Rebecca, and three of my grandkids, Jon Jr., Alvin, and Hope."

Jonathan nodded and shook Kaisa's hand. "It's so... so awesome to meet you."

I continued with introductions. "And this is my daughter, Jenna, and her boyfriend, Roger."

Jenna stepped forward and shook Kaisa's hand but didn't say anything.

"And this is my oldest, Franklin, his wife, Kimberly, and my other four grandkids, Brittany, Chris, Juliette, and Wendy."

Kaisa extended a hand, but Franklin shook his head, stepped around the table, and extended his arms. Kaisa stood and hugged him.

"You don't know what you mean to this family," said Franklin. "I can't tell you how much I thank you for being here. And thank you for being you and for writing your stories. I'm sure you know, like everyone else—my mom committed suicide two-and-half years ago. It tore our family apart. Thank you for bringing our family back together today."

Kaisa bit her lip and appeared on the verge of waterworks. As each of us came around and followed Franklin's lead, she lost it and had to take a break after she signed the old, ragged book with a shaky hand. She wrote:

> *To the Miller Family,*
> *Your words of love heal me in ways you do not know.*
> *Love always,*
> *Kaisa Jännök*

The kids and grandkids left, and I waited until Kaisa finished bringing the last smile to the last child and parent. As Kaisa got up to leave, I approached.

"Kaisa, are you hungry?" I asked. "I'd love to take you out for a bite if you are. Unless, of course, you already have plans."

"En ole. Um. No. I mean, no, I have no other plans. And yes. I would like to eat with you very much. That would be nice."

I smiled. "You like sushi?"

"Yes, I love sushi."

"Great. There's a wonderful place within walking distance. Chefs make it fresh to order right in front of you. They have great sake too, but I don't drink anymore."

"I do not drink much either. I know it is unusual for a Finn, but not as much as it used to be. I just like to be different, I guess," she said with a subtle smile.

At the restaurant, we ate and laughed and even cried a little as we spoke like we had known each other for a lifetime. After we stuffed ourselves with several rolls, we drank green tea.

"I don't mean to pry," I said. "And you don't have to answer if you don't want to. But what did you mean when you wrote, '*Your words of love heal in ways you do not know*'?"

Kaisa paused and stared at seaweed wraps on the sushi prep table as if peering through a window into another time and place. She looked down and then at me with sad eyes.

"I am a very private person. We Finns tend to keep a lot to ourselves. I have never really liked book signings. Not that I do not love Toivo's fans. They are wonderful, and they give me strength. I have never told anyone how I came up with the stories I tell. Only my children know, and my family in Suomi. When I was a young girl, I fell in love with a Saami boy named Toivo Jännök. We had been friends since the first day we went to school. As we got older, there was only one boy I ever loved. I never dated another. I never looked at another. And I do not believe he did either. When we were old enough, we were married. And we loved each other and made love often. Then six months after our wedding, Toivo went walking on the ice in early winter with a friend on the Kemijoki River outside Rovaniemi. They had been drinking. The ice broke." She paused to compose herself. "The friend fell into the ice and was sucked downstream. Toivo tried to save him, but he also drowned. I was at a public sauna with a few cousins when Toivo and his friend were found under the ice. Bystanders told me what happened. I was heartbroken..." She paused again. Her lips quivered.

"... As my ...as my cousins drove me home to the small village of Vikajärvi, I prayed that I was pregnant. Within a month, I started to feel sick. I would learn I was not pregnant with one but three. We were very poor, and it was very difficult raising the triplets, but my family helped all they could. As Paavo, Antti, and Selma grew, I began to tell them stories about their father and what a great boy he was and what a great man he would have been." She paused to collect again and sat up straighter.

"Soon, Toivo began having fantastical adventures and would explore the world around us, making many friends along the way. By the time they could remember the stories, Toivo had become a strong, loving bear, and he had strong, happy friends. Mikko the Moose—Mikko was Toivo's good friend, who he tried to save. Pietari Little Bear from Saint Petersburg and Markus the Puffin from Iceland—those were my two cousins who drove me home that day. Your children saying what they said today touched me deeply, and as I said, their words healed me in ways none of you could have known."

Our eyes connected. I had made love to many women and dishonored Vanessa every time, even as she called me, pleading for a kind word that would've changed her mind. Of course, I knew all the *could-have-beens*, and only a future without me would've saved her from the fate she still suffers because of me. I didn't deserve love, but I felt something as Kaisa continued to hold my eyes. It was something I hadn't felt since seeing Vanessa at the Halloween party so long ago. I melted. I panicked and looked away.

"Kaisa, thank you for having dinner with me. But I think I should go."

She laid a palm against my cheek. I raised my hand and pressed her hand firmly against my skin. She leaned to kiss me.

I saw Delores Destiny *laughing* and Vanessa in anguish, strapped in a straitjacket. I leaned away. "I'm sorry. I can't do this."

She smiled sweetly, trying to hide her embarrassment. "I understand. Thank you for tonight. Telling you my story removed a heavy burden from my heart. I know there is still one on yours. If ever you wish to lighten the load, call me. Or come see me in Helsinki. I will buy dinner next time."

"It's a date. I've always wanted to visit there."

"And now you will have me to be your guide around my favorite city."

Forty-Seven

I was nervous as ever as I sat in the waiting room outside Nate's office in the WNN building. I hadn't spoken with Nate Murphy since he fired me, but I knew I needed to face him. Make him understand that I'd changed. That I had the same fire as before, and most importantly, that I'd been clean for nearly two years—not even a drop of alcohol. I wanted to get back in the field. I missed the adrenaline. Without the drugs, it was all I had. Plus, the world continued to heat up, and sitting and writing on the sidelines was not for me.

After the release of *Ackerman's Curse*, I suffered from severe writer's block. The manuscript of *An Interview with Death* was much the same as it'd been when I left Gladys and Morton's place, except it was now typewritten rather than in its original blood script. Its revelations weren't included in *Ackerman's Curse* and wouldn't be revealed until the writing of this version.

"Nate will see you now," said Patty, his secretary.

I entered, Nate hopped up, and I extended a nervous hand.

He batted it down, hugged me, patted my back, and released. "How about the upcoming election?" asked Nate. "Talk about a dumpster fire."

I sat in front of the desk as Nate returned to his chair. "Yeah. Hell forbid, Cochran gets elected. I was on board at first. Dead Blow is bad news, but she went too far. She's gotta go."

"Tell me about it. But will she?" asked Nate.

"We'll see, won't we?"

"Yes, we will. Nothing we can do now except vote and present the truth of what Cochran's done since Rollins' assassination. The people haven't spoken yet, but polls show a close race, and Bloom has the momentum. He's gained fifteen points in the past few months. I really like Bloom. From research and interviews, he seems legit—a good, honest man but still tough enough and smart enough to handle the shitstorm south of the border. And don't get me started about the rest of the world, but with his military background I believe he'll be able to check Banisadr and Vasily with the help of Emperor Lee. Well, if he wins, he'll be the first Independent in the White House. But you know Cochran—if she goes, she'll go kicking and screaming. But, I know you didn't come here to hear me bitch about fascist Forty-Six. So, you think you're ready to get back on the horse, huh?"

"Yeah, something like that."

"And you're clean and sober?"

"Almost two years. AA meetings every Wednesday."

"Well, I have an assignment for you, but Julie Florid and I will be coming along. She's covering the Helsinki Peace Conference. President Vasily will be there, and I have no doubt he'll be pressing for the removal of sanctions after his invasion of the Donbas and the Crimea. He'll probably ask for the whole of Ukraine and say he'll play nice after that. Not like we haven't heard that before. Anyway, Julie secured an interview with the Federation President."

"That's great for her. So, what will I be doing?"

"Well, granted there's plenty of hot spots I could send you, but you've been out for a while. So, you'll have to earn back my trust before I chance this network's reputation again. I have something a little less intense but no less interesting. You'll be interviewing Jakko Kantelejarvi."

"Ilmarainen Tech, founder and CEO?"

"You got it. I figured after your recent bestseller, you two should talk especially since he appears in the epilogue and is at the forefront of Light Ethereal technology that wouldn't be a thing without the discoveries following the tragic events of 2007. It'll be for a 20/20 episode we'll call *Age of Ethereal* unless we come up with a better title before it airs around the fifth anniversary of the end of those terrible eight weeks. While it won't be a promo for your book, I don't think it'll hurt sales."

"Sounds great. I've been wanting to meet Kantelejarvi or at least speak with him. I tried to contact him for the book but he was never available."

"Well, he is now. And he wanted me to tell you he loved the book."

"So, why are you coming along? You have that little faith in me?"

"No, I trust you. Otherwise, I sure as hell wouldn't be giving you this opportunity to redeem yourself. And what, you don't want me to come along?"

"No. Nothing like that. It's just you never go on assignment anymore. At least you didn't before my downward spiral."

"You ever think I might want to get out of the office every once in a while? Plus, Julie and I have vacation plans after the conference."

"What? You and Julie?" I asked, pointing and squinting incredulously.

"Guess I should've mentioned that while you were off getting your shit together. Julie and I started dating. I plan to propose while we're in Helsinki. Like you, she's obsessed with Hemingway, but she's partial to his third wife, the iconic war correspondent, Martha Gellhorn. She's on a quest to retrace her every step. So, I figured I'd find a footprint, kneel, and see what she says. And I know just the spot. Julie has this black and white photo of Gellhorn on her office wall. She's standing in front of some place called King's Gate. It was taken the day before the Soviets started bombing Helsinki in the opening days of their Winter War in '39. Hemingway was home in Key West writing *For Whom the Bell Tolls*. Or was it Havana or Ketchum?"

"Key West."

Nate chuckled. "Is there any Hemingway trivia you don't know?"

I laughed. "I'm sure there is. Hey, Nate—thanks for this second chance."

"My pleasure. I will always believe in you, Nathan, and have since we first met at that coffee shop down the street... that's now a Charlotte's Café. Hey, you down for a Frespresso?"

"Would love one," I said.

Forty-Eight

Tuesday, September 11, 2012, Helsinki, Finland, EU.

The flight was long, and my legs were stiff even after sitting in first class. I didn't sleep well, and the jet lag was killing me. When Nate, Julie, and I entered the concourse, a limo driver was waiting. A half hour later, the driver dropped us off at the five star Hotel F6 off the Esplanadi.

Once settled in, I took my shoes off and sat on the bed. My thoughts were instantly of Kaisa. The interview with Kantelejarvi was tomorrow and Julie would be speaking with Vasily on Thursday. I reached for my wallet and found her phone number. I looked at the paper with perfect blue-ink handwriting, and almost put it back in my wallet, dismissing the idea of dialing the magic number.

"Fuck it," I said, grabbed my phone, and called. It rang four times, and then I heard that sweet voice.

"Hei, keneltä saan kysyä, puhuu?"

I didn't understand a word except *hei*, but knew it was her. "This is Nathan Miller."

"Oh, sorry, Nathan, I did not know it was you. How is New York?"

"I'm not in New York. I'm in Helsinki, staying at F6."

"Really," she said, her pitch rising slightly, then lowering with regained composure. "That is very nice. I am doing nothing right now. I could come into town and show you around. This is the best time to come to Helsinki. And I know of a nice place we can eat. It is next to the Helsinki Cathedral. I can meet you there or at your hotel."

"Meet me here. We'll walk together. I have a little work to do to get ready for tomorrow. But I'll meet you in the lobby at 18:00."

I went through the questions I'd prepared for the tech mogul plus extra questions for two additional guests, Charlotte's Coffee CEO, Francis T. Pickens, and Hachiman Corp. CEO, Takijirō Sasaki. While I was familiar with Pickens, I knew little about Sasaki or Hachiman Corp. I only knew it was a Japanese defense firm based in Hiroshima with restrictions that were placed on its activities since the end of WWII. It was already 14:27. I had a lot to cram to be ready for a night out with Kaisa and have any hope of pulling off a decent interview in the morning.

When I stepped from the elevator at 18:05, Kaisa was waiting in the open air atrium outside the lobby. She was wearing a colorful floral Marimekko blouse and skirt. Her blonde hair was trimmed short and permed in a wave that curled right. She wore light makeup but little was needed to accent her natural loveliness. Her thin red lips were curled into a subtle smile below alluring green eyes.

"I'm sorry I'm late," I said.

Without warning, she leaned and kissed me, hugged me, and said, "It's okay. It is just so nice to see you again so soon. Let's go. Our reservations are at 18:30."

We strolled briskly through the summer crowds which where paltry compared to Manhattan. The sky was clear with a few fluffy clouds but otherwise Finnish blue. We spoke little which made me feel awkward since Manhattanites rarely shut up. I kept glancing over. She would catch my gaze and smile. We passed the fountains on the east side of the Kauppatori—a famous outdoor market that had just closed for the day. We turned and continued down Sofiankatu—a narrow brick-paved street with its sign written in Finnish, Swedish, and Russian. Like the Kauppatori, the shops we passed were closed.

We turned onto Aleksanterinkatu. Across the street was the large square, known as the Senaatintori, which sprawled in front of the fifty steps to the iconic White Lutheran Cathedral that made Helsinki's skyline memorable. The cathedral was built in the shape of a Greek cross with its large central and four smaller copper domes greened with time like the Statue of Liberty. It was dedicated to Czar Nicholas I and originally named for the not-always-jolly ancient St. Nicholas in the land that boasted Santa Claus's permanent residence outside Rovaniemi. I stopped and admired the statue of Nicholas I's son Alexander II in the center of the Senaatintori. He was considered by many to be an admirable man and was responsible for liberating the Russian serfs before Abraham Lincoln's Emancipation Proclamation. I reached for the door to Ravintola Savotta. Kaisa beat me to the handle and I entered first.

We had a multi-course meal with various Finnish appetizers and a main course of topside roast reindeer and elk sausage. We finished with a crème brûlée and local Frazer's "Blue" milk chocolate. Everything was delicious. We talked and laughed. I was happy, but nagging guilt nipped me. I didn't want the night to end. I was falling in love again, and there was no stopping it.

After Kaisa paid the bill against my protest, we returned to the hotel around 21:00. In the open atrium, I thought about saying goodbye, but grabbed her hand and led her to the elevator and up to my room. Once there, we quickly removed our clothes. I kissed her and caressed her breasts. She kissed me and dropped to her knees. She did what she could, but the machinery wasn't working.

"Is something wrong?" she asked as she stood.

"Not at all. I don't know what's wrong. Hey, don't worry about me."

I laid her on the bed and sank my head into her delightful triangle. She gripped my head and moaned and groaned, her hips gyrating, grinding. I felt blood rushing downward, but my rocket wouldn't take off. I came up for air, inched my tongue and fingers up her smoothness to her breasts, and kissed and gently suckled each. I inched my way to her neck, and continued upward and made love to her lips as my flaccid member glided against her softness. I slid my fingers down, rubbed, then slid a finger inside her warm wetness, then two. She moaned and groaned as my fingers went to work with tender ferocity until she screamed and gripped me close, grinding her fingernails into my back. She relaxed.

194

"I'm sorry. I... I don't know what happened," I said, feeling much less than a man.

"Don't be. That was incredible. You need not worry. I have not made love since Toivo died. It has been far too long." Kaisa kissed me, and I quickly fell asleep, wrapped in her embrace.

Forty-Nine

Kaisa and I met Nate and Julie the next morning at the hotel breakfast bar—traditional Finnish and European continental for the tourists. Nate and Julie smiled at a face they knew well and another they'd never had the pleasure of meeting. Nate and Julie hopped up as we approached the table with full plates and coffee.

"Nate Murphy, WNN News," he said with a hand extended.

Kaisa set her plate and coffee on the table and shook Nate's hand.

"Julie Florid, Reporter for WNN News." She shook Kaisa's hand in turn.

"Let me introduce my friend," I said. "This is Kaisa Jännök. She writes..."

"... Children's stories," Julie finished. "I don't have any kids, but my sister loves your work. Such imagination. Where do you get your inspiration?"

"From a little white bear, I guess," said Kaisa.

Julie smiled. "So, when were you going to tell us, Nathan?"

"About what? I figured we needed a tour guide, and Kaisa knows the area."

"Uh-huh," Julie said with a wicked grin.

Kaisa glanced at me, and we traded confessional lip curls.

"Seriously, though, how did *this* happen?" Julie continued to pry.

"Off the record?" I asked.

"Of course. We're friends."

"We met in June at a mutual book signing at the Westfield Mall."

"Yes, we did. Nathan brought his whole family just to tell me how wonderful I was and what an important part of their lives my sweet little Toivo and his friends were to them. He won my heart, but he was a gentleman after dinner that night. I told him the next meal was on me. We had a nice dinner last night, but that is all I will say," she finished with a barely detectable grin.

"Oh-kay. Sorry for being nosy. It's the reporter in me."

"Yeah, we had a nice night, but we're taking it slow."

Kaisa coughed and tried not to giggle.

Julie glanced at Nate with a smirk. "Yeah, slow. I'm sure."

"Annnyway," Nate butted in to change the subject. "Eat up. Kantelejarvi wants us at Ilmarainen Tech in Espoo around 9:00." He continued, curiously tripping over his words, "And Kaisa, since you're planning to be, uh, Nathan's guide, if it wouldn't be too much trouble... I mean, we don't want to be the third and fourth wheels, or anything... but would you mind if we, uh, tagged along? Would love a local's tour and I'd like to visit Suomenlinna."

Julie regarded Nate suspiciously.

"Oh, of course," said Kaisa. "You cannot come to Helsinki without visiting Sveaborg. And no, I would not mind. The more the merrier, as they say."

196

We finished breakfast and left. Traffic was heavier than usual due to the Peace Conference which would begin that afternoon. Nate called Kantelejarvi to let him know we would be late. He admitted he was running behind as well.

We arrived at the lonely Ilmarainen Tech campus around 09:30. The three-person film crew from the Helsinki's local WNN affiliate was waiting.

It was a gorgeous location built on Lake Bodom's southwestern shore, surrounded by birch and pine woods with scattered moss-covered boulders (some quite massive) left behind from the great Ice Age. The main building was a thirteen-storied, four-pointed star, topped with a glass pyramid. It looked identical to photos I'd seen of the new Charlotte's Coffee headquarters in Packer City, Colorado—a definite upgrade from the quaint aquamarine-colored café where the late Charlotte Lee founded her coffee empire. The old café was still there and a major tourist draw to the once tiny town which was not nearly as tiny as the last time I visited with Ryan's family—a bitter-sweet memory as I write this volume.

Stepping through the glass front doors was like stepping into a Finnish forest and wasn't much different than the woods outside. There was natural greenery, moss-covered rocks, birch and pine trees, and a variety of berry bushes brimming with ripe fruit. And the place smelled amazingly natural with no elevator music or bad renditions of pop favorites. The only sounds were bird songs and the gentle whistle of wind through the trees.

Nate stopped at the security station. "We are here to see Mr. Kantelejarvi," he said to the guard at the desk. "I'm Nate Murphy from WNN, and this is Julie Florid, Nathan Miller, Kaisa Jännök, and my film crew."

The guard spoke in perfect English with a slight Finnish twang. "Yes, Mr. Kantelejarvi is expecting you. I will let him know you are here." The guard buzzed Mr. Kantelejarvi. "Mr. Kantelejarvi will be down momentarily. Please help yourself to our Charlotte's Coffee Bar. Light Ethereal is legal in Suomi, so enjoy an original Charlotte's Frespresso."

Julie's eyes went wide. She smiled wide and skipped to the barista. The film crew followed with no less enthusiasm.

The guard's voice rose as I walked off. "Oh, and I encourage you to visit the company exhibit beyond the bar."

Julie ordered two Frespressos. I skipped coffee, and went straight to the exhibit with Kaisa. It was mostly photos. I stopped at a picture of Francis Pickens in October 2007, holding a metal canister filled with Dark Ethereal. I licked my lips and felt the twinge, burn, and itch. I took a deep breath.

"Are you alright?" asked Kaisa.

"Yeah. I'll tell you about it later."

"Okei," she said, grabbed my hand, and squeezed.

The urge melted away as I gently clutched Kaisa's hand. I kissed the side of her head.

The next photo was of a bush burning with light blue fire. Flakes of Light Ethereal sparkled in the air. Posing and smiling next to it was the Mears County Sheriff and one of his deputies. The photo was taken in November 2007 outside Packer City. The sheriff would go on to become Governor of Colorado but the events that sealed the deal are revealed in a later tale.

The next photos revealed some of what was discovered within the bowels of Lester Ackerman's Fallout Shelter. The last was of a very happy Francis Pickens and Jakko Kantelejarvi. Each had one arm draped over the other's shoulder. The opposite arm was extended with a palmful of icy blue gold. The luminance around them had an aquarium appearance. The exhibit continued with the various products that Kantelejarvi designed from the more stable aquarium-colored Light Ethereal. Absent was any mention of the horrors that preceded these innovations. I was disgusted by the omissions that cost so many lives, including Ryan Mender's.

"Let's get a cup of coffee," said Kaisa, sensing the tension.

"Sounds good."

Kaisa ordered a Light Charlotte, and I had an Americano, *hold the Ethereal*. I was done with that evil shit in any form.

Mr. Kantelejarvi stepped from the elevator with open arms.

"Tervetuloa. Welcome, welcome. It is so good to finally meet you all, especially you, Nathan Miller. *Ackerman's Curse* was remarkable."

Jakko Kantelejarvi was a sharp-dressed, striking man with piercing light blue eyes. He was taller than most Finns, clean shaven with silver hair pulled into a pony tail. He was a timeless older gentleman with smooth skin of a much younger man. I suspected Botox and a top plastic surgeon was to thank for that since he looked as natural as the nature outside the entrance doors.

"Thank you, Mr. Kantelejarvi," I said.

"No, no, no. Call me Jakko. And thank you for another masterpiece. It was almost as good as *The Menders: A First American Story*. I was devastated when I learned of your friend Ryan's death. Absolute tragedy like much of what happened in 2007. Francis and I both grieved when we heard the news. But it is fortunate that at least some good things grew from that soil of tragedy. That is why I had you come. Oh, and Francis Pickens and Takijirō Sasaki will arrive here soon. They are still in Packer City and Hiroshima. Both are looking forward to speaking with you."

The four of us traded quizzical glances. What did he mean *arrive here* if they were a third of the way around the globe going west and east? Whatever he meant, it didn't matter. I was prepared for anything.

I extended my hand.

Jakko shook it firmly and regarded Kaisa. "Kaisa Jännök. What brings you here?"

"I am with Nathan. He is a friend of mine. I am his tour guide of our fine city while he is here."

"Well, it is good to see you. It has been a long time. I doubt you remember."

"Oh, I remember. You brought your little boy to meet me at Stockmann's bookstore. I signed his first-edition copy of the *Adventures of Toivo the Bear*. He brought his little white bear that day. He told me he named it Toivo because you told him that my stories were about hope. Actually, you gave me the idea to have those bears produced en masse. Now they are all over the world."

Jakko placed fingers lightly on his chest. "Wow. Really? I did not know that."

"I guess I owe you some royalties," said Kaisa.

Jakko laughed. "It is very nice to see you again. I still have that bear and that book. They are two of my most prized possessions."

Kaisa smiled. "So, how is your son, Thomas?"

Jakko's aspect changed from sunny afternoon to dusk. "You remembered his name. He is gone. He was killed in a motorcycle accident on his eighteenth birthday."

"I am so sorry," said Kaisa.

Nate and Julie's expressions matched Kaisa's as the mood shifted.

"It is okay. How could you have known? Like you, my private life belongs to me. And there is nothing like time and new love to heal wounds," said Jakko, glancing at me.

"Yes. I know," said Kaisa as she squeezed my arm.

"Just a tour guide, huh?" Jakko said with a smile that Kaisa returned.

I changed the subject. "I have to say, it's amazing what you and Pickens have accomplished in such a short time."

"Ah, yes. And you will not be disappointed you came all this way. Come, come. We go to the penthouse. We will do the interview there."

We nodded and entered a roomy glass elevator that comfortably accommodated the eight of us plus video equipment. It rose, giving us a breathtaking view of each floor, which together, might give the Hanging Gardens of Babylon a run for the title of Wonder of the World. The doors opened into a spacious birchwood forest with mossy rocks and a creek that flowed into a small pond. Unlike the ground level, the floor was made of natural earth. Along the trail leading to the pond were mushrooms and more bushes brimming with strawberries, blueberries, red and black currants, and various other berries. Out of place were two columned glass cases by the elevator. One contained the lower jaw of a large fish with strings tied across it like a harp. The second case contained a wooden five-stringed instrument I recognized as a kantele.

"Sorry, it is not very realistic. I decided to skip the mosquitoes," Jakko said with a subtle chuckle and a lip curl. "Pick some berries. No doubt, you will find them delicious. Also, the mushrooms are edible."

Julie, Nate, and the film crew indulged.

"Wow. These are the sweetest currants I've ever tasted," said Julie.

"These strawberries and blueberries aren't too bad, either," said Nate.

"Glad you like them. Would you like an apple or peach?"

We looked around and didn't see any apple or peach trees, then suddenly one of each, heavy with fruit, materialized a dozen feet from us.

"Holy sh..." Julie started to say. "How, how'd you do that?"

"It's all technology from Ackerman's Fallout Shelter. This glass pyramid, like the one atop the Charlotte's Coffee Headquarters, is equipped with the same environmental controls discovered at the shelter. If you like, I can make it snow or rain. Sun—you want sun and a nice beach—I can do that, too. It seems there is nothing impossible with *Terrarium Tech* which will be available to the public within a few years."

"Was this what you brought us here for?" said Nate.

"No, but it is cool. No?"

"Yes, very," said Kaisa. She picked two peaches, handed me one, and sank her teeth into the fruit.

Jakko headed into the imaginary forest and stopped near the pond's edge. A large paper-thin screen materialized and hovered in the air. Kantelejarvi nodded at the film crew. They set up at three angles around the screen. It reminded me of a Reality Window that separated me from Aunt Dorothy and my parents when the Blue Dragon took me to Paradise.

"Sit," Jakko said, motioning to the floor. "Francis and Takijirō will join us shortly."

There were no chairs. Not wanting to hesitate or offend, I crouched to sit on the ground, but before I could, roots erupted from the soil. They rapidly twisted and morphed into ergonomically balanced throne-like seats for three guests to the right of the screen and one for me facing the others. The film crew adjusted their angles and started filming. Three additional root thrones formed on the left side of the makeshift studio. As soon as Nate, Julie, and Kaisa rehinged their jaws, they sat in those.

The camerapersons panned to take in the wonders like children standing in a dream. I was less impressed. Maybe I was jaded after visiting Gladys and Morton. Still, it was a sight to experience considering what reality was like before 2007.

I sat in the interviewer's throne and Jakko sat in the one by the screen, angled to face Pickens and Sasaki when they joined the interview. I wondered why there were two empty seats.

Francis appeared on the left side of the screen. He was clean shaven, in business attire, and wore stylish round-rimmed glasses. From the waist up he appeared slim and buff with short cut white hair that seemed fuller than it should be. He sort of reminded me of Andy Warhol. He looked nothing like the heavy-set balding coroner with thick plastic-framed glasses who was on the scene at the beginning of the 2007 shitstorm. He was the same man who coined the term *Ethereal* and first recognized the dangers of the darker version. No one imagined then that he was heir to what was now a one hundred billion dollar company.

"Hi, guys. How's the weather in HEL?" Pickens said in a cartoonish high pitch, that would've been unexpected for anyone who hadn't heard the coffee mogul speak. He snort-laughed. And HEL... that was the abbreviation for the nearby Vantaa airport. It was a tiresome jest for newcomers to the Finland's capitol and a cause of rolling eyes for locals.

"Actually, we are in Espoo, and currently we are not living up to our reputation for ice and snow, snow, snow, and more snow. It is quite beautiful outside. How is Packer City?"

"It's dark and the view of the Milky Way above the pyramid reminds me why I love living here. Is Takijirō there?"

"No. But you know him. He will be late to his funeral if he ever has one."

"I heard that," came a gruff voice with a harsh Asian accent. A second man appeared on the floating screen's right half. His face was pudgy and the left eye was covered with a black patch.

Jakko laughed with a convincing smile. "Good to see you, old friend."

"Yes. Always a pleasure, my old, *old* friend," said Takijirō Sasaki, his demeanor stormy and devoid of cheer.

"Takijirō and I go way back," said Jakko. "So, are you two just going to stand there, or are you planning to join us?"

I looked at the studio audience. Nate and Julie were looking at each other while Kaisa was watching with rapt anticipation for what was coming next, clearly taken aback by the amazing sights so far.

"Are you ready for the transfer?" asked Jakko.

"Absolutamente. Beam me up, Scotty," said Francis.

Mr. Sasaki rolled his right eye as his lips pursed.

Whoever was controlling the cameras in Packer City and Hiroshima pulled back for a wide angle. The two men stood on three-foot round blue disks atop a much larger disk swirling with aquarium-colored liquid that reminded me of Morton Death's holograph table. The light around the men darkened and the larger disk began to shimmer, shading Pickens and Sasaki in aquarium-like effects.

"Watch the pond," said Kantelejarvi.

We did. Two cameras panned to Nate, Julie, Kaisa, and me to capture our expressions for whatever was about to happen. The last camera was directed toward the screen and the pond behind it. The Reality Window dissolved into light blue mist and the pond began to ripple. A large swirling disk of Light Ethereal emerged from the center followed by two smaller disks from that surface. A pleasant humming like an angelic choir interrupted the birds and the breeze soundtrack. Seconds later a pair of swirling spectral columns appeared atop the smaller blue disks and took shape. Like clay being molded by the maker, the column took human form. It became solid as finer features became recognizable and skin and clothing was painted onto mannequin-like apparitions. The aquarium light faded to the natural luminance within the pyramid forest. Atop the small disks, Francis Pickens' lips spread into a wide grin while Takijirō Sasaki's remained a thin line.

Fifty

The cameraman caught my O mouth. As a kid growing up in the sixties and early seventies, I loved Star Trek. The show challenged my imagination and made me wonder what was beyond my reality's narrow confines. I loved the show's communicators and thought it was so cool when Finland-based Nokia came out with flip phones. They were now old technology, replaced by smarter phones for zombies. But the transporters—that was something I never for a second imagined was possible. I'd just witnessed it was.

"Hello, hello, everyone," Francis said like a Stooge as he stepped off the larger disk and into the pond. He didn't sink and walked on water to the shore. He sat on the root throne next to Jakko.

Takijirō followed and sat in the last throne. He wore an emerald suit over a lemon-yellow shirt and a green tie with yellow polka dots. The suit looked tacky, just short of pimpish. The man was short, maybe five feet tall, frumpy, but not fat. As mentioned, a black patch covered his left eye. On his hands, he wore eight alternating emerald and amber rings with petrified insects within the amber.

"Wow," was all I could muster.

"Yup, it's pretty amazing and scary as heck the first time you ride the Ether-*Unreal* Airways," Pickens said and chuckled with a snort.

I had questions but my mind went temporarily blank as a camera focused for my response. "So... So, uh, tell me about this transporter. I mean, this could... no, it *will* revolutionize travel as we know it."

206

"You betcha," said Francis. "But this is only one of the many Ethereal-based innovations Jakko and Mr. Sasaki have perfected or are currently working on."

"That it is," said Jakko. "The transporter was quite simple to design with the knowledge gained within Ackerman's Fallout Shelter. Unfortunately, I cannot give further details concerning how the transporter works since those details are among my company's most closely guarded secrets—almost as secret as the recipe for *Coca Cola*."

I laughed along with the studio audience of three.

Jakko continued without cracking a grin. "For now, just know that it works and that it has been well tested. Of course, Francis and I did not start with living things. We initially saw it as a means to transport freight, but we were obviously curious what else could be moved. So, Francis sent his pet rat, Freddie, to me. It arrived alive and in one piece. I kidded with him about coming over for a drink at *Hemingway's* that night. Well, I went to the bathroom, and returned to find Francis sporting a Cheshire grin, sitting on a couch holding Freddie."

Francis laughed. "Oh, your face. You were so mad. Nathan, you know, I loved Star Trek and always dreamed of doing that for real."

"Me, too," I said, unable to contain myself.

"Hasn't any Trekkie?"

"I admit—I was furious with Francis for risking his life," said Jakko. "But he seemed well enough after the transfer. I calmed down after a few drinks, but insisted Francis have a full physical the next day. I ordered full chemistries, ultrasound, echo, CT, MRI, and a stress test. Well, he turned out to have all his molecules in their proper places and appeared as healthy as a coffee mogul."

Francis chimed in. "That night after dinner at Ravintola Savotta..."

I glanced at Kaisa. She grinned back.

"...Jakko agreed to let me take the Light EtheRail home. I called him several minutes later after I got back to Packer City. It would've been sooner, but I couldn't find my phone and had to use an employee's."

"You had me worried," said Jakko. "Well, after that, we did more tests and found organic transfer accuracy to be one hundred percent over several hundred transfers of various species. True, had anything gone wrong we might have heard from animal rights groups—but nothing did. In the coming years we plan to release the technology for multiple applications and even for home use for delivery of Charlotte's World Famous Frespressos straight to your transporter disk."

Mr. Sasaki fiddled with his tie then scratched under his eye patch.

I asked the next question. "What else does Ilmarainen Tech have in its pipeline for the Age of Ethereal?"

Jakko looked at Mr. Sasaki. He seemed to be zoned out, his mind somewhere, anywhere, but there for the interview. "I'll let Francis answer this one since our first product was his *vauva*."

"Yes, it was my baby," said Francis as Mr. Sasaki chewed a fingernail. "Nathan, I won't steal your thunder," he said, then leaned forward and slapped my leg. He looked into the camera like he was doing an infomercial. "I recommend picking up a copy of *Ackerman's Curse* if you haven't already. Pick up two or three and give them as gifts this Christmas or Halloween. My part in the 2007 ordeal is well documented in its pages."

Jakko produced a hardback special edition seemingly out of nowhere to show the cameras. Mr. Sasaki rolled his right eye again.

Francis continued. "As you know, my first experience with Ethereal was with the dark stuff. I mean, I didn't actually take Dead Blow. No, I saw right away that this stuff was unstable. But it was my late Aunt Charlotte who discovered the lighter stuff some time back. She lived as long as she did because of it. She had breast cancer, and Light Ethereal kept her cancer in remission. The dark stuff was the curse, but the light stuff has been a blessing for everyone. That dark stuff is only good for destroying lives and families. Oh, and it's a great flame retardant, too."

I hoped the camera didn't catch my shakes as Francis spoke the truth.

He continued, "But the effect wasn't unique to Dark Ethereal. We found we could get the same fire retardant effect from the light stuff my Aunt—bless her heart—was spiking her World Famous Frespressos with before it was cool."

The Reality Window reappeared as if on cue with a video of a lumber mill and planks of wood being sprayed with an aquamarine mist that turned clear on contact.

"Already new homes are being built with the *Ethertardent Technology*. Even President Cochran has allowed its special use to continue. Unfortunately, it's highly regulated which is driving up housing costs in the States. But it's best not to talk about politics these days," Francis added with a concerned look as if he'd said too much.

Jakko picked up where Francis left off. "But *Ethertardent Technology*—trademark Ilmarainen Tech—was just the beginning. Due to the low to nonexistent cancer rates among Light Ethereal consumers in Packer City, medical applications were immediately recognized."

"It even made my hair grow back. And look at these guns," said Francis, flexing his arms with a comical expression.

Everyone chuckled, except Mr. Sasaki, who was looking increasingly annoyed.

"But seriously," Francis continued, "before Light Ethereal, people like me couldn't see cuts like these unless they took anabolic steroids which made some things get big and other things, well..." He held up a hand with the tips of the index finger and thumb close but not touching.

I shook my head and laughed again.

Jakko rolled his eyes and picked up the thread. "But seriously, life-saving and life-extending medications are already on the market or in Ilmarainen Medical's pipeline which could potentially cure all forms of cancer, immune mediated conditions, you name it, or at least drive these illnesses into remission for decades. It is a brave new world ahead of us. And beyond pharmaceuticals, there is limb replacement therapy."

The Reality Window switched from a pharmaceutical conveyor belt to a pair of War on Terrorism veterans, a young man missing an arm and an early middle-aged woman without legs. Each stub was wrapped with luminescent aquamarine-colored tape.

"These videos were taken immediately after application of *RegenerTech Gel*—trademark Ilmarainen Medical. This is six weeks later."

The bandages were gone and fetus-sized appendages had sprouted like seedlings.

"Twelve weeks."

The appendages were child-size and both veterans were doing light weight exercises.

"Six months."

The young man was bench pressing his body weight and the woman was running on a treadmill at top speed at full incline.

"Holy shit. I'm sorry," I said.

"Don't be. If anything deserves a *pyhä paska*, this does. These are only two of the three hundred veterans in our phase two trial who have gotten their old lives back with limbs better than the ones they were born with. Plus, we have begun studies for use for acute battlefield injuries that could save countless lives in the ongoing worldwide conflicts. Unfortunately, President Cochran and Prime Minister Lord Byron Smythe will not allow their Veterans Administrations access to the limb regeneration therapy until phase four trials are complete..."

Francis looked uncomfortable with the freedom of Jakko's speech.

"... Most other countries have not been resistant and pre-orders are already maxing our production. The gel will start shipping in the second half of 2013."

"That's... wow... truly revolutionary. If only we had RegenerTech a decade ago," I said as my mind drifted to memories of the dying and the dead.

"Yes, indeed. It's a very different world we live in now, for better and for worse," said Jakko.

211

I turned to Takijirō Sasaki. "I'm glad you took time out of your busy schedule at Hachiman Corp to be here. And that entrance. Wow. Well, *wow* to everything."

"Yes, I do suppose it is eye opening the first time you see such things," Mr. Sasaki said as if this was nothing new in a tone that was anything but jovial.

I awkwardly lowered my own tone a few notches toward reticent and asked something broad to get him to open up and hopefully loosen up. "So, uh, could you tell us about the Hachiman Corporation and how your defense firm is utilizing the light blue miracle?"

He hesitated, took a breath, and said, "I apologize if I have not been a good guest. But what I have to say is something I do not like to speak of and a subject that has weighed on me for a very long time, as Jakko knows."

Jakko nodded solemnly. Francis rubbed his chin pensively.

"As I am sure you are aware—Hachiman Corporation has a checkered past for which I am not proud. My uncle Eiichirō was party to human experimentation at Unit 731 in Manchuria during World War II as well as many other atrocities the Japanese would like to forget. But I cannot. I will not," he said with a simmering voice. "The bomb erased his life and his former headquarters from the face of this Earth, but I survived with the loss of an eye. With the eye that remained, I witnessed the aftermath following the incineration of virtually every living thing within a half-mile and the suffering and slow death of those exposed to nuclear radiation. Two hundred thousand lives with one bomb. There was a girl—a cousin of mine—who was among the victims. Her name was Sasaki

Sadako. Have you heard of her, Nathan Miller?" Mr. Sasaki asked, choking out the question.

"Yes. Yes, I have," I said reverently.

"Then indulge me, so I may tell her story to those who do not."

"Yes. Yes, please. By all means."

"Sadako was two-years-old the day the bomb was dropped. She suffered greatly from radiation sickness but she never lost her smile. She died of leukemia when she was twelve. In the year of her death, her father told her the one who folds one thousand paper cranes will be granted a wish. She folded six-hundred-forty-four before she died. Since then, children from all over the world have folded the rest, thousands of times over, and placed them in glass cases around the monument next to the Genbaku Dome and the Peace Memorial. There, her statue stands upon a bomb-like platform with her arms raised holding the skeleton of a paper crane. At the base is a black marble slab with the inscription: *This is our cry, this is our prayer: for building peace in the world.* Her monument is dedicated to all the children like her who died in the days and years that followed the dropping of the first atomic bomb."

I glanced at Kaisa. She was wiping her eyes with a tissue.

Mr. Sasaki continued. "The flames of the nearby Peace Memorial have burned since its dedication in 1964 and will continue to do so until nuclear weapons have vanished from this earth. As you know, General Cornelius Adamson's actions in Almawt Lilkifaar did nothing to bring lasting peace and brought more suffering on the guilty and innocent alike. Curse his damned soul. His actions have increased the likelihood for a long-feared apocalypse and the unlikelihood that the monument's flames will ever be extinguished while life remains on this planet. And that was true… before the discovery of Ethereal."

The Reality Window showed a photo-realistic animation of a large city underneath a semi-transparent dome of swirling aquarium blue. A portion of the mock-up was removed to show the thriving city within the shield. Outside the dome was utter desolation.

"What are we looking at?" I asked.

"The Sky Forge."

"Sky Forge? What is it?"

"It is part of a dream to produce a defense network that, when perfected, will, hopefully, make war obsolete, but at the very least neutralize the threat of nuclear weapons once and for all."

"Like Ronald Reagan's Star Wars project?"

"Yes, and no. Yes, the Sky Forge will stop nuclear weapons. But unlike Reagan's unworkable fantasy meant to bankrupt the former Soviet Union, the energy of the blasts will be neutralized. In fact, all energy that comes in contact with the shield will be neutralized and converted into harmless, usable kinetic energy, making the shield stronger with every attack. In doing so, nuclear weapons or any missile will be made pointless."

"So, what's stopping Hachiman Corp. from moving forward with the Sky Forge?"

"I will let Jakko answer that," said Mr. Sasaki.

"It is simple—we are yet to create a power source which can generate the energy needed to initiate and sustain the shields. Our goal must be to shield countries, continents, the whole planet, if possible. The power source is the Holy Grail that Takijirō and I seek.

We call it the *Sampo* and I fear it will take Ilmarinen himself to make it real in this Age of Ethereal."

Fifty-One

I ended the interview after a closing round of questions. I motioned *cut* and Mr. Sasaki said he was thirsty. Jakko handed him a bottle of water, but he said that wasn't what he had in mind. Julie, who had red eyes after shedding tears for Sasaki Sadako, suggested we go to Hemingway's in downtown Helsinki. Mr. Sasaki cracked his first smile.

Jakko, Francis, and Mr. Sasaki changed into casual clothes Jakko had stashed in the penthouse dreamland to blend in with the average dressed Finn. Once ready, Jakko ordered a driver to take us to the metro so the newcomers could enjoy a scenic ride and avoid downtown traffic. Jakko revealed that the Helsinki/Espoo/Vantaa area would soon be driverless with the growing transit infrastructure and automated cars technology accelerated by Ethereal-assisted artificial intelligence.

On the way, I asked Kaisa about Ilmarainen and the Sampo references. I could've looked it up but I wanted to hear it from a local and I loved to hear her voice. The names came from the Kalevala which was the Finnish National Epic written by Elias Lönnrot. It was a collection of folktales that gave the Finnish people of Finland, Estonia, and Karelia their cultural identity. Many Finns even named their children for characters from the epic, like her cousin, Kalevi. Kaisa also took pride in the fact the Kalevala was one of the major inspirations for J.R.R. Tolkien's Lord of the Rings saga.

The national treasure was named for an ancient Finnic ruler who lived in what is now Estonia before the sixth or seventh century. He was an enormous giant, and when he died, his wife, Linda, buried him, creating a massive burial mound that is now called the Toompea upon which Tallinn was built by Danish conquerors.

"...But the mound is far too large for any mortal or even giant man to have been buried. It is probably just a legend... or maybe not," Kaisa said with her precious smile as her green eyes sparkled. "As for Ilmarainen—it is best you read the epic. It is... different, I will admit. It contains many tales about him. He was a blacksmith. He is sometimes mistakenly compared to Thor, but Thor is mistakenly confused for a blacksmith. Our Ukko, the Thunder God, is our version of Thor. But Ilmarainen is most famous for forging the Sampo, a mystical item that brings wealth to the one who possesses it. If what Mr. Sasaki and Jakko say is true about the Sky Forge and that the Sampo is needed to power it, I can think of no better name. After all, what is more valuable than peace?"

We got to Hemingway's around noon at the location around the corner from Helsinki Rail Station. Mr. Sasaki started with double whisky twins straight up and then we ordered a bite to eat. A drink sounded nice, but I stayed dry as usual, and Kaisa refrained in support. Nate and Julie enjoyed Lonkeros while Jakko and Francis kept us in stitches. Funny what a little liquid lubrication can do. Even Takijirō was relaxed, smiling, and talkative, insisting that we stop calling him Mr. Sasaki, and to please call him Takijirō.

Nate finished his third glass of the Original Lonkero and said, "Julie and I are new to Helsinki. What do you suggest we do this afternoon?"

Kaisa looked at Jakko. "Suomenlinna," they said at the same time.

216

Nate raised his eyebrows and looked at Julie, then glanced at me.

"What?" asked Julie.

"Oh, nothing," Nate and I said.

"Well, let's go then. I assume you all are coming," said Kaisa, eyeing Jakko, Francis, and Takijirō.

The three traded glances. Takijirō answered with barely a lisp, "Sure, why not," and slammed his fifth double whisky.

After a short ride in Jakko's boat past a few islands, we docked by a convenience store on one of Suomenlinna's eight islands where the Swedes built the Sveaborg fortress in 1748. The fortress's history was long but it was now the residence of eight hundred Finns and a favorite spot for the others to visit at least once a year, or when they could. It was also the city's most popular tourist attraction. While the weather this time of year was often cloudy and cool, we were enjoying a second day of sun and reasonably warm temperatures.

Nate stopped by the market, picked up some champagne, and then we set off to explore the bridge-connected islands. Sunbathers and picnickers were everywhere, taking advantage of the final warm days before the wet fall and harsh winter. We followed Kaisa and Jakko. They appeared to be getting on well. I'll admit—I found myself getting a little jealous. But whenever that doubt monster crept in, Kaisa would shoot me a reassuring glance that I had nothing to worry about. I hadn't felt that way in years—probably not since the day I fell in love with Vanessa. Kaisa was my second chance, and to be honest—I was terrified of losing her, and my performance the night before didn't help.

We walked along the trail above flattened rocks that disappeared into the Baltic. Finns laid out soaking up the sun like solar panels for the shortening days. Some were wading and splashing in the water in a small cove below us.

"That looks fun," Kaisa said and ran down the steps.

I followed and tried to keep up.

She took off her shoes and coaxed me into the water.

I took mine off, rolled up my pants, and stepped into cool water. I glanced at the others. They didn't need an invitation.

We waded like kids or locals and were seemingly invisible among the families in the water around us. It amazed me that no one recognized us or accosted us for autographs. I thought it hubris to think it unusual, but our collection of faces, with the exception of Takijirō, were some of the most recognizable on the planet (or at least in the West). Kaisa and Jakko said it was just the way Finns are. They respected privacy and private time of even the most famous. It was nice to feel invisible.

We continued past cannons, bunkers, and battlements. A Finnish battle flag, with the lion crest centered on the blue cross, fluttered in the wind over a brick building. The King's Gate lay ahead. Julie picked up her pace, passed underneath, and stopped at the fortress's rounded entrance steps.

Julie spun around to face Nate. "It was right here. This is where Gellhorn stood for that photo the day before the Soviets started bombing in '39."

"Yeah. It is, isn't it? Totally forgot about that photo on your office wall. Hey, think you can take a photo of Julie and me together?" Nate said as he handed me his smartphone.

I stood far enough back to catch the entire gate. I waited until the stream of people thinned to get them alone and snapped a shot.

Nate suddenly knelt. "Hold on a second," he said.

I zoomed in for a close up.

Nate acted like he was tying his shoes. He looked up at Julie, lifted his hand, and revealed a little black box. He opened it. Inside was a ring and a rock that could feed a lot of rabbits.

Julie's hand flew to her mouth. "Yes, yes, yes," she said.

"Shouldn't I pop the question first?"

"Yes, yes. Ask, ask, ask."

"Julie Annette Florid, will you marry me and make me the happiest man in the world?"

"What do you think?"

We laughed as Nate slipped the promise onto Julie's finger. There were a few Finnish grins but otherwise everyone passed like Nate was any other Paavo, Pekka, or Pietari proposing at the King's Gate. Takijirō uncorked the champagne. The cork flew from sight and landed on the gate's mossy roof. Everyone but Kaisa and I took a plastic champagne glass. Takijirō filled each.

Before they drank, Jakko said, "Hölkyn kölkyn." We repeated the cheer and those drinking drank up.

Fifty-Two

After seeing us to our hotel, Jakko, Francis, and Takijirō took the metro to Espoo where Francis and Takijirō returned to Colorado and Japan in the manner they came. After a quick stop by the rooms, our group remained at the Ravintola Savotta to celebrate Nate and

Julie's engagement. Kaisa spent the night. I had the same difficulties as before. And like an angel, she was just as understanding, patient, and seemed to enjoy what I did for her (or lied convincingly well).

Julie's interview went well the next day but the same couldn't be said for Russian Federation President Vladimir Vasily. If his purpose was to fool hearts or minds of his true intentions, he failed miserably. Vasily wasn't one to give interviews outside his state-controlled echo chamber and likely assumed he could steamroll Julie. She quickly squashed that notion, giving him nothing but a smiling, diplomatic inch.

She refused to let him dodge, or drown the viewer in rhetorical bullshit, or allow him to what-about anything. She asked pointed, direct questions concerning disappearances and unsolved murders of opposition leaders. Vasily dodged but she countered with crosses that had him stuttering for plausible lies. When she asked about the one hundred thousand Russian troops sitting on the Ukrainian border, he said he was performing military exercises like NATOs forty thousand in Poland. Julie countered that they were only placed there after the start of said *"exercises."* Then he went into the pointlessness of NATO's *"aggressive expansion"* and its continued existence as the reason for said *"exercises."* Julie countered with questions about the Federation's invasions and genocides in Georgia, Chechnya, the current occupation of Donbass and Crimea, and his provocative alliance with the bloodthirsty Iranian Shahanshah Banisadr. Vasily dodged the Banisadr question and corrected Julie that *"Donbass and Crimea chose to rejoin Mother Russia."* She retorted with questions concerning the details of said *"choice,"* violations of international treaties, and other border countries with Russian populations that were compelled to *"choose"* to join Mother Russia at the point of a gun. Vasily vacillated back to

NATO's aggressive expansion. She countered with the step by step process required to become a member nation, a process many former members of *"Mother Russia"* happily complied with to prevent being *"liberated"* again after years of oppression by their *"Mother."* At that, President Vasily removed his mic, said the interview is over, and stormed out of the studio red-faced and cursing in Russian.

On the flight home, Julie expressed regret that the big man, "bitched out before *this* malyshka nailed him to Red Square about Banisadr, Georgia, and Chechnya." But all in all, the interview was what WNN viewers had come to expect from the iconic Julie Florid.

Fifty-Three

September-December 2012.

My schedule was insanity after returning from Helsinki. Over the next three months I longed for Kaisa's embrace and her soft red lips. True, we spoke every morning, remembering the seven hour time difference. But I wanted—no, I ached to be with her. But there wasn't enough time for us to get together with the lake between us. It made the wait for Kantelejarvi's new transportation system that much harder.

While working on the 20/20 *Age of Ethereal Special*, I felt like a kid again, floating on cloud nine. Focus was a challenge but there was a lot on the line and I didn't want to let Nate down. Occasionally, I thought about having a drink to calm my nerves... just one... or maybe a joint or a bump of Coke... a little H... some Dead Blow, maybe, just a little? Then I would think about what Gladys and

Morton had done for me. It helped but I missed Gladys's special cookies that made the lies in my head a little bit easier to ignore. Still, nothing could sway my determination to stay on track and be the man Frank and Dorothy wanted me to be. Stand on my own but not be an island. I wanted to make the living proud of me again, but moreover I wanted to be proud of myself and to be the best man for Kaisa. Be the hero with a history in my story. Be the phoenix that rose from the ashes of my self-destruction.

During that five week period, I had frequent conference calls with Jakko, Francis, and Takijirō for additional content. I also started writing a new book. I was fascinated with Kalevala. Jakko knew the stories well. He also had incredible insight into the origins behind them, the history of the semi-legendary land known as Väinölä, and the Baltic Vikings. Takijirō had his tales as well from the East that would feed later projects. Over that five weeks, the four of us remotely became good friends and remained so until they were gone.

What we created aired Friday, October 19, 2012, three days shy of the fifth anniversary of the horrendous revelations that set the new age in motion. The episode would go down as 20/20's most watched episode at a time when my country braced for an election like nothing we'd seen before.

Cochran lost by a sizable margin, but immediately after, she claimed there was wide-spread voter fraud and vowed not to accept the results. This spurred violent riots among her supporters. The death toll and property damage eclipsed the nationwide riots of November 2007. As Christmas neared, all was not calm and the future looked anything but bright.

Fifty-Four

I went to the office early on December 23 to finish a few things. My work carried over into the afternoon, but I still got back to the Village in time for the Giants/Ravens game.

An unexpected visitor awaited in my apartment. After two years, Death had returned, but he was just Morton to me now. There he was—boots off with his feet propped on the coffee table next to his black Stetson. He was watching football with the volume up and didn't notice me come in. The Saints were beating the Cowboys in OT, thirty-one to twenty-eight. I set my bag on the floor.

Morton turned. "Sorry, I let myself in. I wasn't sure how long you'd be. And I needed a break."

"No problem. I was starting to wonder if you were ever coming back."

"What do you mean? I was only… Oh. Never mind. I forget about the whole mortal Timethy concept. In my head, I was gone for what might seem to you like a couple of minutes, or if I stretch it, maybe an hour. Yeah, when you've existed as long as I have and pop in and out of multiple dimensions and multiple, fairly repetitive realities of countless individual mortal lives, your concept of Timethy can get away from you. Anyway, you look well. I might even go out on a limb and say you look happy."

"Yeah, I am. I had a good time in Helsinki."

"I should say so. Things going well with you and Kaisa?"

"Not bad. You haven't been spying on us, have you?"

"Of course not. I'm far too busy with all that's going on in the world, especially in Marduk's old stomping grounds. I tell you, genocides are the worst. And always for the same reasons. But I can't blame Marduk this go around. Nope, it's just a bunch of asshole mortals making the lives of good ones difficult. Keeps me running non-stop. I just needed a break to watch some football. I've always hated the Cowboys and love to see them lose."

"That's funny. I figured you liked the Cowboys," I said and reminisced about a Philly loss to the Cowboys long ago. I sighed inside.

"Why, because I wear a cowboy hat? Yes, I do, but I hate the Cowboys."

"Good. Me too."

"You know, Gladys is gonna be all over my ass with the Underspirit backlog, but the game's almost over."

"*Interception Antonio Long! Long is running up the sideline,*" the announcer belted with unbridled excitement.

"No. No. No, No, Noooo," cried Morton as Cowboy defensive end Antonio Long bobbed and weaved and jumped and spun as the Saints' offense tried to stop a ninety-yard run.

Five yards from the goal, a wide receiver dove for Antonio's legs, tripping him and sending him stumbling forward with his arms outstretched. He hit the ground with the ball possibly short of the goal with two seconds remaining.

"You're killing me," said Morton as he chewed his fingernails and leaned forward with elbows on thighs. He anxiously watched as the officials conferred.

The head referee raised both hands and announced, "Touchdown, Cowboys."

"Goddammit!" Morton yelled and threw his hat at the TV. He huffed, sighed, and shook his head. "Damn. Well, you ready to start your training?" he asked unpleasantly.

Death likes his football. Who'd have thought? Not me. "I'm pretty beat. Can we start tomorrow?" I asked.

"Pretty beat. Seriously? You've had over two mortal years to rest and get well. You can sleep when you're dead if you don't have my job. I thought you said you were interested in being my relief Reaper, because I really need your help now," he said with growing agitation. He sighed. "I'm sorry. I'm just a little flustered over the game. And... well, I'm dreading heading back to the once fertile crescent. I've returned there so many times in the past, but this is the worst it's been. On top of that, I have to deal with the crap going on in South America, where someone slipped a new cartel the secret of siphoning Dark Ethereal from the Afterworld. But there's not much I can do about it until whoever is responsible dies. Then I can review their life, but there's no telling how long that'll be, and Gladys can't give me that information."

"I thought you didn't interfere."

"I, I don't... well, not usually. Well, not 'til lately. Look, sometimes the Burden gets too heavy. I feel if I don't do something, then I'm part of the problem. My programming screams for me to do my job, but it's getting harder with the shenanigans going down in the Afterworld that directly affect my job. But I'm not gonna get into that now. It just pisses me off, even more than seeing the Cowboys win."

I raised an eyebrow and regarded him with a wry expression.

"That was a joke. It's much worse than the Cowboys winning."

"I understand."

"Good."

"You're right," I said. "Maybe I can catch some Z's in your realm."

"Good idea. Alright, let's head over to my place. Gladys will have milk and cookies ready for you," Morton said as he pulled on his boots.

"Oh, about your sister's special recipe," I said. "She should think about revealing it to my world. The Dead Blow problem is getting out of hand, and I know what Fate's tears have done for me."

Morton stood and reached for his hat. It spun into his hand. "That's a good idea and you're a good soul, Charlie Black. I think Gladys would be agreeable to that. Who would distribute the cure?"

He patted his silver frizz and put on his hat.

"I have someone in mind," I said, thinking of Francis.

"Hmmm." Morton snapped his fingers. The television blackened. He placed a hand on my shoulder.

I blinked.

Fifty-Five

We stood in front of the Home of Fate and Death on a cobbled walkway of alternating aqua, cobalt, and black stones. Above was a swirling cobalt and aquarium-colored sky. I looked around. That

226

was something I didn't do on my first visit. What can I say? I was a bit overwhelmed.

Curiosity transported me to the edge of the realm. Below was a vast ocean of churning aquamarine, cobalt, and oily black. Hanging in the air above and below were many islands of land, like flat-topped stationary comets, that seemed close but imperceptibly far away. I suspected I was standing on one as Morton and I gazed into the vastness of another dimension.

In the distance was a slowly rotating cyclotron made up of mostly aquamarine spheres. The spheres looked like thousands of beads or marbles held together by a tortuous network of black mesh-like vines. The cyclotron appeared to be hanging from aquamarine threads attached to each sphere. The threads darkened as they rose and became cobalt, coalescing around a black and blue spot in the eye of the swirling sky, and then fanned out and blended with the canopy overhead.

In the cyclotron's center was a single black marble fed by three spouts from the Ethereal ocean. One was aquamarine. One was cobalt. And one was black. The aquamarine spout fanned out at the black pearl into thirteen threads that connected with thirteen aquamarine spheres before splitting into many more threads that connected all spheres to the central black one. The cobalt and black spouts passed through blackened marble and continued upward, adding to the black and blue eye in the sky. Beyond the cyclotron was a limitless black.

"Sometimes, I stand or sit here and try to make sense of why Marduk and Gaia designed their creation the way they did," said Morton. "By the way, the Afterworld is above the swirly sky. And that black and blue eye at the center—that's the Abyss of Non. It's a recycling center where all Afterworld creations can be disposed of

227

including Eternals, Immortals, and Imaginaries. I'll have to tell you sometime about Imaginaries. Oh, and those blue spheres bound together are the Realities. All two-thousand one-hundred and ninety-seven of them, including the Blackened."

"The Blackened?"

"Yes. Dead realities. For a long time, there were only two. That one in the center there." He pointed to the black pearl. "That one died after my siblings and I came into existence. A natural disaster destroyed the other. But recently, several more have burned out."

I looked at the black marbles among aquamarine spheres. "What happened to those?"

"Nuclear wars, pandemics, famine, ecological collapse. You know, the usual stuff. Complete annihilation of all life on its mortal world of that universe."

"But that's just one planet, out of what… billions, trillions?"

"Yes, something like that. But all those planets are and have always been dead. They're just for mortal imaginations. Your ancients got it right. Everything does revolve around the mortal world, and when all life dies, so goes that universe… Like it was all a dream."

Life is but a dream, I thought and nodded as if I comprehended what I was seeing and hearing. "Why so many realities?"

"Oh, that. I think that was Gaia and Marduk's Eternal fuck up. Something called a *Reverberating Bang*. The central blackened reality was where the Mortal Project took place and my siblings and I came into being. Shortly after, there was a *big bang*. It destroyed that universe and sent out echoes, so to speak, creating near-duplicate copies of the first reality and all spirits contained therein. Before we knew what happened, my siblings and I had been copied into each reality. But our essences were one and many at the same time, and we existed as one in all realities simultaneously. I mean, how else could I service so many mortal worlds?"

My head hurt as I struggled to grasp what Death was revealing.

"So, there are multiple copies of me?"

"Why, yes, and not exactly. There are copies of your *Underspirit* and together they make up the *Wholespirit*. But what a particular Underspirit inhabits might vary, but not rocks. I think I already told you the *what* has to be living with a few exceptions. I have to say, of all the versions of you—even with your failings—I like this one the best."

"Uh, thanks. I guess."

"You know, as mortally mind-bending as this probably seems, think about this. I believe there's a level of creation above the Afterworld, an Upper Realm, where a Master Creator, far greater than Marduk or Gaia, watches over this craziness. I just don't understand why he or she or it lets this nonsense continue that keeps me running. I mean, even Death deserves a break every once in a while. Well, I guess this is a break, but I think you know what I mean."

My brain was trying but failing.

"Speechless, huh?" Morton laughed. "I guess I would be, too. We can stay here a little longer if you'd like or head up to the house."

"Uhh, if you want to relax here, I wouldn't mind taking in all of creation for a few more... umm, well, whatever," I said, unable to describe what passed for time in the Realm of Fate and Death.

Morton and I stood silent for what seemed like several minutes as my brain recorded the impossibly possible.

"Where is your White Room Realm in all of this?" I asked. "And which one of those spheres is my reality?"

"Well, first, it's hard to call the White Room a place. That would be like calling one's reflection a twin. It is the world the Underspirit lives in until it's released. The Underspirit has no perception of the White Room until Gladys unlocks its awareness of the Overspirit it is destined to become. The Overspirit is the Immortal you will become when your Wholespirit reunites the many Overspirits to make up a many-faceted being. That Essence of life will exist with the memory of you for an eternity. Oh, and your reality. It's... right... over... there," he said as his pointing finger found the right one. "The one connected to the sky by the cobalt string. Reality Three-Thirteen." Among the many aqua threads, its single cobalt thread had blended with the others.

"As you can see, one thread is not like the others. Someone in your reality opened a conduit for Dark Ethereal and I think I know who."

I did and they were revealed in *Ackerman's Curse* and further exposed in later volumes of these chronicles from the all-seeing knowledge gained before and after I was among the dead.

"So, you seen enough?" asked Morton.

"Yeah," I said.

He nodded and we returned to the cobblestone pathway.

"So, tell me more about you and Kaisa. I know she's been hurting since I led Toivo away. He was so young then, and they loved each other so. Just glad he was able to lay that seed for those three great kids of theirs. Next time you see her, tell her Toivo's doing fine and waiting for her in the Lutheran district of the Heavens of Christ."

"I will, but she'll probably think I'm crazy."

Morton chuckled. "Yes, you're probably right. He'll be there waiting for her if Kaisa gets through this life without any hiccups. She's made it this far, so I think they have a good chance of finding each other again. I just wish Gladys would tell me how it turns out. The suspense kills me sometimes. I wish I could just do my job and not care, but I can't help it. I'm an old softy, I guess. So, you said things were going 'Not bad' between you two. Does that mean things are good? Or is there something else I sensed in your voice?"

"You don't let up, do you?"

"No, I don't. It's just that I like you both and think you make a nice couple. I know you're having trouble forgiving yourself for what happened to Vanessa, but you have to learn to live and love again. That is unless you want to end up going through the Middle Door and doing this over again as Karma knows what, or take a chance of going through the Left Door your next revolution around."

"Okay. The truth is, I think I love her. No, I know I love her, but... well, it's personal."

Morton looked at me with a wry grin. "Hmmm. Things not working like they used to, huh?"

I rolled my eyes and nodded.

"You know, there are pills for that problem."

"Yeah, I know, but it's more than that. I believe it's a punishment to remind me of something unforgivably horrible I did."

"What did you do?"

"I, I never told you what happened the night Vanessa killed herself."

"Then, do tell. Otherwise, I won't know until we take our final walk with you as an Underspirit."

A tear escaped as I took a deep, shaky breath. "There was a woman at a book signing that day. She gave me her hotel room number, and, uh…" I paused as my lips trembled. I sighed. "I was a different man then."

Morton nodded, stopped walking, and peered into my eyes, looking like someone just died.

"Well, I slept with her the night you came for Vanessa. But she wasn't a normal woman and looked like a younger version of Gladys."

Morton lowered and shook his head. He rubbed his forehead, lifted his face, and met my gaze.

Another tear trickled down my cheek.

"Yeah, buddy, you screwed up one too many times. There's a reason she looked like Gladys, and you already know why. That was my sister, Delores. You made love to a god, and once you've gone god, no mortal will do, even if you want them to."

I nodded. I'm sure I looked as ill as I felt.

"So, what did my charming sister call herself?"

"Delores Destiny."

"Wow. *Wow*. She didn't even hide her identity. That's strange. You know, she hates mortal men. I think it's because of Marduk. As I may have mentioned, they've been a thing since the dark one fell out with Gaia. He's cheated on my sister so many times. You know how many gods and godlets he's produced? Honestly, I've lost count. No, wait—I haven't, but I won't labor you with the number. It's a big one. But Delores always returns to that Devil. Does his will.

Does his dirty work. No doubt, Marduk has his eyes on you, or why else would Delores curse you like that and why would my brother bother to protect you? Not sure what the game is, but there's always a game. Walk with me, let me show you around the outside of my place. Maybe you can give me some suggestions to *liven* it up a bit."

Strangely, talking about Delores Destiny didn't set me off. Maybe realizing a larger multiverse existed, filled with infinite possibilities, realities, and outcomes, gave me a sliver of hope for Vanessa and Frank. As crazy as it sounds, I pitied Delores. Not a lot, but a little. Compassion for that evil bitch must've been a symptom of what I caught from Kaisa. And besides, the she-devil didn't make me do it. It was my choice and the consequences were something I had to live with—my burden to bear. And I deserved to live on to bear it like a man and be a better one from now through eternity.

We continued down the cobblestone path past several statues of the mortal conceptions of Death. Each sculpture was centered around fountains and pools filled with jet-black koi fish.

"Nathan," Morton said to get my attention, his eyes wide with exasperation.

"Yeah, yeah. If you want, I can bring Kaisa here sometime. I'm sure she'll have some ideas."

"Yes, Kaisa. That might be nice, but the visit will need to wait until I'm sure you're the right soul for this job."

We walked quietly and continued until we reached a rose garden where every imaginable color bloomed.

"Kaisa would love this," I said.

"That's all Gladys's work, but she's too busy with every mortal's fate to do much more than maintain this garden. But back to what I was saying about my sister, Delores. There has to be some game going on here. As I told you, the *Gavin* you knew after the mortal year 2000 CE is my brother, Frederick. The real Gavrilo Haus fell climbing Mt. Elbrus on July 23, 1999. His mortal shell still rests deep in a crevasse. Soon after that, Frederick took his form and assumed his identity. If I know my brother, and of course I do, the God of Chance allowed Gavin's luck to run out."

"He killed him?"

"Yes, most likely. I believe he did it as part of whatever scheme Marduk has him mixed up in. I'm even a little curious whether he had a hand in that illusion in Kirkuk that cost the lives of those eight Kurdish boys. Had more of Ryan Mender's men survived, I have no doubt I would've been dealing with a few disqualified suicides. I still would've had to damn them through the Left Door, rather than the Middle because of the damn Black and White Rule."

I closed my eyes and thought of Gavrilo, the killing field, and the Man in White. "That sonuvabitch. That *fuckin'* sonuvabitch."

"Have you heard from my brother?"

"No... I haven't. I haven't seen the Man in White since the day you and I first spoke. But I've also ignored his calls like you told me to."

"Really? He tried to contact you?" Morton asked acidly.

"Yes. Several times."

He shook his head and pursed his lips as anger lines added to his wrinkles. "That little fucker. I found him in a Macao casino and warned him *nicely* that if he ever contacted you again, I would haul his ass to the Abyss and throw him in, damn the rules. It still burns me that he got you hooked on Dead Blow when he knows what it does to mortals."

"Don't worry about me. It was too hard getting clean. There's no way I'm going back there."

"Good. Good boy." Morton leaned forward and smelled a rose, then stood straight. "We should head inside. Gladys will have plenty for me to do, and it'd be nice for you to come along on my rounds. You can pick out an outfit that fits you best and can choose any color you like as long as it's black," Morton said with a wink and a smile. "Well, if you're ready, I'd like to get my tongue lashing out of the way and then get some work done."

Fifty-Six

Gladys was on Morton's ass like an angry beehive. "Where have you been? Seriously, you know I can't do this without you. The White Rooms are loading up, and I can only let so many in before I have to keep them waiting outside. And you know what happens then."

"Yes, yes, I know, Gladys, but sometimes I need a damn break!"

"Break? Break? Does Fate take a break? No. I'm here endlessly working to make sure your schedule is up to date..."

Gladys paused when she saw me. Her face softened. "Oh, sorry for my outburst. Morton doesn't think sometimes. He thinks he can just stop and watch American Football anytime he wants. He knows I can record it, but he insists on watching the Dallas Cowboys get their butts kicked live."

"Well, they won," Morton said with a pout. "So, can we move on? I'm sure Nathan doesn't want to hear any of this."

"Well, sweet brother o' mine, he needs to if he takes this job. Nathan, if we hire you, you have to understand that you cannot be spending time in the mortal world while you're on duty. If you need a break, come here. You can make this place into whatever you desire. I admit, this is a lonely job, but it's the job we were programmed to do. And it is the job we will do to the best of our Eternal ability, so help me, Gaia."

"Well, Gladys, we could talk about this for an eternity, but I caused quite a backlog, didn't I, and Nathan's going to help me catch up." Death's eyes fixed on me. "No way to know if a job's right for you until you've jumped in the fire, wouldn't you say?"

I felt nervous and was probably a little green in the pale light.

"I know you're nervous. And I won't lie, it's a tough job, but in the White Room, you are all-powerful. So, let's go to my wardrobe—pick you out something to wear."

We passed through the library and entered a small study with a desk covered with scattered parchment, an inkwell, and a few quills (where I would eventually sit and write this volume long after I was among the dead). Above the desk in a glass case was my A+/Wow essay, *Interview with Death*.

We continued and stepped into a large closet with costumes from every imaginable culture, religion, and mythology. Before perusing my choices, I turned back to the study.

"You write?" I asked.

"I try but can never seem to find the right words to describe the things I have seen and done. They always come up short of the true horror of it all. Every mortal shell's story ends the same way, but how can I put a life into words that are completely true or draw an image of suffering that does justice to the one who suffered? And

236

there are so many stories. Which do I pick? Which do I ignore? If I write about one death, does that diminish another? So, every time I try, I don't get very far."

"I totally understand."

"Do you really? Do you *really* understand? I don't think you do, but before I'm done with you, I think you will. We can talk about this later. For now, hurry up and pick something."

I nodded and walked along the uniforms displayed on the long wall. Not all were black. In fact, many weren't. "I thought black was the only color I could choose from."

"I was just kidding. You can choose whatever you like, or Gladys can conjure something custom-made as she did for me."

I studied each uniform. Each one had a title underneath. Many I'd never heard of, and some had forms I couldn't put into words. I passed the Dog-headed Anubis, the Yoruba orisha Eshu, the Greek god Charon, various Aztecan, and other Native American Reaper uniforms. I passed the fearsome Canaanite Mot, the Caucasian Aminon, and various eastern Asian, Indian, Norse, and Mesopotamian Deaths. If I wanted to go out in drag I could be the Spanish Lady. There was even a cliché black robe covering a skeletal Grim Reaper with a decorative razor-sharp scythe. I tested it. It sliced my finger. How would I choose?

Morton smiled. "Overwhelming, huh?"

"Why don't I just wear what you're wearing? I don't care for any of the other choices. You're the only Death I've ever known."

Morton rubbed his chin and thoughtfully gazed at his old Grim Reaper uniform. "Alright then. I can't see why that would be a problem. Gladys, can you put a *Man in Black* together for Nathan? And he'll need a Scythe access ring, too."

Gladys appeared outside the door with a starched black suit, matching shirt, boots, and Stetson hat. She handed me the outfit and stood watching as I dressed.

"Oh, sorry." She turned away.

I put on the uniform. When dressed, I looked like a younger version of Death in a mirrored obsidian column. Gladys handed me a platinum ring with a skull overlying a scythe. It looked like a miniature version of the Burden talisman without the cobblestone background. I slid it on my right ring finger since my wedding ring was on the left.

Gladys smiled proudly. "Well, aren't you two just the dapper Men in Black?"

We chuckled.

"Okay, here's your itinerary," she said and handed us two tablet-like devices. "You have quite the backlog. I advise exponential splicing, or you two will never catch up."

"What's exponential splicing?" I asked.

"I guess Morton got off on a tangent like he's known to do and didn't quite explain the *how* beyond the *Burden*." Gladys pointed at the case above the desk and said, "You asked in that essay how my brother does what he does and Santa does what he does every Christmas Eve at midnight."

"Santa's real?" I asked.

"Uh, no. Not in the mortal realities, at least. There is one for the children in the Afterworld that doesn't skip the poor houses or give more to the ones who were well-off when they were mortal. Santa was just an example. The concept is the same, though. It's the only way Morton can service all those realities outside our door filled

238

with numerous but finite numbers of living shells, all dying at different Timethies. Your reality is quite busy right now, so you'll recognize many of the places you see. The ring is bound to the Burden of the Scythe and will allow you to splice with Morton. But don't take that ring off outside our realm. If you do, you'll be stuck in an infinite number of White Rooms, and Morton will have to waste time he doesn't have, finding you and splicing you back together one version at a time."

I looked at the ring. It felt loose around my finger. I closed the hand into a fist.

We left the library and headed to the front door.

Morton asked, "You ready for this?"

"Would you believe me if I said yes?"

"No. No, I wouldn't. You are about to experience what no mortal has experienced before."

I swallowed hard, feeling anxious and queasy. I wasn't the indestructible Nathan Miller I once was. I was scared shitless, but more excited than any Christmas morning back in Oak Park. I had never felt more alive as I stood in the Home of Fate and Death.

"Let's do this," I said with a hint of bravado.

Morton nodded.

Gladys smiled.

We put on our hats and strolled outside. Morton looked at me and touched his shirt over the talisman.

Fifty-Seven

The world turned sepia. Bodies, parts of bodies, viscera, and odd chunks of this and that were strewn everywhere in a destroyed marketplace. Many bloodied victims were still alive, missing some of those body parts. I stood like a stone.

"Don't just stand there—give me a hand!" barked Morton. "I don't like newly dead to see their bodies. With so many dead and dying, they won't all get a personal White Room."

I snapped into action. We cleaned the area with tools that appeared in my hands. We swept and mopped quickly, then stood to the side as three black doors appeared along with six Arab children (two boys and four girls), two women in hijabs, and a man wearing a bomb vest. They looked disoriented. Then they saw us.

In unison, they spoke Arabic which I understood. "Who are you?"

"I am Morton Death, and this is my assistant, Nathan Reaper. We're here to guide you to Paradise, where all good servants of Allah go when they die. You may take off the hijabs and proceed to Paradise. It's down the hall through the Right Door."

The children smiled, and the women removed their head coverings and crossed the threshold. The suicide bomber followed.

Morton straight armed, barring the killer's entry. "But not you," he said in a loathsome tone as the door slammed shut.

"But... but I was promised if I died killing the unholy for Allah, I would be welcomed into Paradise."

"Son, you were lied to, and… and you disgust me. Your door is the one on the left."

The Left Door creaked open.

"There you will meet your true master and pay for what you've done."

"But, but Paradise. Seventy-two virgins…"

"Only virgins you'll be seeing are those kids you just murdered—through their eyes and feeling what you just did to them. Now go!" Death said, pointing at the open door. "I'm not arguing with garbage like you. If you don't go on your own, I'll drag your ass to Hell myself."

The suicide bomber gave Morton a defiant glance, glowered at me, and looked at the open door. He mumbled a curse as he stepped through. The door hit him where Allah split him.

"Okay, we gotta move. I figured I'd start you out with something easy, but we're going to have to split up to get the rest done."

Morton touched his chest again, and my perception shattered into millions of multi-faceted shards of crystalline glass. It was like the screen I watched in the waiting room the first time I visited Gladys and Morton's place. Only now, I was in each facet of every shard simultaneously, seeing all the others and experiencing everything from both my perspective and Morton's. Numerous murders. Multiple suicides. Battle deaths in hot spots around the globe. A genocide in progress. Drug overdoses. A school shooting. Several more suicide bombings. Car crashes. Heart attacks. A plane crash. Several young kids accidentally blowing their heads off. And touching deaths, like Uncle Frank's, surrounded by loved ones.

Several White Rooms were crowded, and we were late to many others. I saw the effect on those that entered the White Rooms and

241

saw their corpses. I worked quickly to clean my rooms and did my best to apologize for the wait. Some refused to go through the doors. Morton didn't argue with the ones destined for the Middle and the Right Door who wished to wait on loved ones or weren't ready to cross over after a life poorly lived. He also didn't push the ones who refused on account of suicide. Morton felt they had suffered enough. And since he couldn't tell them what Karma had in store for them, he left them to haunt the living and become chindi, yurei, ghosts, or the many other names mortals came up with to describe wandering Underspirits.

When we weren't cleaning up and directing mortal shells to their final destinations, we dealt with non-mortals and spirits that dwelled within animals or plants. Those cases were much easier since they didn't argue, and I didn't have to deal with the Left Door.

It seemed the shift would never end as my sanity stretched to its limits. The files in my mortal mind were overloaded, and papers exploded from cabinets I pictured in my head. Then we were done.

Morton clapped his hands.

My splinters reunited and I was standing next to Morton in an empty White Room.

"Let's head back to the house. Like always, Gladys will have some milk and cookies ready. She's making peanut butter ones, and those monsters with the M&M's—love those." Morton patted me on the back. "You did good, kid." He touched his chest.

242

Fifty-Eight

We were back in front of the Home of Fate and Death. I dragged myself up the steps to the front door. I was shaking and wanted to vomit. *How the hell can I ever do this job?* I thought. I had to tell Morton I'd reconsidered, but then I thought about all Gladys and Morton had done for me, how they gave me back my life. But I was just a mortal. How could he expect me to carry his Burden alone for even a single day, much less more than that? I had to be honest with him. Morton was used to this. He had been doing this since Abel.

We stepped through the door. Gladys was waiting with a smile and a silver tray with two glasses of milk and a range of cookies.

"Made a variety for you two. So, how did it go?" Gladys asked, a bit overly giddy for the task completed.

"The kid has a knack for this. I would've never expected a mortal to hang with me, but he did. I can tell you without us going out again, Nathan is our mortalberry," Morton said as he took a glass of milk and a monster cookie.

Gladys tenderly studied me. "Nathan looks a little worn around the edges. Maybe we should ask him how he thought it went."

Morton nodded, looked at me, and asked, "Well, how do you think it went?"

"Umm… It was something else, that's for sure," I said with little enthusiasm as I grabbed a glass and gulped. I took several peanut butter cookies and devoured one.

"Good, aren't they?" asked Morton.

"Yeah, they are," I said shakily.

"Are you alright?" asked Gladys.

"No. Not really. I don't think I can do this, but I don't want to disappoint you guys after everything you've done."

"Totally understandable after the first day," said Morton. "And I can only imagine, since on my first day I was able to sit back and talk to Abel. Even when Cain died, I got to hear his side of the story even though I already knew it. So, don't you worry. No pressure. It's not like I haven't been waiting for someone I could trust since the Great Flood. That was my first big rush and my first rough day." He scoffed. "And all because of a practical joke that my stupid brother played on Gaia."

"Really? What happened?"

Morton huffed. "What always happens with Frederick—he doesn't think about anyone but himself. He thought it would be funny to turn up the rain controls to the Realities. Gaia learned Marduk was in on the joke. When confronted, he blamed it on Frederick. Gaia didn't believe him since Marduk had been gunning for mortalkind since Cain killed Abel. That was pretty much the beginning of all the trouble between those two that has continued all the way up to what happened in your 2007. Yes. It was terrible. White Rooms packed. You know, those rooms didn't have the capacity they have now, and several Underspirits had to wait in their shells until Gladys let them in. Imagine drowning but not being able to die. Lungs burning filled with water. Choking. Brain cells exploding. Dreadful. And when they finally got into the White Room, damn, they were pissed. Got a lot of bad reviews, that's for sure. But I did the best I could. After that, the weather controls for the Realities were set to self-sustaining. Still, up until recently, mortals blamed the weather on the will of the gods. Marduk even got the nickname the God of Thunder in the Mesopotamian

244

pantheon. Now, *'god of thunder'* is a cliché in almost every other one. Hey, why don't we go to the library where we can talk some more?"

I sat on the couch in the library while Morton sat in the recliner. Gladys set the tray of cookies on the coffee table and sat next to me. She picked up a peanut butter cookie, took a bite, crossed her legs, and turned toward Morton.

Morton reclined and held his hands together, formed a triangle, and feverishly tapped with thumbs and index fingers together. "I wish I could say that was my worst day," he said, stopped tapping, and dropped the triangle. "No, that was just my first of many worst days. When the Red Horseman, War, entered the picture, that's when things got bad. He was Marduk's general in the mortal worlds and fomented conflict for no other reason than Marduk's sadistic pleasure. War kept me busy, and once he got the ball rolling, the cycle of violence and revenge pretty much maintained itself. And whenever things started to slow down, Marduk would send War in to stir things up. You realize who War is, don't you?"

"No. Who?"

"Cain, the son of Adam and Eve."

"Wait. What about killing Abel and the Black and White Rule?"

"Yes. What about it? Marduk does as Marduk pleases inside his Prison of Homicide. Always has. As I understand it, he let Cain suffer for centuries before offering him the job. Yes. Cain jumped at the chance to stop having to stare at himself through Abel's eyes as everything kept fading to black. And Cain has done a *stellar* job as War ever since."

Morton stared at something (or nothing) across the library. "I have met the greatest and lowliest of your kind. Few avoid meeting me during their existence. I have walked many a battlefield and cried alone next to mothers, fathers, sons, and daughters—always mistaken for the wind. I have walked with mass murderers, serial killers, school shooters—they kill, you name them. I have observed and been a party to their crimes, standing and watching until I could send them through the Left Door with prejudice. I have also been a party to the injustices done to the righteous that I have sent to Marduk's Hell. I have guided the downtrodden to Samara Station and sent those who did not wish to continue their existence to Karma's Asylum. I believed you were the one I'd been searching for when I saw you in that killing field. Your words in *Ghosts of Bosnia* captured what I could not. I haven't read the whole book, but I've read enough to know you have the heart for my job. But I realize now what I request is too much for any mortal to bear. I know it was foolish to ask you in the first place, and I will not forsake you when you decline my offer. The Burden of the Scythe is mine to carry and mine alone."

I swallowed hard, breathed in and out a few times, and said, "I'm sorry. I really am. It's just too much."

Morton nodded with an understanding, sad-eyed grin.

Gladys put an arm around me and leaned her head on my shoulder. I smelled roses.

"It's okay, dear," she said. "No need to be sorry. We understand. I've said it before and I'll say it again. If you ever stumble or need to visit us for whatever reason, we will always have a room ready for you, along with all the warm milk you can drink and all the cookies you can eat. And if I sense you need it, I might drop by your place with a special delivery from time to time. Just think of me as your cookie lady."

"I do. And thanks, Gladys."

Though I wanted to, I didn't feel up to asking for her secret recipe to save the world from the Blue Dragon. It could wait. Fate and her tears would still be around when I recovered from the trauma of a single shift as Nathan Reaper.

"And thank you, Morton."

Morton nodded, smiled, leaned, and slapped my knee. "So, we down to watch the Cowboys lose to the Eagles in two weeks? Last game of the season. I mean, of course, if it's okay with my sister here."

"We'll make do. You're the one who'll have to play catch-up and listen to whiny spirits."

I chuckled and said, "Morton, I look forward to it."

We stood and headed to the front door. Once outside, I hugged Gladys on the porch and shook Morton's hand. I saw the Scythe ring on mine. "Oh, I almost forgot." I went to take it off.

Morton cupped my hand with both of his. His hands were warm.

"No. You keep it. It'll be a souvenir from your day as a Reaper of Souls. You earned it. Plus, it doesn't work without the Burden that comes along with it."

I nodded with a soulful smile. Morton snapped his fingers, and I was back in my apartment.

Fifty-Nine

I collapsed into my recliner and turned to WNN. I sat stunned. Russian Federation President Vladimir Vasily had finally done it. He had launched the long anticipated blitzkrieg into Ukraine from the east, the Black Sea from the south, and Belarus from the north. It was a surprise attack since the invasion was not expected until spring.

Due to the early cold winter, the ground was already frozen, allowing the movement of tanks and other heavy equipment. Targeted missile strikes had already destroyed much of the Ukrainian power grid. More missiles were hitting civilian targets and infrastructure. From first contact, rumors swirled that Russian troops had sparkling cobalt eyes, super strength, and speed, leading to speculation that President Vasily was using Dark Ethereal to enhance military performance. There was no mystery where Vasily had gotten the Dead Blow. The same thing had been reported by the National Guard troops, Homeland Security, CIA, and DEA agents fighting cartel guerrillas south of the border.

The Ukrainian death toll from the opening salvo was unknown but expected to be in the tens of thousands. The outlook was bleak and Ukraine's surrender appeared imminent by month's end if their forces could resist that long. NATO was on high alert. The Baltic States were bracing for what would come next: the invasion of Poland, Lithuania, Latvia, Estonia, and Finland. Of the five, Finland was the only non-NATO member, and its 1,340 kilometer border was Russia's northern flank. All indications pointed that it would be Vasily's next target.

My thoughts were of Kaisa when the phone rang. It was her.

"Are you watching the news?" she asked.

"Yes."

"People are getting nervous over here. I was thinking about spending time in New York while my family waits to see how the situation plays out."

"Uhh, that… that would be great. Th-that would be wonderful," I stammered. "When were you thinking?"

"Very soon, but current events are not the only reason I am coming to your Big Apple. It has been months since we were together, and I… I really miss you. The phone calls are nice, but I want to be with you."

"I feel the same way. Where you planning to stay? I mean, if you don't have a place, you can stay at my apartment. It's small, but it's located in a nice spot in Greenwich Village."

"I was hoping you would offer. I love you, Nathan, and I have not stopped thinking of you. Not even for a minute. And… and I know when I see you again, I will want to be with you as your friend, or, maybe even your wife, if you want. I am sorry. Excuse me if I move too fast."

I paused and breathed a little heavier.

"Oh, I should not have said that."

"No, no, don't be. I'd love to marry you. It's just… it's just…"

"It is just what?"

"It's my kids—Jonathan, especially. And, and I don't deserve you, not like that, and not after the things I've done. Not after what happened to Vanessa which I know was my fault," I said, my voice cracking as I looked at my wedding ring and caressed it with my left thumb.

"Nathan, we have spoke of this already. I have seen your heart, and whatever you did or think you did, I know you are not that man anymore. And don't think because you love me that I expect you to stop loving Vanessa or love me more. I will tell you this—I will never stop loving Toivo, and you will never replace him in my heart

249

if we both live forever. But you have healed me and made me whole again. And I believe I have done the same for you—or at least a small slice from being whole. And we can work on the other thing. There are medications for that."

I chuckled and smiled, sensed her warmth, and her soft, thin lips curling into a sexy pose.

"So, tell me, when will you be here?" I asked.

"Monday, January seventh at two P.M. I am flying into JFK. My sweet and not-so-little triplets, Paavo, Antti, and Selma will arrive later in the week. They are bringing all their little bears. Everyone is excited to meet you. I guess they love seeing their äiti and isoäiti happy."

"Who?"

"Mother and grandmother. I need to teach you some Finnish."

"I'm sure you'll be a great teacher, and I'll be your hungry pupil."

"God, I can't wait to see you, Nathan."

"Samoin."

"Ahh, you do know a little suomen kielen."

"A little, but 'likewise' and 'mita kuuluu?', *how are you*, push my limits. Look, why don't I call Franklin, Jenna, and Jonathan and see if we can all get together Saturday after next. I think they need to know what's going on between us. I care about you, but after what happened with Vanessa, I want them on board, especially if we're talking about ringing church bells."

"That is a good idea. It would be nice for our children to meet."

"Then it's settled. I'll call Franklin and Jenna and see if they'll host the get-together. My place is too small for so many people."

"But Nathan, it would be cozy like the little cottage I grew up in. I guess you have not seen most houses in Finland?"

"Alright, we'll have it at my place."

We said our sweet goodbyes. I hung up with Kaisa and Nate Murphy called.

"Nathan, you watching the news?"

"Yeah."

"Then I need to ask you—you ready to get back on the horse? Because I need you in the Baltics soon."

"Yes. Definitely. When do I need to leave?"

"Well, I heard through the grapevine Vasily may move sooner than expected into Finland and possibly Estonia. NATO is about to announce a resolution condemning Vasily's attack on Ukraine. My source tells me the resolution has teeth. All the member nations have secretly agreed to commit significant resources and troops to check the Russians. When the shit hits the fan, you'll need to be ready to go on a moment's notice."

"Alright, but I'm planning a family get-together Saturday after next. Kaisa and her family are coming to New York. As you can imagine, everyone's on edge over there, and she wants them out of harm's way if the bombs start dropping. Also, Kaisa and I are getting serious and wanted our families to meet before we took it further."

"I understand, but if I need you to go, I need you to go."

I sighed. "All right. I'll let Kaisa know."

"Nathan, you shouldn't have too much to worry about. It's unlikely this mess will blow up for several weeks, and it's more likely it'll be a couple of months. I can't imagine Vasily will want to over-extend supply lines in the middle of winter. But come spring, things are gonna get uglier. So, who do you want to work with on this assignment?"

"Who else? I'd like Travis to go with me. He's always been my wingman, but we haven't spoken for a few years."

"Well, why don't you call him? I mean, if you need me to, I can vouch that you're not the same asshole you once were. And if he tells you to piss off, I have another cameraman with balls as big as Travis's."

I laughed.

Nate chuckled.

"Okay, okay. I'll call him. Bye, Nate. Talk to you soon."

"I know you will."

I dialed Travis's number. He didn't answer. I left a message, then turned off the television, leaned back in the recliner, and closed my eyes for the first time in what seemed like—like a really long time. As nod land approached, the phone rang. It was Travis.

"So, you need me for a job?" Travis said without formality.

"Yes, but it's more than that. I want to say I'm sorry for everything. Sorry for forgetting who my real friends are. And sorry for just being a general douchebag. I guess what I'm trying to say is… I want my brother back." There was a pause. A long one. "Hello?"

"Yeah, I'm here. I'm texting Candy. We were both just talking about you. She wants to know… if you would like to go out… with us Saturday night?"

"Yeah. Yeah, sure. That'd be great."

"Man, I've missed you. I know you went through a pretty rough patch. I just… I just hope you found some peace after Vanessa… whew…" Travis swallowed loud enough to hear.

"Yeah. I miss her so much, and my feelings about what happened are still raw. It's getting easier to wake up each morning, but I still have a long way to go. Hey, I'm seeing someone. She's a widower like me."

"Really? Anyone I know?"

"You read children's books?"

"Of course, I read a few every time the grandkids are over."

"You heard of Kaisa Jännök?"

"No shit. She's hot. Grrrr—cougar hot."

"Yeah, she is, and she's mine. And I'm hers. And if it's okay with the kids, we'll be getting married soon."

"Fuckin' A. Congratulations, brother. This calls for a drink with Candy and me."

"I'll let you guys have one for me. I'm clean and sober. No alcohol or drugs for over two years now."

"Really? That's awesome. I'm proud of you, man."

"Thanks. I love you, brother," I said as I teared up.

"Same to you. I'm glad to have you back."

Sixty

Saturday, December 29, 2012.

I met Travis and Candy for dinner at *il forno Hell's Kitchen* on Eighth Avenue. It was a block from Times Square where preparations for the annual (albeit toned down) New Year's Eve insanity were underway with the typical heavy military presence of a burgeoning fascist state. But when I saw them sitting at our reserved table at Candy's favorite Italian restaurant, it felt like old times even though everything around us screamed that it wasn't.

Dinner was great. The three of us laughed and cried a little as we talked about college memories, the double wedding on the Rocky Steps, funny stories about Vanessa, and how much we missed her. At that point, I desperately wanted a drink but stayed strong and thought of the hell I had put Vanessa through, and, as always, what Morton and Gladys did for me. The fear of a sip that would make me slip into the need for something more kept me sober as the iceberg continued melting away, and the Tiramisu was served.

After dinner, we headed to Queens and spent the night at Travis and Candy's place. It was Candy's idea. We stayed up all night watching a Rocky marathon on DVD which was no small feat with the original and five sequels that had come out since 1976. We didn't quote the lines like old times and more than once we shed tears in Vanessa's memory.

Rocky Balboa's credits rolled after dawn. We yawned like a choir then Travis made breakfast while I called Kaisa. After waffles and bacon, Candy refused to let me go home without sleeping first and put me up in the guest room. I slept until midafternoon, had a quick lunch, then headed back to Manhattan.

Sixty-One

Most people were on edge as that dreaded Monday neared. Cochran hadn't backed down from her claims that her re-election was stolen and doubled down on her refusal to accept the results. She'd even threatened with loosely veiled rhetoric to incite violence among her radical supporters if Independent Orville Bloom was confirmed as the next President. There was also increased street presence of Cochran's black and white clad HSC enforcers. They now dressed like the infamous Black Berets who won that infamy in 2007.

Slain President Rollins had formed the elite corps for special Homeland Security operations related to the War on Ethereal. After Cochran was sworn in following Rollins' assassination, she expanded the Homeland Security Corps (HSC) to assist police departments overwhelmed by the cobalt crime wave. Since then, the HSC had become Cochran's personal police force used to ferret out threats to her growing power. With the nation under martial law, she gave them authority to be judge, jury, and executioner in cases of Dead Blow-related crime. Their abuses of power became an everyday occurrence across the nation, but reports were censored, and reporters jailed for reporting their jack boot tactics. In fact, on my way to dinner with Travis and Candy I'd watched the summary judgement of two flyers and a homeless man with a positive retinal scan. They were shot in the head and their bodies left on Broadway as a warning to others to just say no to Ethereal. This wasn't a topic of our dinner discussion that Saturday night.

Sixty-Two

It was a busy week as I counted the hours and minutes until Kaisa arrival at JFK. Most of my time was spent writing copy, preparing for my upcoming assignment, and doing interviews with talking heads about the Russia-Ukrainian conflict that appeared darker every day as the Ukrainian death toll soared. The Russian Federation seemed unstoppable as the ancient city of Kiev suffered under siege and constant bombardment which mainly targeted civilians. I felt bad for Morton.

That Saturday I took another break and went out again with Travis and Candy to a restaurant in Queens, but I declined Candy's movie night/sleep over offer. I had work to do before Kaisa arrived on Monday.

I caught a taxi back to the Village and stumbled into my apartment, dead tired. The television was on, and peeking above the recliner was a white Stetson.

"Gavin? Is that you?" My question seeped like acid from my lips.

The Man in White stood and faced me. "Damn, it's so good to see you, Nathan. I waited and waited for you to call me back but, but you never did."

"Why no disguise, Frederick?"

"Oh, you see me, don't you? I guess you've been talking to my brother. So, you know who I am. But that's okay. We can work this out. I forgive you for not calling me back. I know you've been through a lot. That was dumb of me giving you Dark Ethereal. I know that now. You have to understand—I'm just figuring out how to be a mortal. I'm so sick of this Eternal coil. What I wouldn't do to just shed it and live one good life as a mortal, die, and be thrown into the Abyss of Non and cease to exist. I will assume my brother told you about the Abyss and a good many other things if you know who I really am." He paused for a response.

I just glared.

He rubbed his chin. "Ohh-kay. Well, I've thought about taking the dive. Even more so, after my brother threatened me—told me to keep away from you… *or else*. But my programming refuses to let me take the plunge into that swirling pool of peace."

"That's a fuckin' pity," I said.

"That… that's cold, my brother."

"I'm not your brother, and I'm not your friend. I know who you are now and what you've done. I know all the suffering you've caused. I also know you had a hand in what happened in Almawt Lilkifaar, and, I believe, probably well before that."

"Hey, I saved your life, and also your *wingman*, Travis. And I saved Ryan Mender, John Smith, Toby Almaraz, and Kyle Wheeler, too."

"Kyle jumped on a grenade to save our lives. Toby was killed by a sniper, and John almost died after we fought our way back to base."

"But, but those deaths weren't my fault. I… you wouldn't have made it out at all if it wasn't for me."

"Yeah, *we* wouldn't have, would we?"

The Man in White smiled as his cobalt eyes sparkled.

"So, why were you there?" I asked, my eyes narrowing with contempt. "And how'd you know the ambush was going to happen?"

"Um, um, that... well, I didn't know you, uh, like... like I know you now. I was, I was..."

"Your brother tells me you were working with Marduk playing some game you started years before. He also told me that Almawt Lilkafaar wasn't your first rodeo riding with the Devil."

"Damn, you know about that, too?"

"I know enough."

"Okay, I messed up. I messed up bad. It was my damn sister, Delores, and Marduk. They used me. They... they lied to me."

I scowled.

Frederick nodded.

"And did you kill Gavrilo?" I asked.

The Man in White looked down.

"You did. You sick murdering piece of shit. He was my friend. He suffered so much, and you killed him for *what* reason?"

"I'd rather not say."

"It doesn't matter. Tell me—did your creator give you any sense of right and wrong? Any sense of decency? Anything to give anyone a reason to remotely give a shit about you? So where is Gavrilo now? And I'm not talking about his corpse. Morton told me where that was. And what of Ryan, Toby, Kyle, and the rest of the guys? I already know where my uncle Frank is, thanks to you and the Dead Blow."

Frederick's face soured. He didn't answer.

"Frederick, you are an irredeemable piece of shit. You need to work on your programming and take that plunge because the Abyss is the only place for you."

The Man in White's lips quivered. He shook his head and replied, breathing loudly through his nose for the first few sentences. "You want me gone? You want me gone? After every time I've saved your life? You would be dead now if not for me. Yeah, I may have messed up giving you Dark Ethereal, but I did it because I didn't like to see you suffer. I see now you can't handle having a god as a friend. Well, let's see how long you survive without your lucky charm," he said as he gritted his teeth and his eyes narrowed into a drop-dead glower.

I matched his hate as neither of us blinked.

The Man in White nodded, tipped his hat, and lifted his arm toward the door, flat hand out. The door blew off its hinges and slammed into the wall across the hall, cracking it and creating a dust cloud. He turned his head and said, "Have a nice death, Nathan Miller," and stormed out.

I watched him stomp down the hall, unseen by the collection of tenants pouring from their apartments. All eyes were on me.

I returned an awkward smirk, picked up the door, and carried it back inside. I dropped the door on the floor with a *THUD*, went to the bedroom, and fell face forward into the heavenly mattress.

Sixty-Three

When I lifted my head again, it was still night, then I realized it was the next day. I sensed someone watching me and looked to my bedroom door. The Man in Black was standing there.

"You seem to have had a problem with your door. It's fixed now. You were asleep when I got here, so I figured I'd repair it before the game. I brought some milk and cookies, too."

I smirked and chuckled as I turned over and sat up. *So much for getting any work done,* I thought. I rubbed my face and scratched my scalp. "Do you ever get sick of milk and cookies?" I asked.

"Does Santa?" asked Morton.

"He's not real."

"Yes, point taken, at least in the mortal realities, that is. And no, I don't have any vices except milk and cookies. And with my job, I can't help but keep the gut off. Now Santa, he only makes deliveries in the Afterworld once a cycle, so he's a little jollier and rounder than Death here," Morton said, patting his washboard. "Get up, or we'll miss the kick-off. Cowboys are gonna lose to the Eagles tonight. I have a good feeling about this one. If I were a gambling man like my brother, I'd bet on it. Oh, and I told Gladys about your cookie venture. She liked the idea. And if Francis Pickens is who you have in mind to distribute her sweets, we are A-Okay with that. Francis is a good egg, and she thinks Charlotte's Café's would be a perfect place to roll out her culinary delights. We even came up with branding. *Fate's Best Cookies. They're to die for,*" Morton said, spreading his hands for emphasis.

"That... that sounds great," I said.

"Glad you think so. I'll pay Jakko and Francis a visit and bring some samples. Haven't had the pleasure of meeting Francis yet, but Jakko and I go way back. *Way, way* back," Morton said with a smirk and a wink.

"Huh?"

"Yes. I'll tell you about Jakko sometime, but later. Cowboys are about to lose so let's go turn the game on."

I was curious about Death's connection with Jakko Kantelejarvi, but not curious enough to interrupt Morton's brief respite from his hellish existence. I also didn't mention Frederick's visit. I knew it would only upset him. And during the game, Morton never mentioned the job proposal or my refusal. No. We only spoke the language of football as we watched Philly ruin Dallas's wildcard shot.

It was nice seeing Morton smile as the Eagles scored touchdown after touchdown in a beatdown that I hoped my father was watching through his Reality Window. Yeah, Death deserved a break. I only hoped the White Rooms weren't overflowing, but of course, they would be. It was funny. Minus the alcohol, it felt like how Travis and I used to be—how I hoped we could be again. I wished Travis had been here. Me, my best friend, and the Grim Reaper. Milk mustaches, profanity, hooting, and hollering. I'd hoped we could set a date, but never got the chance.

When the final score was displayed—Eagles forty-nine/Cowboys nineteen—Morton looked sad.

"What's wrong? The Cowboys lost."

"I know, but now I have to wait until next season to see them lose again."

Morton didn't say it, but I knew what he had to do now that the game was over. I sort of wished Death was cold and horrific like I'd always been led to believe. A skull-faced reaper in a black robe who viciously strikes us down with a razor-sharp scythe before extending a skeletal hand for a final walk into eternity. No, Morton Death was a kind creation, and his job, a cursed abomination had it been given to any Eternal or Immortal, much less one with a mindheart as big as his.

Morton put on his boots, stood, and grabbed his hat. "It might be a while before I see you again. I'll still be around, and maybe we can do this next season. I know you carry a great burden, but you need to forgive yourself and love the one you're with and don't let her go."

"I'm not planning on it. I just hope Jon, Jr. will be okay with us getting married. If not, Kaisa will be my best friend."

"I have a good feeling that everything will work out for the best. You may feel you don't deserve it, but life goes on until the final walk and talk with me. Enjoy what Timethy you have left in that shell of yours. It'll be over in less than a blink of an eye, and then eternity begins for better or for worse."

I nodded and man-hugged Morton. He patted my back. I thought of my father again. My mother. Of Frank and Dorothy.

Morton let go and placed his hands on my shoulders. "Look, it won't be long before we see each other again." He removed his hands and glanced at the scythe ring on my right ring finger. "And if you ever have trouble, make a fist with that hand and think of my place, and you'll be there. Gladys will be waiting with your room ready."

"Thanks. But I'm going to try to stand on my own. If I stumble, I know Kaisa will catch me or else Travis, or Candy, or Nate, or Julie will. And I also have Jakko, Francis, and Takijirō now."

"Good. That's what I wanna hear. Well, I gotta go. You know better than any mortal the diabolical schedule Gladys has waiting for me. The only reason she let me do this is… well, she's sweet on you like a meema."

I'd never known my grandmothers. "Yeah, she's pretty awesome," I said with a warm smile, and thought of Aunt Dorothy.

"Yeah, Gladys is a good one. Well, I gotta go." He returned the kindly smile. He put on his hat, tipped it, touched his chest, and vanished into mist.

Sixty-Four

I watched WNN while waiting for Kaisa at baggage claim on what would become another day of infamy among many others since 2007. Earlier that morning, President-elect Orville Bloom, his wife, and three children were found dead at their Portland, Maine, residence. It was an apparent assassination on the eve of his congressional confirmation as the Forty-Seventh President of the United States of America. The family had been killed in similar fashion to what was first witnessed on September 2, 2007. Like victim zero, the Bloom family was found in advanced stages of decomposition with no signs of trauma.

The death of President-elect Bloom was unprecedented, and VP-elect Cyrus Vance was slated for confirmation. But in a move similar to the 1876 Election between Rutherford Hayes and Samuel Tilden, the electors for Bloom in closely contested Georgia, Nevada, and Pennsylvania refused to cast their votes for Vance and changed their vote to Cochran. As a result, the nightmare of a Cochran second term became a reality, as she was confirmed with two-hundred-seventy electoral votes, the bare minimum for victory.

I turned from the television, put on my headphones, and pressed play on my phone and listened to some peaceful Saami music Kaisa had turned me onto. I wasn't going to let events beyond my control sour the reunion. I wasn't listening long before Kaisa stepped through the security doors, picked up her pace, and raced into my open arms.

We ate a nice steak near the airport, then returned to my apartment where Kaisa surprised me with a little blue pill. We tried, but again, nothing. Still, Kaisa didn't make me feel like less of a man.

Sixty-Five

I went to the office early on Tuesday for a conference with Nate and Travis. Julie was already on assignment in Poland, covering the rising tension on their eastern border. NATO had deployed more troops to add to the forty thousand already there and was moving defensive hardware to the border as Ukraine teetered on collapse. All eyes were on the heightened tension in the northeast Baltic as Vladimir Vasily closed Ingria and Karelia to non-Russians. Finland, who once had little interest in NATO membership, were now on the fast track, along with Sweden, to secure the defensive alliance's northern flank. Nate believed Travis and I would be heading east sooner than expected. I only prayed it would be after Saturday when

I planned to officially propose to Kaisa if the kids gave the green light.

During the meeting, the Man in White's taunting presence sat across the table from me. I acted like I didn't see him. I guess Frederick believed he could still stalk me like he had since I was a kid. I stared through him so he wouldn't realize he was no longer invisible when he wanted to be.

I glanced at my Scythe ring under the table. I slid it off, looked up, and the Man in White was gone. I slid it back on, and he reappeared. Morton hadn't mentioned that his ring would reveal his brother to me. I wondered if Morton even knew, since I was the first mortal to wear it. Frederick looked bitter, and he often glanced, glared, or glowered at Travis with envious eyes.

Travis and I left and the Man in White followed but Chance still appeared unaware that I sensed his every move. I wondered if I could detect other apparitions around me, like the Underspirits who refused to step through Morton's doors.

I ignored the Eternal following us as I walked, talked, and laughed with my oldest friend, until we met Candy and Kaisa for lunch at *il forno Hell's Kitchen*. They already acted like they'd known each other for a lifetime. Kaisa was magical like that—as magical as the ring. Everyone she met loved her. And I was hers, and she was mine. I could see it in her eyes as she spoke, and we exchanged glances known only to young lovers. She was alive again, and so was I. And we were here with Travis and Candy. The world was perfect again. Well, not really, but close enough for us.

Candy told Kaisa about Vanessa, but Kaisa didn't appear uncomfortable talking about my former love whose wedding ring was on my finger. They spoke of when Vanessa was alive, not after she died. Kaisa opened up and told them the true story of Toivo the Bear. Like Franklin, Jenna, and Jonathan, the little white bear had been a part of Travis and Candy's two girls' childhoods and was now a tradition with the grandkids. I could see Kaisa's burden lighten as she told the story of the man she would always love more than me, as I would always love Vanessa more than her, no matter how much I wished otherwise. As she spoke, the Man in White sat, brooding, in a corner.

After a delightful afternoon, Kaisa and I returned to Greenwich Village. The apartment was no longer a man cave, and Kaisa's touch was everywhere. The room now burst with natural color, making our apartment feel like a slice of Suomi.

The next couple of days were some of the best in my life as I showed Kaisa around Manhattan and hung out with Travis and Candy. I got reacquainted with their girls and met their grandkids. They were thrilled to spend time with Kaisa and hear her tell new stories of Toivo and his friends that had never been written. She even pulled me aside and asked if she could invite them to the party on Saturday.

I said, "Why not? I'm sure we can squeeze in eight more and have room for an elbow or two."

Travis and Candy thought it sounded fun and said they'd be there. Plus, Travis knew Nate might call any time, and we would be on a red-eye, regardless of when we left for the Baltics. We'd been lucky so many times, and every time we knew our luck might run out. Mine... well, I'd just kicked him out of my life. But for some reason, Chance still stalked me. I suspected it was part of the game he was playing.

266

Thursday night, Jonathan called me. He'd received my two-week-old message and actually apologized for not calling sooner. He said he would *definitely* be there Saturday and asked when Kaisa's kids were flying in so he could greet them at JFK.

I said, "2:25 tomorrow at Terminal 8."

Sixty-Six

Kaisa and I arrived at the airport to find Jonathan smiling next to his wife and my grandkids, Jon, Alvin, and Hope. Jenna, Franklin, and his family were also there, a surprise Jonathan organized. Jon Christian was the first to hug Kaisa.

Paavo, Antti, Selma, and their families arrived together on Finnair and were welcomed by a crowd of Millers. Jonathan instantly bonded with Paavo, who was a fellow snowboarder. Before day's end, they'd planned a trip to the Austrian Alps that March, granted the rest of the world didn't catch fire, the snow melted, or a crazy pandemic closed the lonely planet.

That night, Paavo and his family stayed with Jonathan in Queens, while Antti and Selma's brood stayed with Frank and Jenna whose homes where a few blocks apart in Brooklyn. Back at Hamilton Tower, Kaisa prepared the next day's feast of treats from home. Smoked fish. Karelian Pie with egg butter. Delicious Savonian meat pies. Rye bread and cheeses. Finnish pancakes, which were more like a cakey custardy flan. Fresh berries of whatever variety she could find in Manhattan. And sweet Pulla bread.

Sixty-Seven

Before anyone arrived Saturday morning, Kaisa went to the corner flower shop to fill the tiny one-bedroom flat with fresh bursts of color and fragrant joy. Once accomplished, she placed a Marimekko cloth over the apartment's small dining table, covered it with northern European delights, then set several bottles of champagne and sparkling apple juice in a large ice bucket beside the table.

Jonathan and his family arrived first with Paavo and his clan. Jenna and Roger were next with Selma and her group. Franklin and family arrived uncharacteristically last with Antti and his, followed closely by Travis, Candy, their girls, and grandkids.

We ate and drank—sparkling cider for me, with many Kippis and cheers. The little Finns called me isoisä (grandpa). My heart was full, as was Kaisa's.

Once everyone was settled and getting to know each other, I went to Jonathan and asked him if we could speak privately. He nodded and stopped his conversation with Paavo concerning whether Burton or Neversummer snowboards were better.

I led him into the bedroom, closed the door, and sat. I patted the bed for Jonathan to do the same.

"What is it, Dad?" Jonathan asked as he sat.

I put an arm over his shoulder. He didn't flinch or pull away. "I want you to know, I love you."

"I love you, too, Dad. And I know you've been through a lot. And I know I haven't made it easy for you."

268

"No, you didn't. But I deserved every bit of it. I'm just glad we're a family again. But there's something I have to ask you. I'm asking you first before I…"

"Before what?"

"Kaisa and I, we're… you know," I said, nodding my head sideways.

"No, shit, Dad," he said with a sarcastic bite. "She's awesome and you don't deserve her. But I can tell she loves you, and I can see that you love her. I won't lie—you were an asshole to Mom, and I think you're the reason she killed herself, and I've… and I've…" Jon bit his lip, lost it, and started crying as his lips trembled.

I wrapped my arms around him without permission. He sank into me. "I know. I know," I choked out as I patted his back and tears flowed. "God, how I wish I could have another chance. Just one more chance to make it right. To bring her back." I started sobbing as air snapped in and out of my clenched lips. "Just one more chance. Just one more chance."

Jonathan's spine stiffened, and he held me as I melted. We sat on the bed and couldn't speak for a few minutes.

Jon Christian wiped his eyes and kept an arm over my shoulder. "So, are you going to ask her to marry you?"

"I was thinking about it. If you're okay with it."

"Well, I can tell you I am. I've only known her my whole life. And when she speaks, I hear Mom's voice, like when we used to sit in the apartment down the street holding our Toivo bears while, while those damn neighbors blared their music while we were trying to hear Kaisa's stories." We released cloudy chuckles. "I read what Kaisa wrote, and I know that little bear she wrote about was her way of healing. She's the medicine our family needs to recover from losing Mom. So yeah, you have my blessing, even if it'll be a while before I can call her Mom. And I might not ever be able to, but I don't think I'll love her any less."

"Thank you, Jon." I hugged him.

We stood, wiped our bloodshot eyes, exhaled, and nodded. I opened the door, and we returned to the front room.

Everyone was sitting listening to Kaisa tell a story—ears enchanted by every word.

"Dad, I'll be right back," said Jonathan. "I need to get something out of my car."

"Okay," I said as I surveyed the packed apartment.

Kaisa glanced at me with a cheery smile, then continued weaving a tale about a little white bear.

Several minutes passed before Jon Christian returned with the ragged, now signed, first edition of *The Adventures of Toivo the Bear*. "I brought this along. I figured the little ones would get a kick out of it."

I patted his back. Franklin and Jenna smiled. I put my arm around my baby boy and smiled back as we waited for Kaisa to finish her story.

When she did, Jonathan handed her the book. He whispered, and I could see tears forming in her eyes. They hugged and looked my way.

Jon clapped. "Hey, everybody—my dad has an important announcement to make. Don't you, Papa?"

I grinned. "Yeah. But something's missing."

Jonathan glanced around, then down at his niece, Brittany, who wore a black plastic skull ring from Halloween. He smiled. "Hey, Britt, can Uncle Jon borrow your pretty ring?"

"Sure." She removed the ring and handed it to him.

Jon Christian grabbed my left hand, paused to look at my wedding band, nodded, and placed the toy ring in my palm.

I laughed through another tear, then went to Kaisa and dropped to one knee and looked into those emerald eyes.

She returned a trembling smile and triggered a chorus of tears. Every adult in the room sang along.

"Kaisa Jännök, would you do me the honor and be my wife for as long as we have time left on this earth?"

"Hmmm. Let me think about it." She looked at the ceiling for a few seconds, nodded, then met my eager gaze with glistening eyes. "A little bear said he is okei with it. Yes, Nathan Miller, I would love to be your wife."

I slid the skull ring on her finger, which I planned to replace with gold and diamonds the next day. I stood and kissed her.

The adults clapped, and the young ones said, "Ooohhh, gross."

Then my damn phone rang. It was Nate. "Great. I have to take this." I stepped into the bedroom and closed the door.

"Nathan. Time to go. Vasily took Kyiv, and satellite shows him moving forces toward the Finnish and Estonian borders. NATO is answering and checking his move. I need you and Travis in Narva ASAP."

I knew my history going back to Peter the Great and the significance of Narva, Estonia, and the short bridge across the Narva River to the Ivangorad Fortress. If Vasily were moving into Estonia, securing Narva and the Gulf of Finland's coast would be a prime objective. Plus, the iconic view from Hermann Castle to the Russian fortress across the narrow river would highlight the age-old conflict between east and west.

"When's the flight?" I asked.

"I'll send you the details. You'll be on a red-eye tonight. Enjoy your party until then."

"I guess I'll give you the news before I let you go."

"What news?"

"Kaisa and I are getting married."

"Hey, congratulations. When's the wedding?"

"I have no idea. Haven't even got her a real engagement ring yet."

Sixty-Eight

Monday January 14, 2013.

I didn't sleep on the flight and wasn't prepped for jet lag when we landed in a blistering snowstorm. Tartu was the closest airport to Narva and we'd have to drive there due to weather conditions. On a summer day, the one-hundred-eighty kilometer drive around Lake Peipus took two and half hours. It would take double that today.

A local news crew met us at the terminal to get a few words from the indestructible Nathan Miller, who was on his first assignment in several years. After a quick interview, we left in a forest-camouflage Hummer with a driver who spoke Russian and very little English. Still, he did his best to narrate our driving tour of the eastern lands of Finnic Eesti. Travis spoke Russian and translated as needed to give me the most from the local's history lesson.

On the dash, the outside temperature read -25 C (-13 F). Even with the heater blowing full, the cold still seeped through winter boots and thermal socks and nipped the tips of toes. It was perfect weather for frozen war stories like the tale of the battle on Lake Peipus between Russian Prince Alexander Nevsky and the Teutonic Knights. The driver also told of Czar Peter the Great's loss to King Charles XII's much smaller Swedish Army in icy Narva (like the one we were headed toward). Being as cold as it was, it was conceivable that an attack might come across the lake or over the river, both of which the driver assured was solid enough to hold tanks.

We saw little of the lake's western shore through the snow covered pines and birch trees that lined the two-lane road as we crawled behind Hummers and a few Bradleys. It wasn't until we merged onto the E20 Tallin-Narva Highway that NATO presence became noticeable. At a sign reading *1E20 Peterburi 163/Narva 25*, two missile batteries, possibly in range of St. Petersburg, sat in the field to our right. Next to tree clumps on either side, large cannons were ready to deliver death. And past the city limit sign and through Narva's main artery, military vehicles and tanks were positioned to greet invaders that crossed the bridge or the river.

We continued to the E20/Tallinn Mantee roadblock before the roundabout to the Narva Museum (located inside Hermann Castle) and the Aleksander Puškini roadway. This was the closest those without proper papers could get to the five-hundred thirty-one foot Friendship Bridge that led to the Russian Federation.

One of two shivering British guards in heavy winter clothing stepped from a temporary heated gatehouse as a gas-powered generator roared and large snowflakes fell.

The driver showed our press credentials to a freckled, ginger-haired, red-nosed guard. The guard looked through to the passenger seat. "Hey-ey, ya-ya-you're *The* Nathan Miller," he said.

I smiled. "Yes, yes I am," I said as a frigid whip bit through the car's warmth.

"D-d-do you think you might, uh, maybe, sign my book? Bloody loved *Ackerman's Curse*. It's… it's your best so far. But I did like most of your others, too. Except that one… S-s-sorry," he said, shivering, his teeth chattering between pauses.

I knew the one. "Yeah. Sure. My pleasure. You have a pen?"

"Bloody sure do. Be back in a jiff." Before I could tell him I had one, he was running to the gatehouse. He returned with his copy and came around to my window.

I lowered it, looked at his name tag (*Edmund Weasley PFC*), took the book, opened it, and tried to sign. The ink was frozen.

The guard looked perplexed.

"Don't worry—I got you," I said as Travis handed me a red Sharpee.

The guard smiled, shook his head, and took out his cell phone. "M-m-mind a pic?"

Before I could answer the guard leaned sideways with his back to the car, smiled, and pointed a finger at me.

I smiled.

Click. Click. And *click.* "Th-th-thank you. Thank you very much. Th-th-this means the world to me."

I signed and pretty much repeated what I wrote. "Well, thanks for reading. Wouldn't be anything without fans like you, Edmund. Try to stay warm," I said as I handed his book back.

The guard chuckled and glowed with an *ah-shucks* smile as he opened the gate. Travis grinned. He seemed happy seeing me back on top after being slapped sober by life.

We parked in the castle parking lot. Several military vehicles and two M1 Abrams tanks with turrets and barrels raised and pointed east were parked there. To our left were large, snow-covered white letters that spelled NARVA. The border gates were within sight to the left.

We stepped into the cold as the driver kept the motor running to keep the engine from freezing. Our thick clothing, heated gloves, and mask-covered faces weren't enough, especially with the wind chill. We would have to work fast and find places to thaw in between takes, but first I needed to find the perfect spot for the segment.

We walked through the outer gate into the castle's vacant inner ward. Snow flurries picked up and whipped around us as wind cut exposed skin. We passed a few NATO soldiers chattering in Polish, hurried through the inner gate into the main castle courtyard below the massive pyramid-topped white tower, and headed up the steps to the ramparts. Its parapet was six foot tall, and our view to the other side of the river required tip toes or peering through rectangular cannon ports for a decent view of the frozen river, Ivangorod Fortress, and its city beyond.

Travis knelt and started recording through a port. I looked around and up to the tower and higher walls which would provide a better view of what lay past the Russian fortress. I waved for Travis to follow since the whistling wind made speaking pointless.

We entered the castle museum where it was delightfully warm, disgustingly aseptic, and wouldn't provide the intensity my reports were known for. This was my comeback and had to be extraordinary.

Keeping in mind the Hummer's running engine, we double-stepped to the tower's top level high above the river. From there, I spied the Russian side through binoculars as Travis captured what we needed. There were far more military vehicles in Ivangorod than in Narva, and based on their formations appeared ready to move if President Vasily gave the invasion order. I peered down at the riverside walkway far below and watched the white eddies whirling over the snow-covered river. I imagined Czar Peter's forces crossing that river only to be cut down at the base of Hermann's icy walls. I could see the sheer brutality on their exposure. *Now that's perfect*, I thought and said, "Let's head down there."

"That's what I was thinking," Travis said with a nod and a hungry grin.

We raced to the warm waiting Hummer. "Tell him to take us to the riverside." Travis translated, and we drove past two overgrown and rusting tennis courts and closed shops in the castle's commerce district. We turned left and passed a half dozen M1 Abrams tanks with barrels pointed east, before descending to the castle's southside riverside parking lot. Once parked by the river, Travis and I took a deep breath, braced for the cold, and hopped out. We double-timed to the wide snow-covered riverwalk which provided an iconic visual between the two fortresses separated by the narrow river with so much history. We continued below the massive walls toward the Friendship Bridge which I wanted above me in the background.

Sixty-Nine

As we neared, I saw a lone figure standing mid-bridge. He was dressed in white and not for the weather—nearly invisible in the surrounding flurries against a light-gray backdrop. I raised my binoculars and recognized the figure in white. It was Frederick, unmasked, and wearing his standard anti-Morton uniform. The wind whipped around him, fluttering his trench coat and blond hair as his white Stetson remained glued to his head. His Dead Blow eyes were fixed on me and dripping malevolence as he malignantly grinned. I glanced at Death's ring and thought, *Why is he here?*

Travis tugged on my shoulder. "Nathan, what the hell are those?" he asked, pointing north to Russia where the river bent slightly northwest.

At first, I didn't see anything. Then I saw silhouettes through the flurries and heard buzzing. The buzzing intensified until I could make out small aircraft—drones, dozens of them. But they weren't like the U.S. MQ-1 Predators or MQ-9 Reapers used in the War on Terror. They were much smaller—less than ten feet long—and approaching quickly.

"I got a bad feeling about this," I said.

"Yeah. Me, too," Travis said but continued recording.

The lead drone fired a missile that screamed past the bridge and hit the castle wall. A cobalt and black ringed fireball erupted with a shrill metallic **BANG-GOOONG**. The explosion obliterated the castle's northeast wall, its flagpole that was flying the Estonian blue, black, and white, and the museum courtyard below the tower.

My mouth gaped. The explosion was like nothing I'd seen before. My immediate suspicions were that these were new weapons Vasily had perfected using Ethereal technology. "We gotta move," I said as concrete and various debris rained down. An arm and torso landed near me.

Travis didn't budge and kept filming the Ivangorad Fortress. I looked up as smaller drones poured over its ramparts. "What the fuck, Travis? MOVE!" I yelled. There was no need to holler twice as we started running toward the Hummer.

I glanced back. The Man in White shot into the air as the bridge exploded with another bang-gong. It crumbled, smoking, into the ice. The drone responsible emerged from the explosion's charcoal cloud. It released a second missile into the river, adding ice chunks and frigid rain to the falling debris. More drones targeted the river up and down the Narva, curiously removing any path for the Russians to cross.

More shrill bang-gongs rumbled the ground, but somehow we were unaffected by skull cracking concussions and the deadly downpour that avoided us. I knew my guardian devil was toying with me as we navigated the developing obstacle course and fresh ice around soft snow. Another drone fired a missile into the Ivangorod Fortress, sending additional concrete splashing into the river. I looked back again and saw another drone destroy the building directly adjacent to the fortress on the north side of what remained of the bridge. It was pure chaos, an uncoordinated attack that made no sense since the drones were coming from Vasily's side of the river. I wondered, was this Vasily's attack or someone creating a false flag? If so, who? That answer would be unknown until after the Purge but I'll come to that in a much later volume.

I refocused on getting out of Dodge as more drones flooded over the river. Rather than bang-gong missiles, these spat rapid-fire rounds that punched basketball-sized holes in everything they hit (including the tanks) without a sound as if they were made of tissue paper. The rounds continued on like rail bolts cutting through other vehicles and personnel standing in the cold. We continued our bee-line to the Hummer. A rail went through our ride. The driver exploded, painting the Hummer with dripping gore.

We didn't gawk long enough for gore-cicles to form and ran back toward the river. Our heads darted back and forth for a path out of this mess. A drone swarm appeared from the Russian fortress's south walls and its city. They peppered every living thing, vehicle, and structure to our right where the river bent southeast. Multiple explosions followed. With no good options, I pointed to the best of the bad which was back along the walls and initial destruction to the steps that led to a residential street I hoped would take us back to the main thoroughfare and out of the city, or at least better cover somewhere.

The snow was just deep enough on a non-iced path and wide enough to allow us to sprint without slipping as we navigated debris. I was dying. I wasn't in the best shape anymore, but I also wasn't ready to take that final walk with my friend in black.

We climbed over a portion of the fallen crossing, then floated on adrenaline up several flights to a viewpoint north of the border gates above the broken Friendship Bridge. From there, we ran along a rundown apartment complex with no idea where to go but with no intention to stop until we got there.

On the Russian side, buildings turned to billowing clouds of flame and gray-black smoke. Distant and near *boom*s preceded conventional explosions close and faraway and added to the bang-gongs as each side took the bait. I glanced left as a bang-gong missile hit Hermann's white tower, making it disappear. I didn't look again as artillery rounds exploded behind us. The ground quaked.

We continued toward the roundabout, zigzagging down E20/Tallinn Mantee as destruction followed us and debris fell all around, almost bouncing off of us. A tank to my right was hit by a bang-gong. Its turret rocketed into the air above black and blue explosive corona. The percussion hit me this time and made my ears ring as everything around Travis and I blew apart including the guardhouse. I wondered if PFC Weasley was inside. My right ear felt warm and wet under my mask. I knew it was blood.

I glanced back as a drone zeroed in on us. The Man in White dropped like a meteor out of nowhere, abruptly stopped in its line of fire, and floated several feet above the ground. The drone released a screaming micro-missile. Chance lifted his hands and a dome of barely visible energy formed around Travis and me. The missile passed through my guardian devil. It hit the bubble and veered toward a nearby building which vanished inside another black and blue fireball. A shockwave followed as a shower of bricks, glass, wood, and body parts bounced off the protective shell. Black smoke billowed from where the three story building stood seconds before.

The Man in White's eyes glared as he smiled maliciously to let me know our lives were under his boot to squash if desired. Travis started recording again.

"Travis. Run. Just run. Don't fuck with the camera! Just run!"

The Man in White laughed.

"Fuck you, Frederick!" I screamed, cutting through the whistling wind and crackling flames.

Travis looked at me like I was crazy.

280

"Goddamnit, get the fuck out of here! Go! Go! Go!"

"What about…"

"Just go…"

The Man in White laughed as another micro-missile shrieked toward Travis. Chance lifted an open hand and surrounded Travis with energy. He made a fist, and the bubble collapsed. He snapped his fingers as the explosive round hit Travis in the back. Travis disintegrated into a fiery wave that slammed into me like a truck. I was gone.

Seventy

Flashes of light. Burning. My right hand stinging. My right arm gone—a bloody stump. Blackness again…

Seventy-One

Flashes of faces—faces looking down knowing I was about to die. Darkness again…

Seventy-Two

More light, then sepia black and white. I stood in an operating room, looking at my body. My right arm was gone, and the right side of my face was a blackened mass of flesh. Morton was there, and he was furious.

"It was my brother, wasn't it?"

"Yeah. Frederick killed Travis. He could've saved us like he always did with that magic bubble of his. But he removed it to prove he could, then laughed about it, right before... right before..." My spirit seethed with sorrow, but my immortal eyes were dry.

"That was his luck bubble. It's how he's protected you your whole career. That sonuvabitch! He's gone too far this time. I'm sure he only meant to kill Travis, but you got caught in the blast. Typical Frederick." Morton scoffed. "He's not getting away with this. But for now, you have to live."

Morton reached into my corpse's chest with one hand and stroked my mangled face with the other. The tattered, burnt edges and exposed bone healed into recognizable facial features. My heart began beating and my soul was sucked back into my mortal shell. Everything went black again.

Seventy-Three

I woke up furious and ready to kill. I saw only red and the image of the Man in White. As my bloody eyes cleared, my mind tore apart, splitting into many but all answering to the whole. It felt as if I'd been splintered like when I performed Death's duties on my one and only shift as a relief Reaper in training. Then I realized, I wasn't me and these weren't my eyes. *Am I dreaming?* I wondered until I caught sight of my hands. I had both and there was no skull ring on the right hand and no wedding ring on the left. I never dreamed without my wedding ring. That wasn't my finger, and these weren't my hands, and I wasn't walking. I was being carried along by a force that I knew. I was Death and he was me and we were walking in Macao… and Atlantic City… and Monaco… and Las Vegas… and everywhere casinos could be found—high rolling casinos the Man in White loved to frequent, some we'd visited together in a different life. Death's eyes were searching, searching, searching, for Frederick Chance.

Morton stood in the many gambling strips. I focused on one. He was outside the Mandalay Bay Casino. Everyone gawked at the Man in Black and moved out of the way of the clench-fisted god. Eyes that caught his glower darted away as if a look from the Reaper could kill. Right then, I wondered if it could.

Morton stormed into the Mandalay Bay and yelled, "FREDERICK, WHERE ARE YOU? FACE ME!"

Fearless bouncers moved to remove the Man in Black, thinking he was just another Death-Love Krishna, and pissed themselves before being introduced to the ground and/or unconsciousness. Morton paid no heed to the mortality of anyone in his way. This was the Death that terrified me—the Reaper I feared. There was no milk and cookies on his mind as I sensed the dam breaking that he'd held together for thousands of years. Today, Morton would bring a flood to the desert if he found Frederick here.

By the time he reached Caesar's Palace, the police and HSC units had been called. They fired, but bullets passed through Morton. He waved his hand. Police cars flattened, and officers flew into the fountains and bushes. Morton stormed into the casino. A platoon of security guards rushed him.

Morton changed form. In a mirror, his kindly face melted into a rotten, fleshy skull with flaming eyes. His Stetson, trench coat, and slacks became a black hooded robe. In one maggot-mottled, nearly skeletal hand, he held a razor-sharp scythe. The other was outstretched, index finger beckoning bouncers to bring it on.

The bouncers looked as if they'd soiled themselves. They backed up a few steps, turned, and ran like their lives depended on it.

Morton saw a gambler surrounded by women. He wore a white Stetson, white suit, and matching snakeskin boots. He was leaning over a craps table, oblivious to Morton's antics in the noisy casino.

The casino worker at the table announced, "*He Who Always Wins* wins again. Place your bets."

Several who'd just won after the God of Luck's last roll patted him on the back and threw high-dollar chips on the table.

Morton resumed his Man in Black guise and stepped toward Frederick like a lion preparing to tear open a gazelle.

The Man in White threw the dice as the Man in Black slapped a firm hand on his shoulder.

Frederick turned and started to say, "Hey, bud..."

Morton slammed a fist through his nose and into his skull. Cobalt exploded onto the women surrounding Frederick as he went airborne and hit the other side of the table before the dice stopped rolling. He flipped over the other end.

Above his caved in face, Frederick's terror-streaked eyes caught Morton's homicidal glare. The Man in White bounded to his feet and ran as his face resumed its normal appearance.

Morton pushed his hand forward, and the table flew toward the Man in White.

Frederick yanked a voluminous woman lugging a cup full of coins into the table's path. She caught it, and a shower of quarters scattered as her bones snapped loud enough to be heard over the slot machines. Her Underspirit awoke in its White Room seconds later.

Mad panic ensued as everyone made for the exits.

Frederick frantically waved his hands at passing slot machines, making the bells go off. Coins rained down. Those running for the doors caught a whiff of greed, did a one-eighty, and clogged Morton's path.

The Grim Reaper waved his hands, and slammed people out of the way. They hit the machines as if he had parted the Red Sea.

Frederick was in a dead sprint, but Morton gained on him with every deliberate step.

Closer.

Closer.

Closer.

Death grabbed Chance's collar and threw him through several Roman statues and the front doors. His face smashed and skidded on the roundabout before he cartwheeled like a bad ski run, slammed his head on the fountain lip, and flipped into the water. He cartwheeled a few times before he came to a stop face down. The water around him turned a deeper blue.

Morton moved like a terminator to finish what he started.

Frederick pushed up, shook his head, and staggered to his feet. He shook his head again, spit out more blue blood, and stood his ground.

Morton approached with deliberate fury.

Frederick looked around, grabbed an arm and headless white marble statue. He ripped it from its base like picking a flower and swung for the fences, clocking Morton's head. The statue disintegrated into dust and marble chunks.

Morton's hat fell off, exposing his Einstein frizz. Morton looked at his wet Stetson, then tilted his head and glowered at Frederick. His nose flared over clenched, pursed lips as dark blue trickled and dripped from his chin. He spat out a mouthful of cobalt, snarled, and dove through Frederick, knocking him into the water. Morton jackhammered his face, trading crosses...

Seventy-Four

... I found myself floating above my body. Kaisa was at my side, holding my hand. She was sobbing. I was asleep or in a coma, but I wasn't dead yet. The television was tuned to breaking news from Las Vegas, USA.

A helicopter hovered over the front fountains of Caesar's Palace as an older man in black pummeled a younger one wearing a blue-stained, maybe-white suit. The older man's silver hair swung side to side with each cross to the younger man's face. The fountains swirled with cobalt.

The camera panned to flattened police cars. Paramedics tended the injured as more ambulances raced through traffic to the casino. Images of gurneys carrying white-sheet-covered bodies flashed on the screen. A blonde female reporter spoke.

"This is Kristen Kettlemeyer here at Caesar's Palace in Las Vegas where the fight of the century is currently underway between the fabled Man in Black and a man in white yet to be identified. The rampage has already claimed a dozen lives, and dozens more have been injured. Police and HSC units have been unable to break up the fight, and both sharp-dressed legends appear to be impervious to bullets."

Kettlemeyer was minimized to a picture in picture as the newscast turned to a KNW newsroom where a brown-haired Caucasian male anchor sat behind a desk next to his serious-faced cocoa-skinned female co-anchor. "Does anyone know what might have sparked the altercation?" asked the male anchor, sounding like a sports announcer.

"Well, Roger, right now, it's too soon to know. But the Man in White looks strikingly like the older one. I know it's just speculation, but I suspect they're related. This is likely a domestic squabble."

"Okay. Thanks for the insight, Kristen."

"My pleasure, Roger."

The helicopter continued its live feed as the anchors looked on.

The Man in White kicked the Man in Black in the nuts.

Roger cringed and brought a fist to his mouth.

The blow sent Frederick flying, splashing into the next fountain. The Man in White spat out blue and shook his head. His jaw dropped, releasing a blood-curdling war cry. He ran at lightning speed, grabbed the older man, spun him round and round, and released him like a hammer. The Man in Black arched over buildings, rocketing half a mile, before exploding into a leg of Paris Casino's Eifel Tower.

The helicopter cameraman refocused for a close up.

A massive shockwave of pent-up rage blew out Paris's windows and those across the boulevard at the Bellagio. Anyone caught in the wake was killed or knocked flat.

The helicopter pilot struggled but kept his craft from crashing into an adjacent building as the cameraman continued doing his job.

One of the tower's legs was gone and two of the others were wobbling precariously. The tower tittered for several seconds, craned, and fell across the strip, creating a splash and a small tsunami in the Bellagio's sprawling fountains. Vehicles and surviving pedestrians were crushed, increasing the toll Morton would have to clean up.

Seventy-Five

Again, I found myself looking through Morton's eyes as he emerged from a pile of debris. He struggled to his feet, tapped his chest, and appeared behind Frederick. Morton grabbed his neck.

"Let's go to my White Realm, *brother*. We need to talk." The world turned sepia. "Wait here."

Frederick tried to speak, but before his lips opened, his mouth froze. He tried to move, but stood stiff as rigor mortis. Only his panicked eyes moved, darting back and forth.

Morton vanished and reappeared at the scene of his personal carnage. Three doors appeared as many disoriented Underspirits wandered through the destruction, devoid of life and sound. Morton cleaned up mortal shells then ushered Underspirits into the White Room.

"Where am I?" said one of many with a slight northeastern accent I couldn't place. "I finally won big over at Bellagio and was heading home when I saw the Eifel Tower falling toward my car. Then everything went black."

"Look, I'm really sorry about all this," said Morton. "I was teaching my brother a lesson, and things got out of hand. But hey, I have good news for you. For your inconvenience, I'll let you go wherever you'd like in the world beyond. Trip to Paradise is on me, even though I know you don't deserve it."

"Seriously, you just killed me, motherfucker, and you think that's gonna make it okay? I am definitely filing a complaint with Jesus or Mohammed or who the fuck ever when I get to the other side."

Another said, "Hey, you guys, this yahoo just killed us, and now he's letting this prick that cut me off go to Heaven. Don't let this asshole send any of you to Hell."

Morton sighed and rolled his eyes. "All of you—through the door on the right." Death beckoned to the appropriate exit.

"Well, I don't want to be dead. I'm not going."

"Fine. Stay. Do whatever. I don't care."

Fate invisibly opened a few more White Rooms for Morton to direct dead traffic. Most of the newly dead took Morton's free ride to Paradise, but a few stayed behind to haunt the Vegas Strip. Luckily, none given a free pass had broken the Black and White Rule. And the ones destined for Samara Station, well, Morton would have to deal with Karma's wrath over those.

Morton returned to Frederick and his bobbling dread-struck eyes. "You couldn't do it. You couldn't leave Nathan alone. Like you haven't screwed up his life enough. You killed him. You fuckin' killed him, but I didn't let him die. I couldn't save Travis Wright, and now his wife and girls and grandkids will have to wait a lifetime to be with him again, all because of you. I am sick to shit of all the bullshit of the gods. And I am sick to shit of doing nothing about it while you, Delores, Marduk, and War make these mortal realities living hells. So help me Gaia, if Nathan doesn't pull through, Nathan and I are gonna drag your ass to the Abyss and watch as you're torn apart. No, wait, that's too good for you. I'm not gonna extinguish you. No, I know exactly what to do with you, *brother*."

Morton looked around the White Room within Caesar's Palace. I felt Death's lips curl into a malicious grin. He grabbed the back of Frederick's trench coat and dragged the stiff through the wrecked casino. The door was open to a cozy high-stakes poker room. He pulled Frederick through the threshold and positioned him like an action figure at the table. A mound of chips was piled in the center. Morton looked at his brother's hand that had been dealt. It was an Ace of Spades Royal Flush. Death placed the five cards in Frederick's hands and grinned. He waved and the doors slammed shut.

Chance unfroze. "I don't get it," he said.

"You will. You realize the White Room only extends to closed doors and windows? And do you see any Black Doors?"

"No," Frederick said shakily as it dawned on him what his brother had in mind.

"Enjoy eternity, *He Who Will Never Win Again*."

"No. No. No, no, no. Please, no," Frederick whimpered as Morton tapped his chest.

Seventy-Six

It was strange drifting between life and death, hovering above a room filled with love. After the Man in White was cursed to spend eternity in a small room in the sepia in-between, I no longer saw the world through Morton's eyes. I didn't need to since he stayed by my side, holding my phantom hand with the Scythe ring on a ghost finger. Kaisa held my fleshy one with the wedding ring and rarely left my room.

The kids filtered through the room that I learned was in Tallinn, Estonia. As I floated above, I watched the news and learned that Russian Federation President Vasily's incursion was checked and driven back. Gains in Ukraine were also reversed after President Vasily died of a strange illness. Several in his inner circle also succumbed and many more cases of a yet-to-be-named illness had been reported in Moscow and surrounding towns. The World Health Organization was on high alert for a possible high level contagion from bio-weapons labs which Vasily emphatically denied the existence of during his September 2012 WNN exclusive with Julie Florid. Major speculation pointed to a successful assassination gone wrong. Vasily's successor was yet to be named and the situation in Russia appeared bleak as federation members called for independence from Mother Russia's yoke.

I was in a coma and too fragile to move. Jonathan spent a week with me, giving Kaisa a chance to rest and take a fast ferry back to Helsinki to tend to business. Franklin and Jenna also spent a week each, and Antti and Selma frequently came across the Gulf. Only Paavo hadn't visited. After hearing what happened to me, he volunteered for the Finnish Army to defend his land like generations before.

I listened as they spoke about Candy, who knew Travis would never be coming home. I knew he was in a good place and I looked forward to the day when he could be my wingman again.

As time passed, I floated like a ghost, occasionally stepping into the White Room only to have Morton kick me out. I began to wonder how Gladys was handling Morton's absence. He would have a helluva backlog when he got back to the office.

I watched Morton with a spirited smile as he held my phantom hand and crystal blue tears fell through the ghost arm. I sighed. *Well, I guess I'll be helping him catch up.*

As I drifted, I became sleepy. Why? I didn't know. I was already in a coma. And so far, I hadn't felt tired during my out-of-body experience. But I felt... so sleepy. So very sleepy. And... I felt my spirit drawn back to my body. And... then... I...

Seventy-Seven

... I found myself walking in a hall with many doors, looking for a way out. I grabbed the first knob. It was luke warm. Inside my parents were tucking me into bed.

I closed the door and walked on. I felt the knobs of several more, but each was cold. I continued until I found one that was warmer than the first. Inside, Uncle Frank and Aunt Dorothy were sitting in their Harrisburg living room. A single lamp was on and they were praying with the Bible closed in their hands. They were praying for me.

I closed the door and moved past several before I tested a knob. It was uncomfortably warm as if a fire was burning inside. Everything within me said, *don't open the door*, but I did anyway. Inside was my old Greenwich Village apartment. I was inside sitting at my old typewriter with a stack of typed pages on my left. Vanessa was making dinner. Jenna was young and playing with a Barbie doll while Franklin was fighting with Jonathan, who was crying. I savored the memory as my heart melted. I reluctantly closed the door and walked on.

The knob of the next door was hotter than the one before. Ryan was inside with John, Geno, Toby, Stan, Kyle, Benny, Jesus, Williams, Thomas, Ricky, and Max. Travis and I were in the middle. Everyone was smiling and laughing at one of Toby's dirty jokes.

I closed the door and opened another, enduring the pain as the knob scalded my hand. Inside was Ryan, Suzanne, and little Alex sitting at The Prospector next to Melvin Anderson as we began work on the story of Ryan's family. I sighed, bit my lip, and shut the door.

I walked on and opened one more and nearly screamed from pain as my hand smoked. I smelled burning skin. Inside was a beach. Vanessa was laying, oh, so beautiful on the sand. Her gray eyes said, "I love you, Nathan." I had to let go. *I had to let go.* I had to move on.

I shut the door and ran into Ernest Hemingway (the middle-aged one, circa 1939, not the *Old man and Sea* bearded one). Papa asked, "Did you get a lot of work done?"

I tentatively replied, "Huh. Uh, yeah, yes."

"That's good. Oh, and the exit is right there," said Ernest as he pointed at a neon-red *EXIT* sign above the door at the end of the hall.

"Thanks, Ernest."

"My pleasure. Happy trails."

I looked at Papa, then at the door. I nodded, pushed it open, and light flooded my eyes.

Seventy-Eight

When my eyes adjusted the first thing I saw was Kaisa's smiling face. I looked to my right for Morton, but he wasn't there... but my arm was and the skull ring was still on my finger. I was obviously still dreaming. Or so I thought until I saw Jakko Kantelejarvi and Francis Pickens. Both were smiling as wide as Kaisa.

"Welcome back to the land of the conscious," said Jakko. "How do you like your new arm?"

I flexed it. During our work on the 20/20 *Age of Ethereal* episode, I had signed the appropriate documents to allow Jakko to use me for his phase three and four *RegenerTech* trials, if by chance, luck ran out on me. When he phrased it, I didn't think how oddly ironic his choice of words were when he said them.

I looked at Kaisa, then Jakko and Francis. "Can I have some water?" I asked in a croaky, cotton-mouth voice.

Kaisa poured and handed me a glass.

I drank, then answered. "It's great. How long have you been here?"

"Today? A few hours. But Francis and I have visited several times over the past year."

"What?"

"Yes, Nathan, you've been in a coma," said Kaisa. She wiped a joyful tear. "Several times, the doctors were not sure whether you would pull through."

Francis spoke. "We've come as often as we could. It'll be nice when the EtheRail transfer hubs open in Tallin. Currently the closest is the Helsinki Railway station."

"Where am I?"

"You're in Tallin."

"Still?"

"Yes," Kaisa answered with a look of surprise as if I could've known. "The doctors felt it best not to move you until, and if, you came out of your coma."

Jakko spoke. "We started the RegenerTech gel immediately after you left ICU. We would have started sooner, but the gel was not yet approved for acute battle field injuries. But after what we have learned during your recovery process even President Cochran and Prime Minister Smythe have agreed to allow its use for ABFIs."

I looked at the arm I was born with and saw no evidence of muscle wasting and my legs hadn't shrunk from disuse. I studied my new arm. Its skin tone was slightly paler than the rest of my skin that had lightened over the past year. I looked at the Scythe ring.

Jakko thought he could read minds. "Yes, I know your skin is paler on the new arm but once you get outside it will tan with the rest of your original skin."

"That's not what I was looking at. Where did you find my ring?"

Francis quizzically regarded Jakko.

I glanced at Kaisa, then back at the moguls.

"What ring?" asked Jakko.

They couldn't see it. "Oh, nothing. Just babbling. Whew. Been asleep for a year—what'd you expect?"

"It is okei, Nathan. I am so happy to have you back. I thought I lost you," Kaisa said as she tenderly patted my shoulder.

"I'm not going anywhere except somewhere to marry you if you're ready. Hospital chapel's fine with me unless you want to wait for something fancy."

"The chapel is nice and then we can do something bigger. I always dreamed of being married at White Cathedral."

After a few tests, my doctor gave me the green light. We called a local Lutheran priest that spoke English and Finnish and waited while Jakko and Francis went out to find rings and something for me to wear. Kaisa was already dressed in her best Marimekko dress. It would do until she picked out her gown for what would no doubt be a media event in Helsinki.

Kaisa and I contacted everyone via Skype. The kids were overjoyed to know I was awake from my coma but disappointed that they couldn't be there for the unplanned first of two weddings. They understood why we didn't want to wait. The world had gotten a whole lot darker while I was asleep and tomorrow anywhere was no longer a given. Fortunately, Takijirō's Hachiman Corp had made strides toward forging the Sampo but the Sky Forge was not yet ready to prevent the coming apocalypse. But life goes on even in the darkest days.

The priest arrived a few hours later but we had to wait for Jakko and Francis to arrive with the rings and my tux. Jakko also brought two silver disks. He set one on each side of the small chapel in front of the altar and pressed power on a small fob. Two Reality Windows appeared. Within each were the faces of Kaisa and my children and grandchildren wherever in the world they might be, including Paavo who was stationed in Ukraine as a NATO peace keeper. Takijirō, Nate, Julie, and Candy were also present from Hiroshima and New York for the small ceremony. In the background at WNN, most of the employees were crowded behind Nate and Julie. The newlyweds raised their ringed fingers.

It was a simple ceremony akin to a Vegas chapel wedding, but before I said, "I do," I looked at Jonathan's picture-among-the-pictures. He gave me a reassuring smile and a thumbs up. I removed Vanessa's ring and placed it in my pocket. It was one of the most painful things I've ever done. But I had to move on. I had to live what life I had left. When it was over, maybe, just maybe, I thought there might be a way to save Vanessa from the place I sent her. Maybe I could help change the rules that led to the unjustifiable torment of Frank and so many others in the world after this one that saw only black and white and no gray.

When the ceremony had ended and Kaisa and I were wearing new rings, Jakko and Francis left to catch the fast ferry back to Helsinki. No sooner had they said *moi-moi ystäväni* and *adios amigo* did my head start racing with honeymoon ideas which could wait until I was released in the morning. But I wanted to do something for Kaisa now. Something unconventional, granted the one who might be able to make it happen had the ability to grant my heart's desire.

"Kaisa," I said.

"Yes, Nathan, what is it?"

"I want to take you someplace."

"That's nice. Where?"

"It's a surprise, but you have to trust me."

"Umm, okei. You know I do."

"Then, come close."

She did.

"Place your hand on my shoulder and close your eyes."

She regarded me with narrowed, cautious eyes, but did as I asked.

I blinked.

Seventy-Nine

Kaisa opened her eyes in a different dimension. She looked at me. "What is this place? And why are you dressed that way? How are you dressed that way?"

I looked down. My hospital attire was gone and I was dressed in black. I felt my head and found a Stetson. "Kaisa, this is the Realm of Fate and Death. Here I am known as Nathan Reaper. I'm a relief Reaper of Souls. Or at least I plan to be. Sorry to spring this on you right after the wedding, but I'm here to accept a job."

I waited for a response but she said nothing as her mouth sat slightly ajar. "Follow me. There's no need to fear the Reaper."

She nodded but her mouth didn't close as she regarded me with trusting, but conflicted eyes.

I offered my right hand.

She took it and walked with me past the Reaper statues, the Black Koi pond, the rose garden, and up the steps to Fate and Death's front door. I rang the bell.

Gladys and Morton answered, looking like surprised grandparents who weren't expecting a visit from the grandkids. Morton wasn't wearing his hat and his hair was its usual mess. Gladys looked as refined as ever.

"Nathan, I wasn't expecting you," said Gladys. "I don't have any milk and cookies ready. And might I ask, who is this lovely creature?"

"This is my wife, Kaisa," I said.

"I know, but I always like introductions."

"N-n-nice to meet you," Kaisa said almost as a question.

I looked at Morton. He wore a subtle grin.

"No need to fear the Reaper or his sister. We don't bite. My name is Morton Death. Why don't you two come inside?"

"Okei," Kaisa said and looked to me for reassurance.

I nodded my head once sideways to beckon her in. I followed and placed my hat on a hook next to Morton's as if returning home.

"Gladys, would you mind entertaining Kaisa? I need to speak with Morton."

"Oh, it would be my pleasure. Come with me. Let me show you my kitchen, not that a woman's place is in the kitchen. Do you like cookies?"

"Yes," Kaisa said, again, answering like a question.

"Well, let's make some. I'll even let you in on my secret recipe. I tell you—they're to die for."

They left Death and me alone and returned in what seemed like fifteen minutes, which in reality was no Timethy at all. Kaisa was eating a chocolate chip cookie. From her eyes and exaggerated Finnish smile, she appeared to be enjoying it.

"Kaisa, I have a surprise for you," said Morton. "A wedding present, but it was Nathan's idea. That boy is a good egg that I am proud to have as my relief Reaper of Souls. I mean, I assume you showing up like this means you accepted my offer."

"Yeah. How couldn't I after all you did to save my life so Kaisa and I could have a life together? And thanks for the bedside vigil. I know it put you behind."

"That it did," said Gladys. "But we're slowly working through the backlog. But I'll be honest—we sorely need your help."

"Well, welcome aboard," said Morton. "You know it won't be easy, but it does come with some benefits. Now, mortal legends in some realities…"

"Realities?" asked Kaisa.

"Yes, there are many, but we'll get to that. As I was saying, some legends say I have a brother named the Sandman. If only I had been *so lucky*," he said, shaking his head while looking at me. "I am the closest thing to the Sandman and as such have certain powers in the realm of dreams. Will you follow me?" Morton didn't wait for an answer that would sound like another question.

Kaisa glanced at me as Death walked off. I grabbed her hand and we followed to the room where I found myself again and wrote the first draft of this never-before-released tale. Morton motioned for us to lay on the two twin beds in the otherwise empty room. The high window was open and I could smell the sweetest roses.

"Now relax, this won't hurt a bit," said Morton as he reached for Kaisa's forehead.

She flinched and looked at me.

I nodded and she relaxed.

Morton's fingers touched Kaisa's forehead and she fell asleep. He did the same to me.

Eighty

Kaisa opened her eyes as I stood in the background. We were next to a river. It was a perfect summer day without mosquitos. Hey, it was a dream. By the bank was a handsome young man with blond hair and blue eyes that looked very much like Kaisa's boys.

"Toivo?" she said in what was definitely a question this time.

He turned.

Kaisa looked back at me.

I smiled. "Go. You've been waiting a lifetime for this."

"I love you, Nathan. I love you so much."

I waved for her to stop wasting time with the living when the dead were waiting.

"Kaisa? Is that you?"

"Yes, yes. It's me. It's me, Toivo."

"How have you been?"

"Better now. There is someone I would like you to meet."

I stepped forward.

"You are not the Death I know," said Toivo.

"No, my name is Nathan Rea... I mean, Miller. I'm just here to help out and maybe give Morton a break from time to time."

"And you love my Kaisa?"

"I do... more than you know."

"Good. Please take care of her. She's been alone for so long since I left. That was the hardest part about leaving—watching her suffer until she met you."

"She will be my sacred trust until Morton or I bring her back to you."

"Then you have my blessing."

"Kiitos niin paljon," (thank you so much), I said, somehow knowing the right words to say.

Toivo stepped to Kaisa and ran his fingers through her hair. "Know that I will watch over you like I always have. Maybe we can meet like this again, if Mr. Reaper does not mind sharing you in your dreams."

"Not at all. Her heart will always be yours. And I'm okay with that. I'll leave you two alone now. Kaisa, when you're ready to go, just wake up."

"Okei, Nathan. I'll see you soon."

I opened my eyes, sat up, and watched Kaisa sleep. She had the sweetest smile as she whistled softly with each breath. I waited patiently, enjoying every moment of her happiness until she opened her eyes.

She breathed in and exhaled utter contentment. "I'm ready to return to reality. I will wait for you until you finish what you need to do here."

We stood.

I smiled, albeit grimly, but didn't speak.

Kaisa leaned and kissed me as Fate and Death watched the scene from the doorway. Morton nodded and Gladys held prayer hands to her lips, thoroughly enjoying the happy ending. Then, we walked with Death to the front door. Fate followed.

Morton laid his hand on Kaisa's shoulder.

She smiled at me and turned to mist.

I rubbed my lips, then grabbed my hat, and placed it where it goes.

"You ready for this?" asked Morton.

"No."

He chuckled, patted down his frizz, and put on his hat. Morton opened the door. "You first," he said.

I nodded, stepped outside, and accepted my destiny.

The End
of
Book 1

Nathan Reaper's next tale begins
in
Accidental Healer
Tales from the Afterworld
Book 2